QUILTED CHERRIES

Fourth Novel in the
Door County Quilts Series

ANN HAZELWOOD

Text copyright © 2022 by Ann Hazelwood
Artwork copyright © 2022 by C&T Publishing, Inc.

Publisher: Amy Barrett-Daffin
Creative Director: Gailen Runge
Acquisitions Editor: Roxane Cerda
Executive Book Editor: Karen Davis of Gill Editorial Services
Copyeditor: Managed Editing
Associate Editor: Jennifer Warren
Cover Designer: Michael Buckingham
Book Designer: April Mostek
Production Coordinator: Zinnia Heinzmann
Photography Assistant: Gabriel Martinez
Cover photography by stockfilmstudio / Envato Elements and
KYNASTUDIO / Envato Elements
Portrait photography owned by Michael Schlueter

Published by C&T Publishing, Inc., P.O. Box 1456, Lafayette, CA 94549

Library of Congress Control Number: 2022930609

Printed in the USA
POD Edition

Dedication and Thanks

I can always think of so many people to thank as I continue to write, but none are more important than my readers. Without you and your feedback, my words would have less importance.

My husband, Keith Hazelwood, has worn so many hats as he's helped me through the years. He's there emotionally for me, but more than ever, he's a physical source of assistance as I continue to age. Thank you, Keith, for your love, help, and support.

Patti Williamson of the *Pulse* newspaper wrote a great review of my first book in this series, *Quilters of the Door*. This was so helpful to introduce me to a new state and county that I loved. On one of my recent trips, she and her husband took the time to give us a tour of some of the areas I was less familiar with. This is the kind of hospitality I've found all over Door County. Patti is an amazing historian, writer, civic leader, and friend who deserves my dedication for this book. Thank you, Patti, for all that you and your husband have done to promote my happy place.

—*Ann Hazelwood*

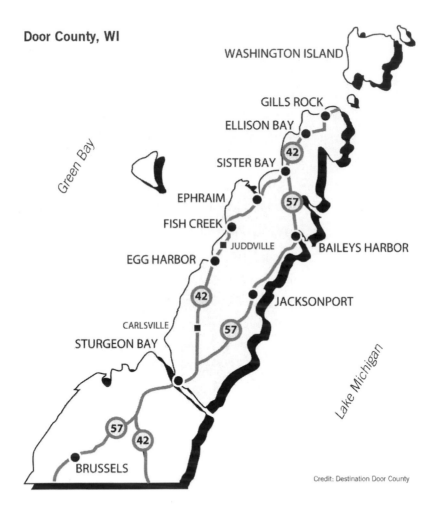

Door County, WI

WASHINGTON ISLAND

GILLS ROCK

ELLISON BAY

Green Bay

SISTER BAY
42

EPHRAIM
57

FISH CREEK

JUDDVILLE

EGG HARBOR

BAILEYS HARBOR

42

JACKSONPORT

CARLSVILLE
57

STURGEON BAY

Lake Michigan

57
42

BRUSSELS

Credit: Destination Door County

WHO ARE THE QUILTERS OF THE DOOR?

CHER CLAMPTON, 56, grew up and attended school with Claire Stewart in Perryville, Missouri. After divorcing her husband, Cher moved from Green Bay to a small cabin in Fish Creek, Wisconsin. When her mother, Hilda, became ill, Cher returned to Perryville to take care of her, and Claire took up residence in her cabin. Cher happily moved back to Door County and rejoined the quilt club after her mother passed.

GRETA GREENSBURG is Swedish, in her sixties, and one of the charter members of the club. She led the group with an iron fist for the first several years, holding firm in keeping to the tradition of only nine members who are diverse in their quilting styles. That is, until Cher and Claire stirred things up. Greta makes quick and easy quilts and is one of the few members in the club who machine quilts.

MARTA BACHMAN is German. She's 58 and lives in Baileys Harbor. She took over as president of the quilt club after Greta stepped down. Her family owns a large orchard and dairy farm. Marta makes traditional quilts by hand. She typically has a large quilt frame set up in her home.

AVA MARIE CHANDLER is 55 and loves any kind of music. She served in the Army, where she sang for anyone who would listen to her. She's blonde, vivacious, and likes to make quilts that tell a story. She loves her alcohol, so no one knows when her flamboyant behavior will erupt. Until recently, she lived in a Victorian house in Egg Harbor.

FRANCES McCRAKEN is the eldest member of the group at 79 years old. She regularly spends time in the local cemetery where her late husband is buried. She lives in the historic Corner House in Sturgeon Bay and has a pristine antique quilt collection that she inherited. The quilts she makes use old blocks to make new designs.

LEE SUE CHAN is Filipina and is married to a cardiologist. The couple live in an ornate home in Ephraim. She is 49 years old and belongs to the Moravian Church, also in Ephraim. Lee is an art quilter who loves flowers and landscapes. She is an award-winning quilter who is known for her fine hand appliqué.

OLIVIA WILLIAMS is Black and lives in an apartment over the Novel Bay Booksellers in Sturgeon Bay. She is 41, single, and likes to tout the styles of the Gee's Bend quilts as well as quilts from the South. She is quiet in nature, but the quilts she makes are scrappy, bright, and bold.

RACHAEL McCARTHY lives on a farm between Egg Harbor and Fish Creek. She is 51 years old and recently widowed. She has a part-time job bartending at Bayside Tavern in Fish Creek, and with the help of her fiancé, Harry, she runs a successful barn quilt business and sells Christmas trees in season. Rachael makes the business unique by giving each customer a small wall quilt to match their purchased barn quilt.

GINGER GREENSBURG, a 40-year-old redhead, is Greta's niece. Recently divorced, she owns a shop in Sister Bay where she sells vintage and antique items. She resides upstairs and has two children. While she works in the shop, Ginger likes to make quilted crafts to sell, and she repurposes old quilt tops.

AMY BURRIS, 41, owns the Jacksonport Cottage in Jacksonport, Wisconsin, where she also lives with her husband. She sells Amish quilts and other items made by the Amish.

ANNA MARIE MEYER, 46, is the niece and goddaughter of Marta. She's single and just moved to Door County from Ludwigsburg, Germany. She does dimensional quilting and is a fabulous baker. She owns a building in Baileys Harbor, where she opened Anna's Bake Shop, and lives upstairs.

CLAIRE STEWART, 56, is single and the main character of the series. She became a member of the quilting club when her friend Cher moved back to Missouri to take care of her mother. Claire was eager to leave Missouri and moved into Cher's cabin in Fish Creek. Greta and the quilt club made a rare exception to let Claire replace Cher until Cher moved back to Door County. Claire, a blonde who is showing some gray streaks, is a quilter and watercolor artist who sells her art-work in galleries and on her website. Claire's brother, a journalist and author, and her mother live in Missouri.

Chapter 1

"I can't possibly marry you!" I told him.

Grayson leaned back in shock but said nothing.

I continued, "First of all, we've never discussed a future life together and what it would even look like. You have a daughter who may never accept me, and that would destroy us as a couple. Please don't get me wrong; I've totally fallen in love with you, but I'm not convinced you have with me. What prompted you to ask me right now?"

Grayson shook his head in disbelief and examined me in silence. His eyes stared right through me. "I truly feel I would like to spend the rest of my life with you, Claire. I know I'm not much for words, and I'm not as gushy as some men, but I always felt you and I were on the same level about our relationship."

"Grayson, in some sense you may be right; but marriage? Kelly doesn't even want to share Christmas brunch with me, much less have me move into her home."

"Kelly will be off to college soon, and she really doesn't know what she wants. One minute I think she's trying to push me to marry again, and then some days she just wants to be that spoiled little girl I raised."

"I can't fault her for that, Grayson. You're all she has. The thought of sharing you with me has to be scary for her. I'm really the first woman you've dated since Marsha died. Life without her is new to both of you. You may even want to date others to make sure I'm the one."

His eyes showed anger and disbelief. "Claire Stewart, we're no longer in high school. I'm a mature adult, and I know what I want. I didn't come on strong in the beginning because I wanted to get to know you first. I know you now. I don't want to waste my time with women I don't know and am uncomfortable with. It took me a while, but I found comfort in you."

"I know. I went through all that as well. After leaving Austen, the last thing I wanted to do was get involved in another relationship."

"Yes, I know," he said sadly.

"The ring you picked out is absolutely gorgeous, but you need to close the box and put it back in your pocket. Did you think I was going to say yes and jump out of this carriage in excitement?"

Grayson looked to the ground in sadness as he put the ring away. "I did think you would accept. I even thought we'd have a conversation about when our wedding should be. I don't want to lose you, Claire."

"I don't want to lose you either, Grayson, but I'm not going to commit to an arrangement I'm not comfortable with."

His look turned to pain. "I get it. Your message has come across loud and clear. I must admit, I need to digest what you've said. You just punched a hole in my ego and my heart. I guess we need to be on our way, then."

"Grayson, look at me," I said, turning his face toward me. "I love you."

He only nodded, and it broke my heart. We got out of the carriage and walked to the car in silence. We remained quiet until we arrived in front of my cabin. Neither of us wanted to speak first.

"This was an incredible evening, Grayson. I thank you so much, and I hope you don't let this refusal come between us."

He nodded without looking at me. Then he leaned over and gave me a light kiss on the cheek, which told me things were definitely different now. I said good night and walked myself to the door.

Chapter 2

Once inside, I wondered if I'd been dreaming. Did I really just refuse a proposal from a man I loved? Did I just imagine the gorgeous, expensive ring that I told him to put away?

Part of me wanted to pat myself on the back for being the grown-up in the carriage, and the other part worried that I may have just made the biggest mistake of my life.

The steps to my bedroom felt larger and looked fuzzy. I was in a daze. Tonight was a New Year's Eve I would always remember, for better or worse.

I woke up the next morning still in my clothes. I must have passed out amidst my dark thoughts. I decided to shed my negativity by showering and letting things wash away. I was the one to decide what my day and my mood would be today. I should be pleased to have received a proposal at all. I would have loved one from Austen when we were together, but instead, I wasted five years without one. If Grayson decided to give me the cold shoulder, so be it. He might be grateful one day that I turned him down. If Kelly knew that he'd proposed, I'm sure she would agree with my decision.

I dressed and drank my first cup of coffee on a positive note. It was a new year, and Cher would have the final papers any day now on the sale of the cabin. It's strange how things work out. I'd moved into the cabin as a favor for Cher when she needed to go back to Missouri to take care of her mother. But I fell in love with it, Door County, and so much more once I settled in.

I went out on the porch to my studio and looked at my latest commissioned piece sitting on the easel. This one was special since it represented a romantic time for my client. It was a scene on the pier at Peninsula State Park, where my client had proposed to his wife many years before. He wanted to give her this painting for their anniversary.

As I was dressing for the day, I heard my cell ringing from the kitchen. I quickly ran down the stairs with hopes of Grayson being on the other end. I was disappointed when I heard Cher's voice.

"Happy New Year, Claire Bear! I didn't wake you, did I? Are you alone?"

"Funny thought, Cher Bear. Happy New Year to you as well. So, were you with Carl last night?"

"I was until three o'clock, when we decided to close the gallery. We had a little New Year's toast with some wine from his stash before I went home. I was okay with that. By the way, can you come by today to sign the papers? My realtor is stopping by around one o'clock."

"Absolutely, with bells on. I love that I'm purchasing the cabin on New Year's Day!"

"That seemed fitting to me, too! You know you can still back out, right?"

"I wouldn't think of it. I should have decided to do this sooner."

"It's awesome that you'll be owning the place so I can still visit. I put so much of myself in it."

"I can tell by that beautiful album you gave me. I will try my best to keep that up. Don't forget—we see the town board this week to get approval for including vendors in our quilt show."

"Oh, I haven't forgotten. I was talking to Carl about it, and he offered to go with us in case we had to argue the case for including vendors."

"It's probably a good idea to include Carl because I can imagine that their first argument will be that including vendors in our show will hurt the local vendors."

"That's what I've been thinking as well, so I'll tell him to join us. So, I take it you had a good New Year's Eve? I remember that Grayson was going to surprise you, so where did you go?"

"The English Inn, which was very nice and private for us. The real surprise was that he had a horse and carriage waiting for us after dinner."

"You've got to be kidding me! How romantic is that!"

"It was very romantic. Hey, I need to get some things done before I join you, so I'd better get going."

"Do you want to come earlier for lunch? I have some ham for sandwiches, if that'll do."

"That sounds great. Should I bring more Christmas cookies?"

Cher chuckled. "Please don't. I'll take care of everything. See you soon."

I hung up feeling proud of myself for not going into the drama of last night. Cher was my very best friend, so she'd find out soon enough. Today was a new day, and I was going to rejoice and be glad in it.

Chapter 3

As I got back to work on my commissioned piece, I remembered that the Quilters of the Door quilt club would be meeting soon for the first time in this new year. I actually looked forward to attending the meetings now that Marta was our leader instead of the previous drill sergeant, Greta. We now could invite new members, which was never allowed before. Cher and I had upset the apple cart by receiving great support for our outdoor quilt show. It had opened the flood gates for change.

I covered my easel for the day to ready myself for Cher's when Mom called.

"Happy New Year, sweetie!" she greeted.

"Happy New Year to you, Mom! Did you stay up until midnight?"

"Oh, gracious, no! I watched TV for a little while and then went to bed at my normal time. There were firecrackers all night long in the neighborhood, so it was hard to get sleep."

"Did Bill stop by?"

"He's coming for lunch, so he should be here soon."

"What are you fixing?"

"I have a baked chicken and decided to make my homemade dressing."

"All for lunch?" I could hear her chuckle.

"Bill and I like our big meal around lunch, and of course he loves home cooking. I almost forgot how to make the dressing. Like you tell me all the time, 'If you don't use it, you lose it.'"

"That's right. Oh, I can just smell that meal now. I wish I could stop by to have some with you."

"I do, too, honey! So did you and Grayson have a nice time last night?"

"We did," I answered simply. "I'm about to leave for Cher's to sign the papers on the cabin and share a little lunch with her."

"Congratulations once again! It's a big day for you. Please wish her a happy New Year for me."

"I will. Enjoy your lunch with Bill, and thanks for the call. It's good to hear your voice."

"I love you, sweetie. Take care."

I took a deep breath as we hung up. It would truly upset her if I told her about refusing Grayson's proposal. When they met last Christmas, they'd really hit it off. I was happy she'd be seeing Bill today. They seemed to enjoy each other's company.

The last thing I did before leaving was write that big check for the cabin. I thought of my inheritance from my dad that I was using for it. He told my brother, Michael, and me to save it for our big dreams, so here was mine. Little did I know when Dad passed that I would be spending my share in Door County, Wisconsin.

Sitting in my Subaru, ready to leave for Cher's, I examined the cabin with admiration but also with my dreams for the future in mind. There were so many things I wanted to improve and add, like a garage for my vehicle. In time, I'd make it my own.

Cher was preparing lunch when I arrived.

"Hey, have you heard from Ericka lately?" I inquired.

"I did! She called to wish me a happy New Year. She seems optimistic about starting chemo next week. I would be a nervous wreck."

"A good attitude helps, and not everyone has the same reaction to treatment."

"It helps that she has a job at the clinic to come back to. I'm sure it provides some peace of mind for her. And all her coworkers have been so supportive."

"Did you tell her I bought the cabin?"

"I did, and she was happy for both of us."

"So do we eat before we sign or what?"

"My realtor should be here any moment, but she can't stay. We may as well eat."

Minutes later, the young, attractive realtor arrived and introduced herself with a card. She was all business, and I could tell she wanted to be on her way.

"You're getting a good buy here, Miss Stewart," she said as she laid the papers on the table for my signature.

"Yes, I realize that. I think she's giving me such a deal because the cabin came with a cat." She didn't appear to know what I meant.

We each signed in three different places, and then I handed her the check.

"Congratulations to the two of you!" she said before she went out the door.

Cher and I looked at each other expecting thunder and lightning.

"You really didn't need a realtor for this, you know."

"I know, but I don't mind her making a little money off of it. So, shall we make a toast with our iced teas?"

We did just that and helped ourselves to the ham sandwiches. Cher received a call from Carl as we finished, and she discretely talked with him for a few minutes.

Chapter 4

"So, what did your boss have to say?" I asked when she rejoined me.

"He was just excited about Foster Collins coming this week to bring another painting. He wants to take us both to lunch. I think Carl sold one of his big paintings, and this is Foster's way of thanking us."

"Was it the one with a $5,000 price tag on it?"

She nodded. "Carl thinks Foster could have gotten even more, if you can believe it. By the way, Carl said if you're free, you're welcome to join us for lunch."

"Me? Why?"

"I didn't ask why, but you said you'd met him before, and you're one of the artists in Carl's gallery. Carl said you went crazy when you met him."

"Oh, I did. Yes, of course I want to go if you don't think it's odd."

"We may not have much notice on a date, but I'll let you know."

"Have you heard from Carole or Linda lately?"

"No, but you have to remember, Claire, that these girls have lives that include a husband," Cher said with sarcasm.

I laughed and nodded as she continued, "So, tell me more about this carriage ride last night."

I took a deep breath. "Cher, I have to confess something, but it's got to be one of those cross-your-heart-and-hope-to-die secrets like we used to have when we were younger. I really don't want this news out there, if you know what I mean."

Cher looked puzzled but nodded in agreement. "What's so secretive about having a romantic carriage ride?" she teased. "Did you do something mischievous?" she snickered.

"Stop! I'm serious."

"Okay, okay. Sorry."

"Cher, Grayson asked me to marry him last night, and I turned him down," I said, not really believing my own words.

"You'd better repeat that, Claire Bear. I think I misheard."

"You heard me correctly."

"I hope you have a really good explanation, my friend."

I began explaining to her about the awkward brunch I had at Grayson's house Christmas morning and how rude Kelly's behavior was. I shared that we'd never once talked about marriage. I tried to explain how bothered Grayson was about all of it and how I felt that his proposal was some way of making it up to me. I told her I felt I did the right thing under the circumstances.

"I think we need to open this bottle of Chardonnay," Cher suggested as she took the bottle off the counter. "So how did he take it?"

"Not well. I think I bruised his ego big-time."

"Oh, I'm sure you did. That's why men don't ask in the first place. Every man is terrified about rejection, and that's the biggest rejection of all."

"So, what makes you such an authority?"

"Carl just said to me the other day that he doesn't know how he would have handled rejection from me, especially since I'm an employee."

"I can imagine. Grayson really did take his time to ask me out, or even to acknowledge me at first. He hasn't dated anyone but me since Marsha died."

"Well, you've got a widower who has put his dead wife on a pedestal for a long time, and he hasn't wanted anyone to replace the mother of his child. What he didn't plan on was falling in love with you. I think it's an important fact that he didn't ask Kelly before proposing to you. That's a good sign."

"Yeah, it was obvious he didn't consult Kelly. He probably knew she would have advised against it, and he didn't want to hear it."

"So, he hasn't called today?"

I shook my head. "I think he's embarrassed and hurt. I don't think I'll hear from him for a while, or maybe ever."

"Ever?"

"I have to prepare myself for that, and it won't be easy. I've really fallen in love with him, but we never once talked about our future together. This proposal was so unexpected."

"That is a bit odd, I have to admit. Man, and to think you would have loved to have had a proposal from Austen."

"I know, but that worked out for the best. I may never get another proposal at my age, but that's okay. I told Grayson early on that I never had plans to marry but that I did want to be in a loving relationship. I decided I would never pressure him on anything permanent."

"No, you wouldn't. That's not your style. At some point, ya know, folks are going to notice that the two of you are no longer together."

"I know, but I'll have to cross that bridge when I come to it. I'm sure Grayson's worried about what I'll tell everyone."

"Well, I crossed my heart and hoped to die, so there won't be anything from me."

"Thanks, Cher Bear. Mom would just die if she knew I did this."

"Maybe not," Cher said, giving me a hug. "She would tell you to go with your heart. Hey, let's get off this topic and toast to that little cabin in the woods."

Chapter 5

The following two weeks were depressing. Besides another big snowfall, not much had been going on, and I hadn't heard a word from Grayson. I was hoping that this morning's quilt club meeting and tomorrow night's town board meeting would cheer me up.

My commissioned painting of the pier in Peninsula Park was complete. I had to stop looking for things to change. I planned to tell Carl it was ready when I saw him at the town board meeting tomorrow.

I loved looking at the *Pulse* newspaper to see what was going on around town. I was tempted to attend one of the Sunday afternoon movies at the library. Meeting new people might get me through to spring when I could putter around in the yard.

At the moment, the most exciting thing for me was looking forward to having lunch with Foster Collins, Cher, and Carl. We'd had an earlier date set up, but it was cancelled when the big snow arrived. Hopefully, Carl would share the new date at tomorrow night's board meeting.

There was still plenty of snow on the ground when I left for the quilt club meeting, but thankfully it didn't take me long to clear off my Subaru. And I didn't have to worry about clearing a path to the car because Tom, the handyman I shared with Dan and Cotsy Bittner next door, took such good care of me.

When I arrived at the library parking lot, there were very few cars. I glanced around for Ava's car. She'd been MIA for a while because of troubles with her husband, whom she was divorcing. I was happy she'd contacted me toward the end of December to tell me she was okay and staying somewhere safe, as we'd been worried about her before that. How would the other quilt members react after her long absence? Would they expel her from the club? If Greta was still in charge, Ava definitely would have been removed by now.

I picked up the mail from my box at the adjoining post office and then met Cher at the library door when she arrived. I could tell from her face what she was going to ask me, so I intercepted.

"I know that look means you're wondering if I've heard from Grayson. The answer is no." She gave me a hand squeeze to show support.

"Good morning, ladies!" our new president, Marta, greeted us. "I'm happy you're here since we had to move our regularly scheduled meeting time a bit later in January. I'm concerned that we may not have a quorum today, but let's wait and see. Anna brought some strudel, so please help yourself until more members arrive."

I was surprised to see Olivia and Frances had made it since they had the longest drives from Sturgeon Bay.

"Olivia, are you still working at the quilt shop?" I asked with interest.

"I am. I tend to work more hours when the weather is bad because I live so close by."

"I'm so glad you're enjoying it," I nodded. "Hopefully after the town board meeting tomorrow, we'll have news regarding vendors at our show. I know Barn Door Quilts is eager to become one."

"I do hope it works out, and of course I'd like to be the one working their booth," Olivia noted. "You're not counting on me doing another exhibit like last year, are you?"

"No, we're not counting on you, but your quilts really were colorful in the park," I complimented. "We want to have new things every year if possible."

In walked Ginger, Lee, and Amy. That was enough for a quorum, so we were able to start the meeting.

"Welcome ladies!" Marta called out. "I'm pleased you all made it safely because Greta happens to have a birthday today, and we can help her celebrate." Greta blushed and seemed surprised. "We've never acknowledged birthdays before like we should, so Greta, I have a nice gift for you that was donated by Nelson's in Fish Creek."

"Oh, my goodness," Greta responded.

"Nelson's gave us several giveaways for later meetings, but here's a lovely garden box with seeds and a gardening apron for you today." Everyone clapped.

"Thank you so much!" Greta stammered. "This is quite a surprise."

"I think everyone is here but Ava and Rachael," Marta noted as she looked about the room. "I hope they're okay. I want to thank Anna, who brought us more calories this morning." Everyone chuckled. "Now Anna has an announcement to make."

"Yes, I do," Marta's German niece blushed with her head hanging down. "I have a house now, close to Aunt Marta, and I hope that in a couple of months or so, I will have a bakery on the first floor." Another round of clapping followed her news.

"Her uncle is working hard with a contractor, and there's so much more red tape than we thought," explained Marta. "Even when we think we will be ready, things have to be inspected, but I guess you all know such things."

"Will we get an invitation when you open?" Ginger asked.

"Oh, yes!" Anna replied cheerfully.

Chapter 6

"Today for our program, I asked Ginger to bring some of the products she makes from old vintage pieces," Marta announced. "I was impressed with some of the clever things she came up with to repurpose linens, so I asked her to speak about how she got started doing this. Ginger, you have the floor."

"Thanks, Marta," she began. "First I have to say how flattered I am that Marta thinks what I do is rather unique. I got started repurposing when my aunt left me with drawers full of linens and doilies. It didn't take me long to recognize that customers were attracted to what I was doing, and my things started selling."

Ginger began passing around her pot holders, collars, pincushions, pillows, and ornaments that were made out of old quilts and dresser scarves. She then showed how she cuts off the ends of linens to use on children's clothing and pillows that need some embellishment. One of her pillows used men's ties to make a Dresden Plate pattern. It reminded me of all Dad's ties that Michael gave me for Christmas. It made me curious what she would suggest if she had the tie collection I now do. Her eyes grew big when I told her I had a large bag full from several generations.

"Oh, Claire, you're so lucky," Ginger praised. "Old ties are fascinating, and some are worth a lot of money. I can show you how to remove their linings for the projects that require a lot of cutting. A Bow Tie quilt pattern is often used for making quilts out of them."

"Thanks, Ginger!" I replied. "If I ever get around to doing something with them, I'm sure I'll have more questions."

There were a couple more questions before we went on to show-and-tell. The best show was Olivia's bold log cabin quilt in bright, solid colors. Greta showed a vintage lavender appliqué quilt top she was working on that had come from a kit. A relative had asked her to finish it.

"I'm not the best person to do appliqué, like some of you ladies," Greta admitted. "Lee, please don't examine it up close," she teased.

Frances showed some beading she was trying out for the first time. Amy presented some small Amish doll quilts she had in the shop for sale. Lee selected one she wanted to purchase.

When Marta asked if there were any announcements, I told them Cher and I were going to the town board to get the permit for our show as well as permission to include vendors this year. I watched Greta look to the floor as if she disapproved of our intentions.

After Marta adjourned the meeting, Amy came up to me and said she was interested in becoming a vendor, if possible.

"Please don't count on anything just yet, Amy," I warned. "This is a touchy issue for the board, but we'll see what happens tomorrow."

"Well, good luck!" she said as she left.

"Do you have time for lunch?" Cher asked.

"I shouldn't take the time, but we do need to go over our talking points for the meeting," I noted.

"Sure!" Cher nodded. "How about just going over to the Blue Horse since it's close?

As we walked over in unshoveled snowy paths, I worried about whether I would run into Grayson. It was at the Blue Horse where I'd first seen the handsome man with the red scarf. Oh, how I missed him. What had I done?

As luck would have it, Grayson was there having lunch with the same attractive girl I'd seen him with months ago.

"Cher, I can't do this," I said, motioning over to where Grayson was sitting. "We have to leave."

"For heaven's sake, Claire, you can't run away from him forever in this small town. Just act like nothing's wrong. He may not even see you."

I took a deep breath and made a quick order for tomato bisque soup and iced tea. Cher led the way as she tried to avoid going near Grayson's table.

I was about to be seated when Grayson looked my way. We stared at each other for what seemed like a lifetime. I finally smiled and gave him a tiny wave. He turned away and didn't respond. I wanted to throw up in my soup as Cher stared at me.

Chapter 7

"Cher, he stared at me and turned away," I said with grave disappointment.

"Well, he just doesn't know what to say or do, that's all. Give him some time. At least he knows you're not ignoring him."

While she dug into her turkey sandwich, I sat there knowing my best friend had a way of making more sense than I did at times. She also was brutally honest with me if she had to be.

"Do you still want me to talk first at the meeting? If I do, then you need to be the one to ask for permission for the vendors. Carl can then follow up with support for your request. Agreed?"

I sat there watching her lips move, but I didn't absorb a word she said.

"Claire? Claire, are you present?" she said as she tapped my hand.

"Sure. Sure."

"Are you going to eat your soup before it gets cold?" I smiled and nodded.

While I force-fed myself, I saw Grayson and his companion get up to leave. He didn't look my way or come over to say hello. It was a clear sign of rejection. Cher was staring at me.

"Claire, relax. Don't make too much of this. So, what did you make of Ava being absent again for quilt club?" I shrugged. Ava was the last person on my mind.

As we left to go back to our cars at the library, we were both silent. Cher knew I was hurting inside, and words were not going to make it better.

Tom was cleaning my steps of leftover snow when I reached the cabin.

"I'm sorry I couldn't get here sooner, Miss Stewart," Tom apologized as he worked.

"It's okay. I understand tomorrow's temperature may melt most of this anyway. By the way, Tom, you may as well know that I purchased this cabin."

"Well, congratulations, Claire! I figured the longer you stayed here, the harder it would be to walk away. Do you still want me to do spring cleanup and mowing?"

"Absolutely! I hope I can make some improvements, like maybe having a garage built for my car."

"A garage?" he said in disbelief.

"I know. A garage is a rare relic around here because everyone goes away for the winter, but I live here all year long."

"You have a point, but you're going to have to jump through some hoops for that. I hope you know someone to advise you on that." I smiled and nodded.

"Say, did you want that shed repaired from the tree damage?"

"Oh, yes, I do."

"I'll get right to it since the Bittners are gone for the winter."

"Wonderful. Come spring, I want to do a bit more landscaping as well."

"Alrighty then, Miss Stewart, I'd better get on it."

I went inside with a smile on my face. I took off my coat and decided to make a fire because I planned to be holed in for the rest of the day. I needed to make some notes on what I was going to say at the town board meeting and do whatever else I could think of to keep my mind off of Grayson.

As the evening wore on, Puff didn't leave my side. It was as if she sensed I was sad. I quilted on one of my *Quilted Snow* pieces until I started to doze off. At nine o'clock, I was startled by my cell phone ringing. It was Rachael.

Chapter 8

"I was missing you, girlfriend," Rachael kindly noted. "I hope you had a good quilt meeting."

"Yeah, I miss you, too. I have to admit, I miss not coming to the barn to work like I did during the Christmas season. How are things going?"

"We've been busy doing what we do when the Christmas trees are gone. I'm focusing now on our wedding plans."

"Of course! Have you decided on a date?"

"Everyone wants to be a June bride, so it will be around that first week, I think."

"That's so exciting! Are you and Harry planning something big or small?"

"We agreed on small, but you know Harry. I've never seen him do anything small!"

I laughed. She continued, "I've been thinking about something, and you don't have to say yes, but I hope you will. Would you be my maid of honor, Claire?"

"Are you serious? Surely there's someone better than me."

"So, is that a yes?"

"Absolutely, Rachael. What an honor."

"Well, girl, you were there from the very beginning of my relationship with Harry, and it means a lot that you also knew Charlie."

"Many knew and loved Charlie."

"I know, but you understand that I didn't intend for this romance to start between Harry and me. It's our love for Charlie that really brought us together."

"I know, and it's beautiful. I love weddings. This will be the wedding of all weddings."

"Well, maybe you'll have one yourself one day soon, the way you and Grayson are going."

I ignored her comment. "So, what else have you planned? Are you getting married in a church?"

"That's still up for discussion, but we did decide that our reception will be here at the farm. Harry had planned to expand the patio anyway for entertainment purposes, so this could be our answer for that."

"Oh, that will be perfect. I have a feeling you have lots of entertainment in store for you, my dear. By the way, has he been out to Washington Island recently to check on his man cave?"

She chuckled. "Not this winter, but he has someone check on it regularly. He likes to tease me by saying that's where we'll end up living one day when we're old and gray."

"I hope you quickly cleared that up."

"I sure did, but he knows how to rile me up."

"How come we missed you at quilt club?"

"Don't tell anyone, but I just forgot. A customer was picking up a barn quilt this morning, and that's where my focus was."

"It was Greta's birthday, and Marta gave her a donated gift from Nelson's. She was mighty surprised."

"Lands! We've never celebrated birthdays before."

"Well, Marta said we're starting now, and what better person to start with than Greta? She was so surprised that she didn't recite any rules we broke!" We both burst into laughter.

"Now I'm sorry I missed it."

"Hey, you didn't tell me who was going to be the best man in the wedding."

"I know you'd love to walk down with Grayson, but Harry's going to ask Kent. They're becoming closer and closer as father and son."

"Aww, Kent's perfect as best man, and I'm happy to hear about their relationship. Thanks for calling, Rachael. I'm looking forward to this."

After we hung up, I put out the fire and went up to bed. Visions of Rachael and Harry's wedding began filling my thoughts. They were a sweet couple who had a lot of fun together. Their love of Charlie, Rachael's first husband and Harry's best friend, had unified them initially. This may be the closest it comes for me to be in a wedding.

The next morning, I woke up with a touch of anxiety thinking about the evening's town board meeting. As I sat at the kitchen table, I read over all my notes. I was hoping I'd see familiar faces at the meeting because last year some members told me how much they enjoyed our show. After this meeting, Cher and I would discuss other ideas about the show. I wanted some changes, but not too many at one time. I had to think of a way to engage more quilters so it would become their show, not just ours. I also hoped we could get all our volunteers back again. Of course, I couldn't count on Grayson or Kelly this year. Just as I thought of Kelly, my cell rang, and her name showed up. What could this be about?

"Claire, this is Kelly," she announced shyly.

"Kelly, what a surprise. How are you?"

"I'm fine. I just wanted to call and apologize for my behavior at Christmas. Dad said I was very rude, and I didn't mean to be."

"Oh, Kelly, your apology is accepted, but I wasn't offended. You have every right to protect your dad."

"Well, that's all I wanted to say. Thanks for being so nice."

"I truly appreciate your call."

She hung up after that. The rest of the day I wondered what on earth was going on over at the Wills household. Did her dad know she called, or was it just her way of fixing things? Maybe Grayson insisted she apologize. Hmm.

Chapter 9

"Hello, ladies," a woman greeted us as we arrived fifteen minutes early at the library.

"You are Miss Bennet, if I remember correctly?" I said with hesitation.

"That's correct. Please have a seat out here, and they will call you when they're ready," she instructed. "You are first on the agenda."

Carl joined us then, so I introduced him to Miss Bennet. We had barely sat down when we heard the call to go into the board room.

The chairman introduced himself, and then it was our turn for introductions.

Cher began talking, as we'd planned. She told them we were pleased with the success of last year's show and hoped we could plan on having the event as we did last year at the same time and place. I got to watch everyone's expressions, and their faces were stone cold.

"Madam Secretary, did you receive any complaints or reported problems from last year?" the chairman asked.

"No, sir," she shook her head with a smile. "There were none reported."

"That's good to hear," the chairman responded.

"I would like Claire to add an additional request for this year, if we may," Cher stated as she looked toward me.

"Thank you, members, for hearing us once again. We're so pleased that not only did we create a wonderful venue for quilters to show their quilts, we entertained the tourists and the local community as well. As a result of this success, we've been contacted by many businesses who would like to become vendors at this event. I know last year you were concerned about taking business away from the local businesses. We took that concern to heart. Because we want this show to represent the whole county, there are businesses like the quilt shops in Jacksonport and Sturgeon Bay that would like to be a part of this event."

"Please let me interrupt you, Miss Stewart," one of the members said. "This board does not represent the whole county. We represent this area—in particular, Fish Creek—and we want to make sure that our businesses are protected as well as the ambiance of the area. Now, when you talk about vendors, where would you put them? You certainly wouldn't want to put them in front of or near our existing businesses."

"I understand your point," I began. "Last year we had exhibits at Noble Park, which worked out nicely. That's where we plan to put any vendors." At that point, Carl stood up.

"If I may address the board," Carl said. "My name is Carl Johnson, and I'm the owner of Art of Door County on Main Street here in Fish Creek. I came this evening to lend support to these ladies, who are requesting that some vendors be allowed to participate. As a business owner, I know vendors add value to the event and increase traffic and profits for all existing businesses. I would personally be interested in having an additional space at the park. As a result of last year's quilt show, I've even expanded my business into the next shop to carry quilts. I'd be willing to pay a fee, as I'm sure others would be, to offset any maintenance involved. I think I know most of our merchants pretty well, and they see the merit in expanding this event."

"Thank you, Mr. Johnson," the chairman said. "Aren't you concerned that having all this activity outdoors will affect your sales inside the store?"

"Not in the least," Carl stated. "I think it will increase the street traffic."

"Miss Stewart, have you thought ahead about what guidelines you would require your vendors to have?" another member of the board asked.

"Somewhat," I reported.

"The director at the Noble House might be concerned that vendors at this event would take away from tourists who would like to visit the museum, just as they could take attention away from your quilts on the street."

"I certainly understand your point," I said graciously. "From what I was told, the attendance inside the museum increased last year when we had the show. It was a good opportunity for them to expose the museum to folks who may have never taken the time to visit." The board member looked surprised by my answer.

"Well, that's all good to hear," he replied. "You know the grass will taking a beating, and there will be significant trash, so I suggest you have a serious conversation with the director there to see what concerns they may have." I nodded.

"As far as last year's show is concerned, I think you surprised us with your creativity and attendance," the chairman said. "My wife was delighted with all of it and wondered if you were going to expand the quilts beyond Main Street."

"We hope so," I responded. "If we have the quilts to expand, I would like to include the shops on the top of the hill. Last year we had requests from them to be included."

"That's interesting," the chairman said, nodding.

Chapter 10

"I think from what I'm hearing, Miss Stewart, I will make a recommendation, supported by a vote, of course, that you once again receive a permit for the quilt show; however, regarding the vendors, I say we recommend this on two conditions. Number one is that you have approval from the Noble House director, and number two is that you don't exceed more than five vendors to see how it works out."

"That doesn't include our exhibits, does it?" Cher interrupted.

"Five vendors," he repeated. "If the director feels you can fit them all in, we'll leave that up to them."

"I'll second that motion," a member to the right of me voiced.

"All in favor say aye," the chairman requested. Everyone said aye, and no one opposed. "Okay, the ayes have it, so we'll be mailing your permit after the clerk makes these conditional use changes."

"Thank you so much," I said sincerely. "We will proceed then."

The three of us walked out of the room in silence. Once in the parking lot, we didn't know whether to cheer or not.

"I say we digest all this with a Bayside Coffee," Carl suggested with a grin.

We headed to the trendy tavern on Main Street, where their popular, potent coffee was waiting for us. I wasn't sure I was up to it, but it appeared I had no choice.

While we waited at the bar for our server, Cher was the first to bring up the meeting.

"So, what do you think?" she began.

"Well, we got our permit," I stated with confidence. "I do worry about what the director will have to say."

"I think you basically got what you wanted," Carl noted. "It's just watered down a bit, and that's not all bad."

"I'm not too worried," Cher added. "I got to know the director a bit last year. She was very supportive of the show and loved the traffic to the museum, so I'll go talk to her if you'd like."

"Oh, Cher, that would be great," I said with relief.

"Now, if you don't think I'm out of line here, this is how I would approach her," Carl offered. "You two lay out exactly what you want and where you would place the vendors. That takes the guesswork out of it for her. You don't want her to be involved with the planning. If she has a simple suggestion or two, jump on it to please her."

"Good idea. Right, Cher?" I said as I looked for her approval.

"By the way, ladies, I withdraw my request to vend at the show," he informed us. "You're going to get so many requests that you can't accommodate. I'm lucky to be located in the area. I think the quilt shops in Door County need to be there."

"Good point, Carl," I nodded. "Thanks for offering to bow out."

Now the bartender had our attention as he began creating the art that is the Bayside Coffee. He told us it was a mix of cordials with just a bit of coffee, topped with whipped cream. He told us to watch for flames to appear as he completed the dazzling drink.

The crowd around us cheered as they watched the process. All their faces were on us as we took our first sips. I wish someone had taken our picture at the moment we toasted our next quilt show. Cher and Carl consumed the drink with gusto. I could see the two of them exchanging looks, which was the cue for me to leave.

"Carl, would you see to it that this lady gets a ride home?" I teased.

"I think I can handle that," he winked.

"Thanks for your support tonight," I said as I patted Carl on the shoulder. "This show never would have happened without your support."

"Now that's a pretty strong statement coming from the two bears," he joked. "This means I'm the one you're coming after if this show fails!" Cher and I laughed and nodded.

As I walked out the door, I could feel the effects of the Bayside coffee. When I arrived home, I looked at my sad Christmas tree that was starting to lose its needles and decided I'd need to find time to take it down. The totality of the entire evening hit me and sent me straight to bed.

Chapter 11

The following week, I finally rid the cabin of the numerous signs of the Christmas holiday. Puff missed her tree, and so did I. I'd be finding stray tree needles in nooks and crannies for a while.

After much discussion, it was time for Cher to take our requests for the quilt show to the director of the Noble House. It remained closed for the season, so Cher had to work around the limited schedule.

Valentine's Day was getting closer, and I'd still received no word from my true valentine. I picked up a card at the Piggly Wiggly that said, "You're not here, but you're still in my heart." It was how I really felt, but if I sent it and got no response from Grayson, it would crush me. Cher believed I had nothing to lose but my pride.

A chamber of commerce breakfast meeting was scheduled for tomorrow at Pelletier's restaurant down the block. Grayson would expect me to be there since I lived so close. I was torn about what to do. Cher offered to accompany me for moral support.

At two o'clock, Cher called, and I still wasn't sure what to tell her.

"Claire, you're not going to believe what happened this morning," she began. "I ran into Barb McKesson at the Fish Creek Market, and I told her I was planning to meet with the Noble House director soon about our show. Barb is the president of the Historical Society there. Well, she said she was on her way there to see the director about a donation that just arrived, so she offered that I could come with her."

"Great! So, did you?"

"I did! I should have stopped by to tell you sooner, but I had to get home to meet with my computer guy. I did something stupid again, I'm sure."

"Well, how'd it go with the director?"

"Let's put it this way: Having Barb with me was half the victory. It took a while, but I was finally able to show Barb and the director the layout we were proposing."

"And then?"

"They both were quiet but nodded now and then. I went ahead and offered the Boy Scouts for cleanup since the town board was concerned about litter."

"Great idea. Are we good to go, then?"

"The only request was that we strictly enforce the hours of the show. They were concerned that the vendors especially would extend their welcome if there still was a crowd. I reminded them it would take them a while to pack up."

"I'll be sure to stress that in the letter to the vendors."

"The director did ask that we keep our vendors and exhibits to a minimum so there would be plenty of green space. I told her that was no problem. Now, what about that chamber meeting in the morning?"

"I suppose I should go because I have to carry on with my business. I'm sure Grayson is expecting me to be there. If he doesn't come, it may be to avoid me."

"I can't believe this is happening with the two of you."

"I thought you supported my decision to refuse his proposal."

"I do support it, but maybe you should have said you'd think it over, or you could have suggested waiting awhile."

"That's all good, except you weren't sitting there in the carriage with him staring at you waiting for an answer."

"Okay, don't get in a huff. So, should I just meet you there tomorrow morning?"

"No, please come get me. I don't want to walk in there alone."

"Now who's acting like we're in high school? Remember when we went to those dances at the KC Hall? We didn't dare walk in by ourselves."

"Some things never change, I suppose. See you tomorrow."

By late afternoon, I had to decide whether to mail Grayson's valentine; otherwise, he wouldn't receive it in time. If I mailed it at the post office, I could stop at the Blue Horse for a cup of coffee. Grayson would never be there this time of day.

I put Puff in her wicker chair so she'd know I'd be gone for a while. When I opened the door to delightful sunshine, I longed for spring and the arrival of the cherry blossoms. On my bucket list was to learn more about the cherry industry in this county.

When I got to the post office, I took a deep breath and dropped the card into the slot.

"Happy Valentine's Day," I whispered to myself.

Chapter 12

The Blue Horse was nearly empty when I arrived, which was rare. There were Valentine decorations here and there reminding everyone about the special holiday. When I received my mocha latte, there was a heart shape on top that just seemed to rub it in. I smiled, but I also wanted to cry. I had to admit, I was a romantic at heart, and it was hard being single right now.

As I enjoyed my chocolate chip bagel, I decided that nothing said love better than chocolate.

Austen came to my mind as I sat there. He loved to make a show at Valentine's Day with a dozen red roses, a box of dark chocolate candy, and dinner at the closest five-star restaurant he could find. He liked to be seen in the right five-star restaurant. He had a sense of flare when he put his mind to it, whereas Grayson tended to be more sensible and conservative. I can only imagine how excited Grayson was to plan our New Year's Eve, and then I spoiled it.

I sat on the porch side of the cafe looking out at the bay. I loved this spot for many reasons, besides the fact it was where Grayson and I met. I felt it captured the charm and scenic views of Door County. I wish I could have moved here sooner. My thoughts were interrupted by a call on my cell. It was Cher again.

"Sorry, Claire Bear, but I have to cancel going to the chamber meeting. George called, and Ericka is really sick from her treatment. He asked if I could stay with her tomorrow, so I'm going to help as I promised to."

"Of course! Oh, my heart goes out to that poor gal. You are her very best friend, and she needs you."

"She's such a proud person, as you know, so accepting help from anyone feels degrading to her. But George said she gets so weak from throwing up."

"I can only imagine. I will pray for both of you. If there's anything I can do, please let me know."

"I'm sorry to disappoint you about the chamber meeting, but I expect you to pull up your big-girl panties and show up by yourself."

I chuckled. "I'll think about it."

"Remember way back when you went to your first chamber meeting with me? It was at the same place."

"I do! Please give Ericka my best, okay?"

"I will."

I sat there thinking of the awful job ahead of Cher. It brought me back to reality pretty quickly. When you don't have your health, you don't have anything.

"Excuse me, but aren't you Claire Stewart?" a young woman asked.

"Yes, that's me," I said with a smile.

"Did you notice that there's a painting that you created on the wall here?"

"No, I hadn't noticed," I said, looking about the room.

"I work here, and when I saw it, I knew they had to have it," she explained. "I purchased it for them because they've been so good to me. It looks nice there, I think."

"Well, thank you so much for buying my painting," I responded. "I'm glad it found a good home."

"My name is Grace Mueller. I've seen you in here many times," she noted.

"It's nice to meet you, Grace. I appreciate your purchase." She nodded and left.

Why didn't I think of that nice gesture myself?

I finished my drink and went over to see the painting up close. I smiled and left the Blue Horse a much happier person than when I'd come in.

The rest of the day and evening I spent curled up in front of the fire, enjoying some of the frozen soup I'd saved for a rainy day. I thought about garage ideas, which circled me back to whether to attend the chamber meeting. If I went, perhaps I could find someone to help me with my garage project.

The only interruption I had was a text from Carole telling me she had heard that Austen had left on a trip.

[Claire]
Thanks for the update. I hope it helps him. I'm still enjoying the cookies I made from your cookie book. What book will come next?

[Carole]
***Coffee with Carole.* You know I'm all about good coffee. Do you like the title?**

[Claire]
It's perfect! You're something else, girlfriend. Keep me posted on it, okay?

[Carole]
Will do! Love you!

[Claire]
Love you too.

Chapter 13

I scrubbed my body nervously in the shower the next morning, feeling anxious about going to the chamber meeting.

I thought I'd dress in red since it was close to Valentine's Day. Grayson would definitely notice me then. I spoke to God before I left. He knew how to keep me calm and wise.

The meeting was better attended than it normally was, but that probably had something to do with one of the topics on the agenda: whether or not the tourism tax should be increased from five cents to eight cents on the dollar.

I took off my coat and stood in the buffet line, forgetting to look for Grayson. I did see some familiar faces. I spotted Carl in the distance if I needed someone to talk to.

I sat down at one of the oblong tables where there was an open seat. I looked at my plate and realized a full breakfast was not what I was used to. The woman next to me said hello but then continued her conversation with the men across the table. I happened to look up as I took my first bite, and there was Grayson helping himself to the coffee bar. As he waited his turn, he looked around and saw me. I smiled at him, but he turned away quickly. Why did he have to ignore me like that in public?

Stirred by a bit of anger, I rose and stood in line to get coffee at the same time. Once he'd filled his cup, I playfully took it from him as my own.

"Thank you, sir," I said politely. He didn't know how to react.

"You're welcome," he said awkwardly.

"How are you?" I asked. He looked down without responding. "I didn't expect this from you, Grayson. Here is your coffee. You can have it back." I handed him his cup and walked back to my table. I was shaking all over and wishing I hadn't come.

Thank goodness the meeting started soon afterward and Grayson's back was toward me. The topic of discussion did interest me, so I managed to forget about the snub I'd received at the coffee bar. The discussion became heated to the point of the president losing control of the meeting. I watched for any reaction or comments from Grayson, but he just sat there like he wasn't even listening. I'm sure he had plenty on his mind.

I left before the meeting was over to avoid any more contact with him.

When I arrived home, I needed something to quickly occupy my mind, so I decided to make my signature brownies. I could take some to Carl when I delivered my commissioned piece for Mr. Adams. Painting was becoming lucrative for me, but I think I really enjoyed making quilts more. The Noble Park piece I was just starting combined my love of quilting with my love of painting, so I was looking forward to digging into it more. Maybe I should donate it to the Noble House instead of selling it. It would be a nice way of thanking them for letting us use their park for our show.

As soon as I packaged the brownies, I headed toward the gallery. Carl always acted happy to see me.

"Hey, Claire! I just heard from Mr. Adams, and he had to cancel coming in today. I hope that doesn't inconvenience you."

"Not at all. However, he missed out on having one of these brownies I brought you."

"Oh no! Just my luck," he said with a chuckle. "I'll let you know when we can do that lunch with Foster Collins. He loves the White Gull Inn, so that's likely where we'll go."

"I'm thrilled to be included."

"I heard from Cher, and she has a tough job there, taking care of Ericka," he noted sadly.

"I know, but I'm glad Cher's there for her."

Chapter 14

Back at home, I decided to ignore the fact that tomorrow was February 14. I needed to focus on the good things in my life, not what was missing. I puffed up my pillow to get comfy when my cell phone rang. It was Cher.

"Claire, I'm sorry to call so late, but I just got home from being with Ericka. She's absolutely miserable. She keeps saying she's going to die, and I can see why she feels that way. I don't know how to make things better for her. I have to help her back to bed after she throws up because she's so weak. I've heard people talk about going through something like this, but seeing it in person is gut wrenching."

"Oh, that poor girl," I responded.

"George agreed to spend the night so I could go home."

"I'm sure he's taking this hard."

"Yes. He wonders whether she made the right decision on the treatment."

"We all know how strong she is, so I have no doubt she'll get through this. On another note, tomorrow is Valentine's Day, and it's bothering me more than I thought it would. Do you have plans?"

Cher chuckled. "If you're referring to Carl, no, I don't have plans. What do you have in mind?"

"Maybe a first-class meal. It'll be my treat. I just got a really nice check from the gallery."

"Well, I guess you've given up on Grayson. A fancy dinner sounds good, but you realize we're going to see a lot of romantic couples, right? I'm used to it, but I'm not sure you are."

"Frankly, it'll be better than sitting in front of the fireplace alone at the cabin. It may be hard to find reservations this late. I could try the inn nearby. Maybe Brenda will be working."

"You don't have to treat, Claire. I don't care where we go. If you have trouble getting reservations, there's always Bayside," she chuckled.

"Okay, then. It's a date. How about coming here at seven o'clock? Now, if you get an offer from Carl, promise me you'll accept."

"No question. I remember the drill. Geez, I can't believe we're still talking this way in our fifties." We both burst into laughter. This was why I wanted to be with Cher on Valentine's Day. We understood each other, and we'd been down this road together before.

When I awoke the next morning, I couldn't believe more snow was covering the ground. When would this winter ever end?

As Puff and I enjoyed our breakfast, I checked my phone for any kind of messages on this somber Valentine's Day. The silence from Grayson was deafening. Why couldn't he text a response to my card? I took a deep breath and called the White Gull Inn, knowing they would be busy with breakfast. An unknown voice answered, and she took no time to tell me they were booked for the evening. She suggested I could get on their waiting list, but I declined.

Now what? Did I really want to call all over town to see what was available in this crazy weather? The idea of walking over to Bayside in the snow was sounding better and better. I wasn't in the mood to fix a special meal for Cher and me. That would be too much like something Grayson and I would have done.

Spending time with Cher tonight would also give me an opportunity to do more planning with her for the quilt show. I picked up the copy of the *Pulse* newspaper lying on my kitchen table and avoided all the ads for special Valentine dinners. A large section fell out that was advertising the Lighthouse Festival taking place in the summer. Visiting all the beautiful lighthouses had also been on my bucket list since arriving in Door County, but other things had taken precedence. First on the agenda had been getting settled and finding a way to make my art a source of income. I got pretty lucky there with Carl and his gallery. Then Cher and I started the outdoor quilt show, which took up a big chunk of time. Someday, hopefully soon, I would be a tourist in my hometown.

I then noticed an article about the cherry season and which orchards needed workers. The cherry business was a happy, fun part of Door County. Everyone capitalized on cherries here because Door County was the fourth-largest producer of cherries in the nation. I still smile at the touches of cherry decor that Cher left in the cabin for me. My kitchen had cherry-print curtains and place mats to match. I even have salt and pepper shakers painted with cherries.

Cherry-picking season would be around the time of our quilt show. Perhaps we should involve the cherry theme this year. Every restaurant has a menu item that includes the Montmorency cherry that Door County is known for. Ideas started flowing that I could present to Cher. If Anna did indeed become one of our vendors, she could have a cherry pie contest. My mouth began to water. Thinking about spring and cherry blossoms brought pleasant thoughts as I watched more snowflakes fall.

Chapter 15

After I dressed for the day, my curiosity got the best of me. I had to know if Grayson had mailed me anything for Valentine's Day. Around noon, I decided to check my box at the post office.

The roads were quite slick, so I took my time and decided not to pick up lunch.

I rushed in and out, hoping I wouldn't slip on the icy spots. I then sat in my car and filed through my mail. The disappointment of not seeing anything that looked like a Valentine put me in a slump.

I was glad to get back home. I started a fire, telling myself I had no reason to feel sorry for myself when Ericka had more serious problems. My phone rang, and it was Carl.

"Happy Valentine's Day!" he said in a joking manner.

"Same to you, Carl. Are you at the studio?"

"No, not with this weather. I just called to tell you that Mr. Adams was quite pleased with your rendition of the park. He got tears in his eyes when he saw it."

"Oh, I'm so glad he likes it. Sometimes it's hard to know what folks have in mind for commissioned work. I've started another quilt building painting. It's of the quilt display in

Noble Park from last year's show. I think I'll donate it to the Historical Society to have for their house."

"That's not a bad idea, Claire. They've been good partners for your show. I haven't heard from Foster Collins, but I'm sure he'll be in next week for a lunch. Cher said you wouldn't miss it for the world," he chuckled.

"That's right! Hey, Cher and I are going to Bayside tonight. If you don't have any plans, why don't you join us?"

"You haven't heard from Grayson?"

"Nope. Cher and I could use a little masculinity so we don't feel so sorry for ourselves."

"I think you two will be just fine, but thanks for the offer. Have fun!"

"We always do!"

When I hung up, I decided I'd better not tell Cher I'd invited Carl and that he passed. I didn't want her to feel any rejection.

The afternoon slipped by as I did a few domestic chores around the cabin. Cher sent a text that she would be by around seven o'clock, which sounded perfect.

I decided my mom needed a phone call in addition to the special valentine card I'd sent. There was no answer. My first thought was that maybe she was with Bill, which would be wonderful. I left her a sweet message and then went up to shower and get ready for the evening.

Cher arrived late because traffic was slow despite the snow letting up in the afternoon. When I saw her pull up, I fastened my coat and went out to meet her. We both agreed it would be safer to walk to Bayside. We both had on high boots and began our trek through the snow.

"Remember as kids, Cher, when neither one of us could get the car, but we were determined to go downtown anyway?"

She laughed and nodded. "And I remember some pretty bad weather."

We stomped off our snowy boots upon entering the tavern. The crowd was light, which surprised me.

"Well, I guess this is where all the losers hang out," Cher joked as we settled on a table. "Do you think Harry is going to let Rachael work here on Saturday nights anymore?"

"He already made it clear to her that he wasn't, but Rachael is pretty stubborn. I think he agreed for her to fill in if they get in a pinch."

"That's a good compromise," Cher thought.

We ordered our usual beers and Bayside burgers before we both started talking at once. Yes, this was much better than sulking at home.

"I think I came up with some good ideas for the show when I was sitting at my kitchen table this morning," I announced.

"Oh no. What am I gonna have to do now?" Cher joked. "Give me a brief clue."

"Cherries," I said simply.

"Cherries?" Cher repeated, choking on her sip of beer. "What's that supposed to mean?"

"I think we're missing the best part of having this show in Door County."

"In what way?" Cher asked, squinting her eyes.

I began my assessment of how so many businesses and events pick up on the cherry theme because it's so happy, colorful, and delicious. Cher listened intently and nodded now and then. When I got to the part about Anna possibly baking things with cherries, she burst with excitement.

"Now you've got my attention!" she yelled out.

Chapter 16

"I don't see why we can't have a theme every year," I suggested. "It would force us to shake it up each year so folks have something new to look forward to."

Cher nodded in agreement. "It would also dictate the quilt challenge each year. The challenge can take the place of Olivia's exhibit this year."

"Don't forget, Amy's going to want to show some Amish quilts if she's one of the vendors."

"That would be awesome."

"Cherries would be a perfect theme, and of course my *Quilted Blossoms* quilt would fit right in. I bet I could sell a lot of those."

"Yes, if you have time," Cher replied.

"With all the cherry-print fabrics out there, it wouldn't be hard for businesses to do something with it."

"Sure. They could offer a discount on any cherry-themed product or have a drawing to win some kind of cherry merchandise."

"I like it!" I said.

"The sooner we wrap this up, the sooner I can meet with our print guy. Gee, I wonder what Carl will think about our theme?"

"Well, as luck would have it, look who just walked in the door!" I announced.

Cher turned around in shock. Her face lit up like she'd just won the lottery.

"Carl, what are you doing here?" Cher quickly asked.

"I heard this was where everyone goes when they don't have a date on Valentine's night," he joked.

"You got that right," I responded. "Why don't you join us? We have a pretty important question to ask you, so your timing is great. Get your drink ordered first."

"It's on my tab," Cher generously offered as she eyed Carl flirtatiously.

"Okay, then!" he said with delight.

After Carl got his beer, we repeated our ideas about having a theme to our show each year. To his credit, he listened without interruption.

"I think you're on to something, especially if the theme pertains to Door County," Carl said, deep in thought. "There are so many possibilities, like lighthouses, Wisconsin barns, apples, boating, and, of course, cherries."

"Exactly!" I agreed with excitement. "Quilted Cherries is a perfect theme title, Cher Bear."

"And a child is born!" Carl shouted out. "Here's a toast to Quilted Cherries being conceived right here at Bayside Tavern." We burst into laughter before clinking our glasses.

After Cher and I finished our hamburgers, I was beginning to feel like a third wheel. It was obvious Carl and Cher had some attraction to each other. Just as I was about to suggest my leave, Carl had an interesting suggestion.

"On my way here, the roads were really getting bad. Cher, if you're smart, you'll spend the night at Claire's. I'm going across the street to the gallery to sleep on my sofa until morning. No one should be out on those roads; you'd be stranded in no time."

"That's a great idea, Carl," I nodded with concern.

"I'll walk you both home because it's the gentlemanly thing to do," Carl winked.

"That's not necessary, Carl," I countered. "We're used to holding each other up. Right, Cher Bear?"

She smiled and nodded. "So true, Claire Bear. Thanks for the offer, Carl. I'm glad you're staying in town. I'll settle up the tab."

We all bundled up to face the cold, snowy night. It actually had turned out to be a fun and productive Valentine's Day. We both gave Carl a hug and then we parted ways, trudging through the snow with each step.

Cher and I nearly slipped a time or two, but we caught each other like always. I teased Cher about making a snow angel, but she wouldn't have it. She did threaten a snowball fight if I didn't quickly unlock the door to the cabin.

Chapter 17

Cher insisted on sleeping on the couch that she used to own and love, so I grabbed some bedding for her. Her night was complete with Carl showing up at the tavern. I was surprised she didn't ask me if I had anything to do with that.

Puff was already asleep on my bed when I got upstairs. She was used to giving up on me in the late hours. I checked my phone before crawling into bed, but there was no sign of my previous love. I wondered if he was thinking of me today. I suppose having Kelly to celebrate with was enough. Was my card just a laughable moment for him, or was it sitting on his bedside table?

I tossed and turned until one o'clock before I went to sleep. My dream was filled with cherries everywhere, with Grayson just observing in the background.

When I rose at four o'clock to get a drink of water, I peeked downstairs to see how Cher was doing. She was snoring just like I remembered from back in the day. It made me smile. We used to tease her about it years ago. I suppose it's something you never outgrow.

I went back to bed and woke up at eight the next morning. I looked out the window to see that the sun was shining, creating crystals everywhere like a snow globe. I checked my phone before going down to breakfast.

I came downstairs and found Cher checking her phone.

"Good morning, friend! I hope you slept okay. I have many flavors of the Door County coffee. Do you have a favorite?"

She perked up. "Do you have amaretto?"

I nodded. "I do! It's one of my favorites also. The cherry crème is my second favorite."

"I see Puff has a routine. She's been waiting to be served." We both chuckled.

"Oh, yes! First things first! I sure saw a lot of cherries in my dreams last night."

"It's no wonder! I'm so glad Carl approved of the cherry idea because marketing is one of his best assets. Hey, I got to thinking. Did you tell him we were going to be there?"

"I can't tell a lie," I blushed. "He called to tell me about Mr. Adams's reaction to my painting, so I mentioned we were going there."

"How nice. I wish I could have seen your painting. You're so good on commissioned pieces. I'm not good at finishing anything of my own to sell, but I love working in the gallery."

"It's a great place, and I'm thrilled you're back here where you belong. Are you hungry? How about a frozen bagel? I have cherry and cinnamon."

"Well, I'd prefer it toasted over frozen, but I'd love cherry if you have it," Cher joked as she joined me at the kitchen table. "You know, you didn't have to keep all the cherry decor I left here."

"Oh, I love the cherries! I guess we should alert all the vendors to our cherry theme for this year."

"Did I share with you that Carol is thinking of selling her quilt shop?"

"No, you didn't. I wonder if Olivia ought to jump on that?"

"Well, I know she loves working there, but I'm sure that would be tough financially. Wouldn't it be great to have one of our quilt club members own it? Say, any word from Ava?"

I shook my head and stayed away from the topic. "So, what do you have planned today?"

"I'm taking over for George this afternoon. He has to leave Ericka's around one o'clock. She'll start feeling better today before she has another treatment. I'm telling you, Claire Bear, if I decide not to take that nasty treatment, you'd better support me."

"The same here, Cher Bear. Do you need some help cleaning off your car?"

"No, the sun is taking care of the windshield. I'm going to move on with this cherry theme for the designer, so don't go changing your mind."

"No, I'm pretty sold on it. I'll come up with some simple rules for the quilt challenge. The sooner our club and others know the rules, the better."

"I don't know what you told Puff about me, but she won't even come to me when I call her."

I chuckled. "It's just a short memory, that's all. Tell Ericka to hang in there. I wish I had something for you to take for her."

"That's okay. She'll get a kick out of hearing about our quilt show plans. She wants everyone to act normal and talk about normal things besides her health. It's pretty hard, though, because half the time she's in the bathroom."

"God bless her. Please give her a hug from me."

I watched as Cher did what she could with her car and drove away.

Chapter 18

As I was folding up Cher's bedding, Mom called.

"Good morning, sweetie," she greeted. "I got your message. I was with Bill at the senior center. They had a little Valentine's Day party."

"Oh, that's great! What was that like?"

"Now, don't be judgmental. We went for the meal, which was quite nice. We always leave before they get ideas about playing games." I chuckled. "Bill hates that nonsense."

"He's pretty intelligent, so I can see why."

"I remind him everyone isn't in the same health condition that we are."

"So true, Mom. You're both very lucky."

"Did you do anything special last night?"

"Not with Grayson, unfortunately. Cher and I went to dinner, and she spent the night since the roads were so bad."

"Yes, I always watch the news for updates about Door County, and you're having quite a winter. How is your friend Ericka doing?"

"She's having a terrible reaction to her treatment. Cher is sitting with her today since her brother can't. Ericka can't be left alone when she's that sick."

"I know very well. It's awful. So, how are the wedding plans coming along with Rachael and Harry?"

"Oh! Did I tell you she asked me to be her maid of honor?"

"No, you didn't, but that's very nice. Tell her to throw her bouquet your way."

"Funny, Mom. Any word from Michael?"

"He's off skiing with his friend Jon, so I assume he's fine. Oh, thank you for the valentine."

"Did you get one from Bill?"

She chuckled. "I got something better than a card!"

"What would that be?" I asked with curiosity.

"A beautiful bouquet of red and white roses."

"Oh, Mom! I'm so happy for you!"

"He said it was a payback for so many home-cooked meals."

"I suppose it could be, but I think that man is quite smitten with you." She chuckled, and then we said goodbye.

When I hung up, I realized my own mother was doing better than I was in the romance department. God bless Bill.

With renewed excitement for our show, I thought about ways that the Quilters of the Door could help. Some would enter the challenge, of course. Hopefully Marta would still take care of registration. Olivia would be working the quilt shop booth, so she wouldn't be available. Amy would be attending to her vending space, and so would Anna. Ginger said she had to stay in her shop because it would be a busy weekend for her. And Rachael, of course, would be busy with wedding stuff. That left Frances, Ava, Lee, and Greta. Greta would likely still grind her teeth about our show, so I couldn't count on her. Ava wouldn't want to expose herself, so that left Frances and Lee.

I was eating a late dinner of grilled cheese and tomato soup when Cher called.

"Oh, Claire, it's about Ericka. I had to call an ambulance for her while I was there."

"No! What happened?"

"She passed out on me, and I didn't know what to do or how to even move her."

"Oh dear. Is she okay?"

"Now she is. I'm just leaving the hospital. They're going to keep her overnight. They say this sometimes happens when someone's blood pressure gets out of whack. George is on his way, so I decided to leave. I'm not very good at this caregiving thing." She started to cry.

"Cher, please don't be hard on yourself. Look what you did for her today. You were there for her and got her to a place she'd be cared for. That's all anyone can ask. She loves and trusts you."

"I think I heard one of the nurses say they were going to adjust her treatment as a result of this."

"It sounds like she needs a break, but what do I know?"

"Maybe so. I'm ready for a drink. I'm not sure I can be helpful to her anymore after this."

"If she's comfortable with me, I'm willing to give it a try."

"She's prideful and independent. It's all very embarrassing for her."

"Go home and relax, Cher. I'll talk to Ericka later."

I sat there with such sadness and worry for Ericka and now, of course, Cher. Ericka's cancer was aggressive, and it was taking its toll on her body.

Chapter 19

I got little sleep thinking about Ericka, and the next morning was difficult. I sat at the breakfast table feeling guilty about making exciting plans for the quilt show while my friend was suffering.

When my cell phone rang and I saw that it was Anna, I smiled.

"Well, good morning!" I greeted.

"I hope I'm not calling too early, Claire."

"Not at all. I'm still enjoying my first cup of coffee."

"I have good news."

"Well, I could use some."

"I'm going to have what they call a soft opening of my new bakery next week. They put in the ovens this week, so I can get to work."

"That's great! I'll be there! What did you name it?"

She chuckled. "My aunt and uncle insisted I call it Anna's Bake Shop. I wanted to call it Strudels, but they felt everyone would think that was all I offered."

"I see. Well, your bakery name is charming, Anna. I like it. I'm so happy for you, but now you won't have much time to quilt."

"Yes, I know, but I told Aunt Marta I wanted to be sure to finish a quilt I started for Billy's graduation. I'll work very hard to make that happen."

"You'll need plenty of help with the bakery opening."

She laughed. "Yeah, but I'm in America now, so anything is possible. Isn't that what you say?"

"That's right! Anything is possible, and I will spread the word on your opening."

"Danke, Claire."

"I hope I'll see you at quilt club."

"Oh, yes. Aunt Marta says I must be there."

When I hung up, I was truly happy for this sweet person who'd been added to my life. So many good things had occurred since Marta had brought her as a guest to the club.

As I finished my coffee, I glanced at the *Pulse* newspaper. The headline read, "Grayson Wills Takes Over as Chamber President." It was hard to believe this busy man I knew had agreed to such a position. But I guess he had more time now that we weren't together, and perhaps he was trying to fill it.

I dressed for the day knowing I had plenty of painting and unfinished quilting to do. Around noon, I received a text from Rachael.

[Rachael]
Hey, gift shop manager. I need you to get in some early orders. Are you free?

[Claire]
Sure. I'll see if I can get out there tomorrow morning.

[Rachael]
Great. About ten o'clock?

[Claire]
Perfect.

I was embarrassed that my boss had to remind me about my commitment to order for the barn gift shop. It seemed early to order for next year's Christmas, but what did I know? I did think I could be an asset to the shop I'd come to love, and Rachael saw that in me. It would give her more time to plan the wedding.

I returned to work on my Noble Park painting. My heart wasn't in it, but I was close to finishing it, so I pressed on. My mind was racing with thoughts of Ericka, Anna, Rachael, and even Grayson. Especially Grayson.

Chapter 20

Around nine thirty the next morning, I left for Rachael's. I stopped to get a coffee to go at the Blue Horse. My mind was training itself to not look for Grayson, so I tried to concentrate on other things.

I placed my order for one of my favorite combinations. When I started to give her my money, she said, "Your order was paid for by the guy sitting over there with the red scarf." She winked like she knew both of us.

I looked Grayson's way in surprise. He wasn't smiling, so I just nodded and left. What was I supposed to do? Run over to him and kiss him? I wondered if this was his awkward way of breaking the ice between us. He must have seen me drive up. The good news was that he wasn't with that attractive woman I'd seen him with before. Maybe the two of us just had to take baby steps to mend our relationship.

My heart was beating rapidly as I drove away toward Rachael's. To get my mind off of Grayson, I tried to think of my job ahead and some of the things the gift shop could use. It was a beautiful day and much warmer than usual, which helped in melting more snow.

Harry and Rachael were outside the barn when I arrived.

"Hey, Miss Claire!" Harry called out. "We were just planning a few new landscaping ideas for next spring."

"Oh, nice!"

"My boss here says we need more flowers to welcome everyone," Harry joked.

"I'm all for that!" I agreed.

"Come on in, Claire," Rachael said, holding the door open for me. "I've got coffee and some chicken noodle soup in the crock pot if you need some lunch."

"Good heavens, Rachael, don't you ever sleep?" She just smiled.

We went to the back room and sat down at the worktable. There sat a stack of what looked to be catalogs.

"Now, I know things are a bit different now, but I'm used to ordering through these catalogs. If you are more comfortable ordering online, I'm sure all of this would be there."

"Oh, how I remember looking at catalogs as a kid and wishing for everything on every page! Do you remember doing that?"

"Oh, I do. I still like to browse through them."

"I've had some time to think about some ideas," I began.

"Shoot!"

"I guess my first dramatic idea is that you start your Christmas season here much earlier and that we get in on some fall merchandise. You could easily get folks here with free hayrides, pumpkin sales, and many other ideas for that time of year. I bet that farmer two miles down the road with all the pumpkins would love to have an outlet here. Halloween is nearly passing Christmas as people's favorite holiday."

"My goodness, you *have* been thinking!"

"Folks are buying Christmas things earlier and earlier. We could carry ornaments for the trees, but they could be specialized, like barn ornaments, for example. An inexpensive idea is to carry all kinds of bows for wreaths and garlands. I could have sold a ton of those if we'd had them this past Christmas."

"Oh, I know!" Rachael nodded in agreement.

"When it's time, bring in some poinsettias, too. And you don't want to forget to have all kinds of lights for both holidays. We need Christmas lights for trees and garlands. The whole idea would be to have a one-stop holiday shop right here at the Christmas tree farm." Rachael's eyes were lit up like the Christmas trees we were discussing.

"You're on it, girlfriend."

"Now, it's not my money I'm spending here. I'm just dreaming."

She chuckled. "Don't worry. Harry said to spend whatever we wanted. Remember how well the watering pipes sold?"

I smiled and nodded. "Exactly. Just please remember you don't need to agree with all my ideas, okay?"

"You make these decisions, and we'll pay you for them. I know this takes you away from your painting and quilting. By the way, if you want to sell any of your work here, that would be just fine also."

"That's very generous of you, but I'm pretty devoted to Carl's gallery. He has given me such great opportunities. I think I'm starting to see some repeat business, which is what every artist hopes for."

"Understood!"

We continued to chat while looking at some of the merchandise in the catalogs and enjoying some hot soup.

Chapter 21

"So, dear Rachael, besides all this, do you have any more news about your big wedding day?"

"Oh, Claire. Please don't say big. That really scares me!"

"Don't be scared. It's all going to turn out just perfect."

"I tease Harry about eloping, but he won't have it. He doesn't do anything small."

I chuckled. "Just let me know what I can do. Thanks for lunch. I'll study these catalogs."

"Claire, before you go, you haven't mentioned Grayson in quite some time. I can't believe the two of you are done. You haven't shared much with me, but if you love that guy, do what you can to get him back."

I nodded. "It's complicated, Rachael."

"If this were me, you'd be lecturing me to go after what I wanted. It's always complicated."

I smiled and nodded. "Maybe I don't know what I want."

"Okay. Enough said, my friend."

"I'll send you my recommendations on the orders."

"Not necessary. I have accounts at all these places, so just copy me on your orders. You're in charge!"

"Oh boy! You may be sorry!"

I left and waved goodbye to Harry from a distance. *Be careful what you wish for,* I told myself as I realized it was up to me to supply the gift shop.

I stopped by the Main Street Market in Egg Harbor to pick up more wine. Somehow, many other goodies filled my cart besides what I'd come in for. Since I was near Cher's place, I gave her a call to see if she'd be home.

"Why, sure, Claire," Cher responded awkwardly when I said I might drop by. "Carl just stopped by with a pizza. You're welcome to join us."

"Oh, no, that won't be necessary. I need to get on home."

"If you're sure, Claire Bear. Thanks for thinking of me."

"Enjoy!"

I continued driving home wondering if the whole world was happily partnered up. I certainly was happy for Cher and Carl, Harry and Rachael, and even Bill and Mom, whatever their relationship was. I suppose at times like this, it was only natural for me to be missing Grayson.

I arrived home just in time to catch the incredible sunset at the beach near my home, which was called Sunset Beach. I drove the circular path so I could get closer. Many cars were pulling over to catch the amazing view. I did the same. I saw some couples holding hands and others snuggled against each other to enjoy this serene moment in their lives. I smiled, watching their happiness, and I drove on to my cabin alone.

I brought in my groceries and opened the new wine Cher had told me about. It was called Velvet Devil. It was delicious, and I paired it with some pepper jack cheese I'd just purchased. My cell began ringing, and I was surprised when I looked to see the call was from Cher.

"Cher, what's up? Isn't Carl still there?"

"Not anymore. He just stopped by to share the pizza and see where I lived."

"That's nice. Are things okay with you two?"

"Oh yeah. I just called to share some good news."

"Lay it on me. I could use some right now."

"Tomorrow is when Foster Collins is taking us to lunch. I hope you'll still be available to join us."

"Well, sure. I wouldn't miss it."

"Carl said for me to tell you to meet us at the White Gull Inn around twelve o'clock. I'll be meeting them also because Foster and Carl will be together."

"I'm happy to be included. I have to admit, I'm a bit nervous."

"You, Claire Bear?" I chuckled. "Foster found you interesting enough to invite you more than once, so there's that."

Chapter 22

As I prepared for bed that night, I felt glad I had something to look forward to. I knew the conversation with Foster about the art world would certainly be interesting. Puff insisted on snuggling up next to me, which was quite unusual. She always seemed to know when I needed a hug, or perhaps she was feeling out of sorts like I was. I accommodated her affection, and both of us traveled to dreamland.

When I awoke the next morning, Puff was back in her usual spot, but as soon as I sat up in bed, she was more than ready to head downstairs.

I sat at the breakfast table watching Puff enjoy her breakfast and thought about my upcoming lunch. The snow had melted and the sun was shining, giving me hopes of an early spring.

I flipped through the stack of catalogs Rachael had given me that awaited my review. It was hard to think of seasons ahead. I turned down the corners of pages that perhaps deserved an order.

As time drew near for lunch, I brushed and brushed my hair, thinking I wanted to do something different with it. I pulled it to the top of my head and let the sides drop near my ears. I wore a black turtleneck to accentuate my turquoise earrings from Linda.

I had to admit, for a lunch date, I looked pretty good. I was careful to leave the cabin at just the right time so I wouldn't be too early or late.

As soon as I peeked in the main dining room, I saw the group seated at the coveted table by the bay window. I particularly loved that table at Christmastime with the white light decor. Cher saw me immediately and motioned for me to join them.

Carl and Foster stood like gentlemen when I approached the table. Foster looked even more handsome than I'd remembered from that day in Carl's shop. As I was seated, I could see that Brenda was working, but not in our section. For a second, I wondered about her and Kent.

"Carl tells me you're quite busy these days, Claire," Foster began.

"I should be more so. I don't feel I've been productive lately," I answered.

"Don't allow yourself to be driven by too many commitments, dear Claire," Foster advised. "One never does their best work under those circumstances."

"Good advice," Carl added. "I don't know how any of you do what you do, but I, for one, am grateful. Foster just brought in another painting I think you'll like, Claire."

"What subject matter?" I asked with interest.

"The cherry fields of Door County in watercolor, which I've never seen done before," Carl said.

"It was fun for a change," Foster added with a smile.

"Cherries must be on many people's minds these days," I said simply, and Cher grinned.

We made our menu choices, and I observed that Cher was being rather quiet. Perhaps she was just happy to be sitting next to Carl.

Our conversation turned to many topics, but Foster kept bringing the conversation back to me. He had so many questions about where I was from and what my background was, which I'm sure was boring for Cher and Carl.

"So, are you still living in Green Bay?" I asked to change the subject. He nodded.

"I'll be going to Florida for an exhibit soon, but when I return, I'll be near the bay again," he explained casually.

"How nice," I responded. "When you're in Florida, will you be painting?"

"I may," he nodded. "If I'm inspired with something, I may stay to do just that. I didn't always have this luxury."

"When Foster brought in the cherry painting, I told him that you and Cher had planned to do the next outdoor quilt show with a cherry theme," Carl interjected.

"You certainly can't go wrong with that," Foster expressed. "Speaking of cherries, I have to have some of the cherry pie here. Will the rest of you join me?"

"Sorry, not today," I responded.

"I'm with you," Carl added.

"I would love to, but I need to be leaving for Ericka's very shortly," Cher explained.

"Has there been any change?" I asked as she buttoned her jacket.

"I can only hope," Cher said sadly. "George was taking her to the doctor to see if there has been any progress from her treatment. I promised I would stay with her today until he returned."

"Thank you for the lunch, Carl. It was good to see you, Foster."

"Give her my best," I said before she left.

Chapter 23

"Next time lunch is on me," Foster claimed as he smiled at me. "Claire, I would like a contact card from you, if you don't mind. Here's one of mine so you can contact me anytime." I just stared at him, not sure if I'd heard him correctly.

"Claire," Carl prompted softly to get my attention.

"Oh, sure," I said as I retrieved a card from my purse.

"Thank you," he said politely. "I'm here for a few days before I head to Florida. Would you be free for dinner, say, tomorrow evening?"

"Sure," I replied, feeling overwhelmed.

"I'll call you in the morning," he promised as we stood up to leave.

"We'll walk you home, Claire," Carl suggested. "When we walked here from the gallery, Foster commented that he was familiar with your cabin."

The three of us made small talk along the way, and when we got to my cabin, Foster just stood there and observed the place.

"I'd like to see the inside sometime," Foster requested. "That glassed-in front porch is where you paint, correct?"

I nodded. I was not about to ask him inside today, or maybe ever.

"Well, thanks for lunch, Carl," I said before going inside.

After they left, I had a strange feeling. I had to rethink this lunch. There was no question that Foster was hitting on me. I was sure that with his looks and reputation, he hit on many women. Would I actually go to dinner with him? I guess I was certainly free to do so since Grayson was no longer in my life. I did have many questions for him if I could keep him from asking about me.

As I changed into jeans to get back to painting, my cell phone rang. When I picked it up, I couldn't believe it was Ava.

"Ava! Ava, where are you?"

"I've got some bad news, Claire," she said sadly.

"What is it? Are you hurt?"

"No, it's not about me. I've been living here with Frances, and she had a stroke early this morning."

"Oh no! Is she okay now?"

"I just left the hospital. She has some paralysis, but the doctor said she came in early enough to recover some of the damage. Her mind is fine, but her speech is still slurred. I feel so bad for her."

"I'm so glad you were there for her. What about you? Are you alright?"

"All this time I've been here with Frances, where I'm very safe. She has been a dear, and very protective of me. She has this big old house, so there's plenty of room for me."

"I'm so glad to know where you are."

"This isn't for anyone else to know, Claire. Please keep this to yourself. I will take care of Frances, as she has no one else. We've become quite close."

"I'm glad. Can the quilt club do anything for her?"

"They should be told, of course, but leave me out of the story. Tell Marta to put the word out and maybe send her flowers."

"What about Olivia?"

"I'm afraid Olivia has figured it out, but she's very dependable. Frances has asked her to be quiet about me being here for my safety."

"I see."

Ava gave me more information, and it sounded like Frances would be home soon.

I got Marta on the phone right away. I gave her a brief update, and she was quite disturbed by the news. She had many questions but agreed she would send flowers right away.

"So is Anna going to keep you busy with the bake shop?"

"Oh my, yes. The whole family is helping where we can. I just hope she can build up some customers. It's a huge investment for her."

"Well, I'll spread the word. Thank you for taking care of getting flowers for Frances."

Chapter 24

It was now six o'clock, and I figured Ericka would be back from the doctor. I gave Cher a ring to find out how it went.

"Claire, it's not a good time. I'm still with Ericka. I'll have to call you back."

I hung up feeling mystified. What was going on? I shrugged it off and proceeded to get a card ready to send to Frances. She was such a sweetheart. I could only imagine how scary this stroke was for her.

I managed to paint on the porch for an hour before calling it quits to have a glass of wine. It was getting hard to concentrate. When my phone rang, I anxiously answered, thinking it was Cher getting back to me.

"Claire, it's Foster."

"Oh, hello again," I replied slowly.

"I couldn't wait until tomorrow to find out whether you'd be joining me for dinner, so I'm calling now to see if you've changed your mind."

"Did you think that might happen?"

"Yes, I'm afraid I did. I don't have much confidence when it comes to women."

"You of all people have confidence issues, being a famous artist and all?"

"I'm supposed to be full of myself, is that it?"

"Perhaps, but you could prove me wrong."

"Challenge on! I'll pick you up at seven o'clock if that's convenient."

"Fine. I'll see you then."

I decided to put any reservations aside about tomorrow's dinner and just see what happened. Wait until Cher finds out I have a date—a date with Foster, no less!

I fixed a salad for my dinner and kept wondering why I had never heard back from Cher. At ten o'clock I went up to shower before bed, and she finally called.

"What's going on?" I asked quickly.

"What a day," she began. "It was nice to have a pleasant lunch to start things off. When I got to Ericka's, it certainly was a different story."

"Was she really sick again or did something else happen?"

"Yes, she was sick, but more so emotionally. The doctor told her that so far there's not been any improvement, but he wants her to continue with the treatments. Trust me: From what I'm hearing from her now, I don't think she'll go back. After this last treatment is over, she said she'll make her own plan going forward."

"Poor thing! What can we do?"

"Good question. I tried to agree with whatever she said. She didn't need to do battle with anyone. She'll feel better after this, but she still has cancer."

"She's more stubborn than I am, so she'll do as she pleases. And who knows, we may do the same if we end up in her situation. Cher, before we hang up, I have something to share with you."

"What's that?"

"Frances has had a stroke, but they hope in time she'll regain what she's lost."

"Oh my. Is she in the hospital?"

"Yes, but there's more to the story. I now know where Ava has been."

"What's Ava got to do with this?"

"She's been living with Frances all this time. She said she feels safe and happy there. It's a good thing, because she got Frances to the hospital quite soon after it happened and says she will take care of her when she comes home."

"Well, I'll be. I wonder how she ended up there?"

"I don't know the details, but it seems to be helpful to both of them. Please keep this under wraps."

"That husband of Ava's must be a real creep for her to go to these measures. Do you think she'll come back to the quilt club anytime soon?"

"I don't think so. Her worries are serious. She feels he'll kill her or take her to the police and tell them about her shoplifting problem."

"That's crazy!"

Chapter 25

"It's crazy, but here's something crazier. Foster called me this evening. He said he couldn't wait until tomorrow to know if I was going to dinner with him."

"Girl, what do you make of that?"

"I have no idea! He even said he was insecure when it came to women. Is that just a line?"

Cher chuckled. "Well, Claire Bear, you're about to find out."

"Why me? I can't figure it out. I wonder how much older than me he is?"

"Google him. Surely you can find out some personal stuff about him on the web."

"I've never dated a guy with a mustache before, have I, Cher?" I asked jokingly. "What does he want with this graying blonde, anyway?"

Cher continued to laugh. "You're always so hard on yourself. He seems to know plenty about you, so don't worry about it."

"What if Grayson gets wind of my date with Foster?"

"It's just having dinner with an acquaintance like he does, right? I know you're not over him, but just enjoy yourself.

What could be bad about being seen having dinner with Foster Collins?"

"This is a small town, and I'm not sure I want anyone thinking I left Grayson for this artist guy."

"Nonsense. You'll be back with Grayson in no time."

"I'm glad you have faith in that scenario."

"I'm beat and need to go to bed. It's been a stressful day."

We hung up with our usual good night, but I had a lot to think about from the day's events. At least we knew Ava was safe.

When I woke the next morning, I lay there continuing to wonder about my day ahead. Was Frances going to be okay? I grabbed my cell phone to see if there were any messages.

There was an email from Marta to the quilt club telling everyone about Frances and that the club was sending flowers. There was no mention of Ava.

I then thought of Ericka. How could she get any sleep? Should I call her? Her choices were so personal that I didn't think I was in any position to give her advice.

As I ventured downstairs for my much-needed coffee, I told myself I needed to be productive today. My Noble Park painting was nearly done, so I could take it to the museum soon.

After I sat down at my breakfast table, I thought about my big dinner date. I really didn't want to go. I had liked the thrill of being asked, but I would much rather be with Grayson right here in front of my fireplace.

I dressed and then went to look at my painting on the easel to see what was missing. The sun peeking through the window brightened it up considerably. The weather today was going to be bright and quite a bit warmer. I saw where I could add a little red on the painting, and that made it look much happier. I needed to stop, as it was complete. It's funny how you know when something is finally done. That goes for many things—even relationships.

At lunchtime, I thought about what my next project would be. I hadn't touched all the ties Michael had given me at Christmas. There were enough for several quilts.

When I finished my sandwich, I went upstairs to rummage through the ties to see if any light bulbs would go off in my head for ideas. The age span of the tie selection was immense. Some of these had to have been my grandfather's ties. Some of the older ones looked more used, which was understandable. I remember my mother teasing my dad about getting his annual Christmas tie. Back then, they dared not show a Christmas theme; it was just a new tie to start the new year. I loved those years when we all seemed to be so happy and carefree.

Chapter 26

I found myself sorting the ties like I used to do with my mother's buttons. Some of the ties complemented each other with colors and prints, so I grouped those together. Ginger had told me how to remove the linings, but I'd probably get on YouTube to refresh my memory. Like any quilter would, I thought about prewashing, but most of the fabrics were questionable.

I chuckled at the few that had soiled spots. Were the stains coffee, spaghetti sauce, or what? It looked like some had never been used. I had a feeling Michael threw some of his unwanted ties in the bag as well. He would flip out if I actually made him a quilt out of these. I'm not sure Mom would find a quilt made from Dad's ties comforting.

I would never use these ties for a bed-sized quilt. Maybe a wall quilt because it would be quicker and more manageable. I could also see doing one of these tie quilts to sell in the gallery. I'm sure many folks would think it unique.

Dad's ties spoke to who he was. I remember him wearing lots of them, though I'm sure he had his favorites. I loved the feel of the more satin-like ones. I wasn't sure I could use some of the ones with rougher textures.

I held one of the ties I remembered him wearing up to my nose. The scent of Dad's Old Spice cologne brought instantaneous tears. Oh, how I missed him and his wonderful hugs. He never quite understood my ambition as an artist like Mom did, but he always looked at me like I was his little girl. Michael had gotten a similar response from Dad when he told him he wanted to be a writer. But Dad looked out for us financially so we could follow our dreams. I'll be forever grateful for that support. I put the Old Spice tie aside. I couldn't cut that one up.

I put all the ties in a plastic clothes bin so they could air out. It was a project in waiting. When I dumped them into the bin, one bow tie fell to the side. Whose was that? It was a paisley print that could have been from the 1970s. I'd have to ask Mom if Dad ever wore a bow tie because I don't remember him doing so.

I went downstairs and decided to call Ericka. I simply couldn't put it off anymore. The phone rang and rang, so I had to leave a message.

"Ericka, it's Claire. I just wanted to call to tell you I'm here for you if you want to talk or need anything. I respect any and all of the decisions you must be making. I also want you to know I believe in miracles. Odd, I know. I love you, girlfriend."

I could only hope the message would make her smile. She needed support right now. I could at least do that for her.

My next call was to Ava. I thought it was going to go to voice mail, but she finally answered.

"Ava, it's Claire. How's Frances today?"

"She's still in the hospital, but when I talked to her on the phone earlier, I thought her speech had improved. She doesn't want me coming to the hospital. She said to just stay put."

"That's probably a good idea, but it's hard on you, I'm sure. When is she coming home? Does she know?"

"They still won't say. She has a car service, so she does have a way home."

"How are you doing?"

"I'm okay, but I'm very worried about her and I hope I'm capable of taking care of her. I worry this could lead someone to my location."

"Mum's the word. Take care and keep me posted, okay?"

"I will. Thanks for being such a good friend."

When I hung up, I wondered what kind of friend I really was. Keeping secrets wasn't making me feel good, but I couldn't imagine what Ava's life was like. Why are some lives so complicated?

Chapter 27

I dressed early for my date with Foster. I kept wondering how judgmental he would be about my appearance and my artwork. I also wondered why he wanted to have dinner with me, of all people? Was he lonely?

It was a warmer-than-usual evening, so I wore a black-and-white jacket to complement my outfit. It was always a safe combination for me.

Foster arrived right on time. He got out of a large, yellow SUV that was almost the size of Harry's Hummer. I was grinning when I met him at the door.

"I could have seen you coming across town in that swanky SUV you have," I teased.

"Do you like it?"

"I do. It makes an artistic statement of some kind," I noted with a grin.

He chuckled. "I leased this, thinking I may change my mind about it, but I rather like the darned thing. I can get most any size painting in it, so it's practical. I keep a little green sports car in Green Bay, but I rarely use it."

"How rude of me, Foster. Please come in." He chuckled.

"Would you just look at this," he said, gazing about the room.

"It's small, as I warned you, but feel free to look around. Puff and I don't allow anyone upstairs, however."

He gave a sheepish grin. "Puff?"

"She's my adopted cat that's sitting in the chair on the front porch. She came with the cabin. It's a long story."

He looked at her sitting in her chair. Puff snarled at him and ran up the stairs. It wasn't a very nice welcome.

"Well, I've not seen that reaction before."

"Maybe she smells my dog, Jasper. He's a greyhound that hangs out at my Green Bay place."

"Owning a greyhound must be interesting."

"I've had him a long time. He's absolutely the best, but he's aging and doesn't get around well anymore."

"Would you like a glass of wine before we go?"

"I would, thank you. I bet you have a fire going in this great fireplace all winter, don't you?"

"I sure do! What do you make of this warmer weather?"

"I like it. I'm ready to get back out on the water."

"Will red wine do?"

"Yes, of course."

He took a sip after his first whiff of it and smiled.

"I like it," he said, picking up the bottle to check out the brand.

"Let's go sit on the porch for a few minutes. I've had the windows open today just to get some fresh air circulating."

"I'm going back to Green Bay tomorrow. I have a show to prepare for in Madison."

"Oh, you should have mentioned that, Foster. We could have put this off."

"Claire, I've wanted to see more of you since the first time I met you at the gallery. I felt I already knew you. Now, you're from Missouri, right?"

I nodded. Then I took a few minutes to explain to him the circumstances of my arrival in Door County. He listened intently until I finished.

"Keep going," he said, staring into my eyes.

"Well, there's a lot to love here in Door County, so it's now my home."

"So, what about that doctor back home, or is that too personal to ask about?"

"That's a story of a whole other kind. Shall we get going?"

"I suppose, but I could sit here all night talking to you. Are you hungry?"

"I may be. Where are we going?"

"Well, typically this time of year, I like to sit in front of a nice warm fire, but tonight, I thought we could experience a bit of the outdoors."

"Sounds good to me. I have a jacket, so I'm okay with being outside."

"Have you been to the Fireside in Egg Harbor?"

"No, but Cher lives near there."

"I have a friend who is invested there, and I like their menu. It has a little kick to it."

"I can handle a kick," I joked. "I do like to try new places."

Chapter 28

I had driven by the Fireside restaurant many times, but I never realized how large it was. Folks were taking advantage of the ample outdoor seating tonight. Fires were burning in the firepits, and it appeared very inviting.

"Let's try sitting by the fire," Foster suggested. "If it's too cool, we'll go inside. There's nice decor in there."

"This will be fine." I nodded with a smile.

Foster knew several people there by name, and he didn't hesitate to introduce me to them. He bragged about the restaurant's French Quarter martini. I told him I'd never had a martini in my life, which was all he needed to hear to start my adventure. I rather enjoyed his positive nature and his beautiful smile.

As we discussed the menu, I was reminded of how little I'd eaten all day. Everything on the menu sounded good.

"I really appreciate good food," he noted. "You must try their lobster hush puppies. They have a bit of a bite afterward that makes you want another drink."

"I'll try them, then."

Foster ordered the bourbon salmon, and I chose the chicken feta Florentine. Then Foster started in on more questions for me. The first one was what I thought of the martini.

"It's quite good but I feel it may be a bit powerful."

"Perfect! Now, if you don't mind, Carl tells me you were recently in a relationship with someone whom I happen to know."

"You know Grayson Wills?"

"Of course. Everyone knows Grayson. If you own a boat around here, Sail Again comes into your life."

"I suppose so," I nodded. "I don't know how much Carl knows, but I didn't break up with Grayson. It's just that we weren't at the same level in the relationship."

"He wanted to marry you, right?"

I looked at him, surprised. "How did you know that?"

"I didn't," he snickered. "Grayson is a wonderful man. From what I understand, he's been single since his wife died in an accident. I hear his father was quite something. I like dealing with family businesses, where they seem to give a hoot about you. Does Grayson have children?"

"Yes, a teenage daughter."

"Ah. That could make things difficult or wonderful."

"Now you're beginning to get the picture."

"I see. By the way, Grayson owns one of my paintings."

"He does?" I asked as I took another sip.

"I think it hangs in his conference room at work."

"What a nice compliment to you." He nodded and smiled in agreement.

As we finished our dinner, it was getting a bit chilly. Foster noticed and suggested we go inside.

"I'd be happy to make a fire at the cabin if you'd like."

He looked at me as if he'd just won a million dollars.

"Are you coming on to me, Claire Stewart?"

I burst into laughter. "You wish! But it is getting late, and you need to travel in the morning."

"Good point, Miss Stewart. Another time, then."

He tucked my jacket around my neck, and off we went to Fish Creek.

When he stopped the car, he paused and looked quite seriously at me.

"You're an interesting, attractive lady, Claire. I knew when we met, we would become friends. It was nice to have a normal conversation with someone like you. You're smart to send me on my way, or I could spoil this evening quite rapidly." I smiled.

"I hope you'll agree to see me again," he said, helping me out of the car.

"That may be possible."

When we got to the door, he kissed me gently on the cheek and told me good night. It was endearing, and I almost hated to see him go. I knew I'd be seeing him again.

Off he went, and I was glad he didn't encourage me to make that fire.

Chapter 29

As I undressed for bed, I was smiling about the fact that we'd discussed Grayson this evening. Everyone liked Grayson, just as I suspected. I was finding that Door County was like a small town.

I picked up a small hint of Foster's cologne, and it was a pleasant smell, fitting for his style and demeanor. I looked at Puff sleeping on my bed and chuckled at her strong reaction to him. Maybe it was his cologne she didn't like.

As I lay there awake, part of me felt a bit guilty about being out with someone new, and the other part of me felt liberated that I could move on. Why couldn't Grayson just accept my feeling that it was too soon to get married? I wonder if he at times regretted his hasty reaction.

Puff walked across my face the next morning. Goofy cat. I decided to lie in bed awhile to plan my day. I hadn't heard back from Ericka and wanted to see her. With her not eating, I couldn't even take her something delicious. Maybe I could entice her to get out of the house.

I gave in to Puff and got up to fill her breakfast bowl. I just wanted coffee after that wonderful dinner last night. I picked up my cell to look at my emails, and Mom called.

"How are you, sweetie?"

"I'm good. We're having some milder weather lately, which I'm happy about. I'm ready for spring, though. How about you?"

"We are, too. My tulips and jonquils are poking out of the ground."

"Lovely. And how's Bill?"

"He has aches and pains just like I do, but he's managing alright. We have a card party at the senior center this afternoon. As far as I know, we'll both be there."

"I forgot that years ago you and Dad played cards with Bill and his wife."

"Those were good days."

"Have you heard from Michael, Mom?"

"Not for some time, but that's not unusual. How are Rachael's wedding plans coming along?"

"Fine. I just saw her, and she's got me ordering things for the barn gift store these days."

"How fun for you, spending other people's money."

"That's what I said. I hope you enjoy the card party, Mom. Please tell Bill hello."

"I will. I just wanted to hear your voice. I sure miss you, honey."

"I miss you too, Mom. Take good care of yourself."

"Not to worry."

I hung up wanting to hug her. Thank goodness she had some kind of life with Bill.

It was ten o'clock, which I decided was a good time to call Ericka.

"Hello," she said in a tiny, weak voice.

"Ericka, it's Claire. I miss you. Are you feeling any better?"

"Most of the time I feel like crap, but you probably know that."

"I'm so sorry. Cher said you might take a break from your treatments so you could feel a bit better."

"Yes. I need a break."

"Can I come to see you?"

"I don't think you really want to do that."

"Why not? I don't care what you look like. You're my friend. Can I bring you anything?"

"Well, I do keep thinking about cherry pie, but I likely wouldn't be able to keep it down."

"Cherry pie it is! I can pick one up at The Cookery. If you can't eat it today, there's always another day. What time is good for you?"

"How about two or three o'clock?"

"Perfect. I'll see you then."

Chapter 30

I was looking forward to seeing Ericka. In some way, I hoped to be helpful. I called The Cookery and asked them to save me a cherry pie.

As I dressed, I gave Cher a call. I had hopes we could attend Anna's bakery opening together.

"Where are you, Cher Bear? I hear some weird noises in the background."

She laughed. "I'm at the laundromat getting some rugs washed. Sorry it's so noisy. My washer went out on me, so here I am until I get a new one."

"I can hardly hear you, so I won't stay on here long, but can we go together to Anna's open house tomorrow?"

"Oh, I forgot about it! Can you pick me up?"

"Sure! I thought I'd stop by Nelson's and get her a plant today."

"Great idea."

"Okay. Happy washing. I'll see you tomorrow."

I left the house refreshed and ready to start my day. I stopped by Nelson's first to get a nice, big fern for Anna. I would have loved to have purchased some things for myself, but I had no room. I'd be back soon for pansies and such for the early spring.

The Cookery had my pie ready to go when I arrived. I grabbed some cherry scones to put in my freezer.

When I got to Ericka's, George was just leaving.

"Hey, George! How's Ericka today?"

He took a deep breath. "She's okay right now. Thanks for coming to see her. I hope she can keep down that great-looking cherry pie you were so kind to bring."

"Me, too! I bet she'll save some for you."

"Hey, Claire, now that you're a free woman, how about we go out for a drink sometime?"

"Word travels quickly. George, don't you ever give up on me?" I joked.

"What's the harm of a drink?"

"Maybe someday. Ericka's waiting."

"I won't hold my breath," he said, getting into his car.

When Ericka opened the door, I was shocked to see her appearance. She had lost a lot of weight, and there were dark circles under her eyes. I gave her a big hug and felt nothing but bones.

"I'll put the pie in the kitchen. Have a seat. I'm sorry the place looks like it does. George did run the vacuum for me this morning."

"Not to worry. I hope you'll have some pie. Have you eaten today?"

"I tried this morning, but I couldn't handle much."

"Well, the cherry pie will add a couple of pounds. Do you like it with coffee?"

"No, coffee is too strong for my system, but I can make you a cup on my Quick Cup maker."

"No, that's alright. I'll cut us a piece of pie, and I can make coffee if you'd like."

Ericka just wasn't herself. I felt so bad for her. I made a cup of coffee and then cut pie for each of us and pulled out a chair at her kitchen table to sit.

"Don't they do a great job with this pie? I bought some scones to take home if you'd like to try one of those."

"Thanks, Claire. I really appreciate your effort and Cher's. She's been a godsend to me lately."

"I talked to her while she was at the laundromat this morning. Her washer is broken, so I guess she'll have to get a new one. Here, now try the pie."

Ericka picked up her fork and took a bit of the crust first. Not wanting to stare, I also took a bite. I noticed she took a second bite as I sipped my coffee.

"Does it taste good to you?" She nodded but had no smile on her face.

"So, tell me about Anna's Bake Shop. Cher mentioned it briefly to me."

"Well, we're all so excited about this single, talented woman from Germany starting her own business."

"Cher said she's a new member of your quilt club."

"Yes. She's really talented. You should see all her work. She also showed us her family's Tannenbaum quilt, which Rachael tried to duplicate."

"Please excuse me, Claire," Ericka said as she went to the restroom.

I wondered if I had pushed too hard for her to eat the pie.

Chapter 31

I kept on eating until she returned.

"Are you okay, Ericka?"

She nodded. "I think I'll save my piece until later, but it truly is delicious. I could taste it just fine. Some things I can't."

"This must be so awful for you, my friend," I said, shaking my head.

"I would see cancer patients at work occasionally, but I never realized what they were going through until experiencing it for myself. Now that I know the chemo isn't working, I have to plan for the worst. I have enough of a medical background to know what all can happen."

"I can't even imagine. What's your biggest fear? Do you feel like talking about it?"

"Thank you for asking, Claire. Cher doesn't want to talk about it. She said it's too painful. I'm a realist, and I don't like sugarcoating anything."

"It's hard on Cher because she's been your friend for so long. She really thinks the world of you. It's hard on our closest loved ones."

She nodded. "I know it is. No one wants to face death, no matter how old they are. I guess I was hoping I'd meet the love of my life before I died, but it doesn't look like that's going to happen. I never had the desire to have children, but I did hope to have a romantic partner and to be a department head at work. My parents are gone, so all I have is George and a brother in Utah who doesn't give a hoot about me."

"Do you tell George how you feel?"

"What good would that do? I hear from the Utah clan every time there's a new grandkid, but that's it."

"Don't give up on your family, Ericka." She looked at me oddly. "Do you think you'll be strong enough to return to work soon?"

"That's my goal, but it's hard to say. If I can control the cancer, I'll be there."

"George is quite shaken up about your condition, Ericka. Does he communicate with the brother in Utah?"

"Nope. They had a falling out many years ago. Maybe once I'm gone, they will."

"Are you afraid of dying?" I paused for a bit. "No one wants to die, of course, but for me it's always been about my faith. It has sustained me all my life, and I know I'm in God's hands. I never feel alone, and that's such a comfort to me. My mom made sure we had a religious education even after my dad passed away. I'm so thankful for that."

"I wish I had that. I feel like a fish out of water sometimes. I always thought this kind of stuff happened to others, not to me."

"I know. I'd be happy to put you in touch with a minister or a layperson to visit with you about things. All it takes is for you to accept Christ in your heart." I could tell she was about to cry. "You have a lot on your mind, and these folks know how to comfort you though this."

"I don't know. You're such a sweetheart, Claire."

"Well, maybe I'm supposed to be here for you now. Remember how you were there for me when I arrived in Door County? I'll never forget that."

"Well, any friend of Cher's is a friend of mine. That Christmas visit from you and Cher saved the day. I thought I'd never get through the holidays."

"I can only imagine," I said with a smile. "I'm so happy that Cher and Carl are getting closer."

"I am, too, Claire. It's like watching a bud opening on a flower. They're good for each other."

"Now, on the domestic side of things, how can I be helpful?"

"Just your being here has been most helpful, and I look forward to eating more of that pie."

"If you have a yearning for anything else, just holler. All I bake from scratch is brownies, but I can bring you most anything."

"Oh, I've had your brownies. Maybe I'll be ready for them the next time you visit. They're so good."

We soon said goodbye and I gave her a big hug.

Chapter 32

I had to take a deep breath when I got back to my car. Poor Ericka. I felt so sad for my dear friend. I could only hope she would be open to having a visit from someone who could speak to her spiritual needs.

When I got home, I watered the fern for Anna and started some cleaning, thoughts of Ericka on my mind.

I ate some soup for dinner, put on music, and continued quilting on one of my wholecloth quilts. The repeated stitching was therapeutic. It's too bad Ericka wasn't a quilter because it could be comforting to her and would help pass the time while she wasn't working. Ericka's medical knowledge was likely a curse right now. I did believe in miracles, and I wouldn't give up on her. I was getting tired, so I went up to bed.

I had just pulled the covers back when my cell phone rang. It was Foster.

"I'm not calling too late, am I?"

"No, it's fine. How's Madison?"

"It's good. How's that sweet cabin in Fish Creek?"

I grinned to myself. "It's the same, which is comforting. I had a pretty rough day."

"How so?"

"I visited a dear friend who isn't likely to recover from cancer."

"That's tough. I'm sorry about your friend. I watched my brother die from it. It's a terrible, terrible curse."

"So, are you ready to open the exhibit?"

"Yes, thanks for asking. I can't tell you how much I enjoyed our evening together, Claire."

"I agree that it was very nice. I'm glad I was able to experience the restaurant."

"We had so much to talk about, and all I can think of is how I'd like to continue our conversation."

"You can call me anytime," I said with a chuckle.

"Is that a green light that we can see each other again?"

"It might be. Good luck with the show, Foster. I hope you sell many pieces."

"You're indeed a question mark, Miss Stewart. I wish you could be here right now."

"How long will you be there?"

"Not long, but then I need to go to Green Bay before I return to Fish Creek to see you."

"Well, it's nice talking with you. Good luck tomorrow," I said, ending the call.

I wasn't sure how I felt after this rather assertive call from Foster. Did I really want to see him on a regular basis? Somehow, I couldn't see it happening. I did want to remain his friend, however. If Grayson would just give me a call, I wouldn't have to even think about this.

The next morning, I was excited to only have to think about Anna's open house. I fed Puff and then dressed for the day. Puff knew something was up when I put her in her wicker chair on the porch. She knew I'd be gone a good while.

I carefully put the fern in the back of my Subaru and then texted Cher that I was on my way. The air was warmer once again, but cloudy with the threat of rain.

Cher was eagerly awaiting me in the parking lot.

"Oh, I can taste that strudel now," she joked. "I didn't have breakfast, so I'm hoping she's prepared for my appetite. I'm not counting calories today."

"When have you ever?" I teased.

She chuckled. "I checked in with Ericka this morning, and she said the two of you had a really nice visit yesterday."

"Yes, we did."

"She said she had a slice of the cherry pie for breakfast this morning, so it must have been a big hit."

"I'm glad. She was only able to take a couple bites yesterday. So, she's feeling okay this morning?"

"Yes, I think so. I plan to take her some of Anna's strudel when I get back."

"Great idea. I hope Anna doesn't run out of strudel like she did at the Tannenbaum party."

Chapter 33

I loved driving over to the Lake Michigan side of the peninsula. It was beautiful, just like the other side, yet different. Some say it isn't as touristy as the bay side. The last time I came this direction was when the chamber met at the Chives restaurant.

"Isn't this where we turned in to Marta's farm?" Cher asked.

"Yes, I believe so. It's supposed to be along here shortly."

"Oh, look. That must be it coming up. I see some balloons tied to something."

"Yup, there's the sign."

"What a great location! I guess the second floor is her living quarters. Nice!"

"I'll park here. Look at all the cars!"

There were many familiar faces crowded into the shop. Anna's red-and-white decor was charming, and over her counter she had a red-and-white awning, reminding me of Wilson's ice cream place. I looked around to see red leather chairs and just a few tables, which were filled, of course. We squirmed our way to the counter where Marta, Anna, and

Billy stood to help folks. I got a glimpse of Marta's husband back in the kitchen.

"Can you believe all this?" Cher asked in disbelief. "Do you see any club members?"

"Over there is Lee and her husband, the doctor. He sure is handsome. Oh, Ginger just walked in the door."

We motioned for her to join us.

"Looks like Anna's Bake Shop is a hit!" Ginger said as she looked about. "They need something like this in Baileys Harbor. Hey, is there any word on Frances?"

"Yes, I hear she may have a full recovery," I noted simply.

"Who told you that?"

I paused. "I can't remember. Look, there's Amy sitting at one of tables."

"Well, let's go say hello."

"The Quilters of the Door will never have a shortage of goodies from now on," Ginger joked.

"So, how are you doing, Ginger?" I asked with interest.

"Business is picking up with this warmer weather," she said with a smile. "What about you? How are plans coming on the quilt show? Your debut show was such a hit!"

"Good! The word is *cherries*!" Cher said in a joking manner.

"What's that supposed to mean?"

"It means we're having a cherries theme for the show this year, so you may want to carry that theme in your store as well."

"Ooh, I love it!" she responded. "Have you told Lee? Because she has a spectacular cherry tree quilt."

"Oh, my goodness!" I said in surprise. "No, we haven't said anything to her yet, but I certainly will today."

"What a perfect time and place for Lee to show her quilt," Cher noted. "Let's be sure to talk to her before we leave."

"Thanks for letting us know, Ginger," I said with sincerity.

It was our turn to order our coffees and strudels. We both ordered extra strudel, and I purchased a cherry stollen, like my mother used to bake. This place was going to be dangerous!

All the tables were filled, but Cher and I maneuvered over to where Lee and her husband were sitting. Lee was glad to see us and immediately introduced us to her husband. He was very polite and didn't have the strong Filipino accent that Lee had.

"Hello, ladies. I know all about the Quilters of the Door," he said with a big grin.

"And we're thrilled to have such a celebrity quilter in our group," I said, looking at Lee. "Lee, when you get home, can you call me? I have something I'd like to discuss with you."

"Why, sure. Has anyone heard how Frances is doing?" Lee asked.

"She's slowly improving is what we're hearing," I said briefly.

"That's good to hear."

Chapter 34

It was another forty minutes before we had a chance to say hello to Anna and wish her well. I asked Billy to get the fern we had for her out of the car.

"Oh, that's so good of you," Anna responded when I presented it to her. "I feel blessed, as Aunt Marta says. Danke."

"You're welcome. I thought it would be a nice addition to your shop," I responded.

Marta was running the ship, just like she did at the quilt show, so we didn't want to bother her. I was taking for granted that she would do the same for us this year, but I hadn't had a chance to talk to her about it yet.

When we left, the crowd was thinning out. Anna placed the fern right near the front counter as if she was really proud of it. Anna's Bake Shop was a perfect example of community support making something big happen. The fact that Anna was so talented helped, too, of course.

It was a fun morning that continued into the afternoon. On the way home, Cher asked more about my visit with Ericka.

"Did she say anything?" I asked.

"She said you've turned out to be a better friend than she ever imagined you would be. She wondered if you'd said anything to me about her hair falling out."

"I did notice, of course, but I didn't want to stare. It must be such a terrible feeling. She's pretty convinced she can't beat this cancer."

"Everyone reacts differently," Cher said, shaking her head. "Cancer knows no age, and since her mother died from cancer, she feels she has a death sentence."

"I forgot you'd told me that. I feel so lucky to still have my mom."

"And I'm grateful my mom still knew me when she died."

"No one could ever forget you, Cher Bear." We both laughed with teary eyes.

Before Cher got out of the car, I asked her if she knew anyone who could speak to Ericka about her spirituality. At first Cher was taken aback by my question, but then she said she might have someone in mind.

"You don't think that kind of visit would scare her even more, do you?" Cher wondered.

"I think she might find it comforting. She said she was envious of my faith, so I think she would be willing to listen to someone."

"Well, thanks, Claire. I really appreciate all you do for her."

"She has helped me a lot. I'll let you know what Lee has to say about us using her cherry tree quilt."

We waved goodbye with the same love for each other we've had since we were kids. Who knows what the two of us would have to face with our health as we aged?

I carried in all the pastries I'd bought and put most of them in the freezer.

I opened my quilt show folder on the kitchen table and made a note about Lee's cherry tree quilt. I was interrupted by a text from Linda.

[Linda]
Hey, Carole is too proud to tell you, but she's going to have knee surgery this week. She's worried you'll count her out of the quilt show because of it. She'll kill me if she finds out I told you, but I knew you'd want to know.

[Claire]
Thanks for telling me. I thought of something you might be great at contributing for the quilt show. The theme is cherries. Can you make any cherry jewelry?

[Linda]
I'm on it. Thanks for the heads-up.

[Claire]
Don't worry about Carole. She'll be fine by the show.

I was sure of that. Nothing ever kept Carole down. I sure wished the two of them lived closer to Fish Creek. The good part about them living in Perryville was having them near Mom.

Chapter 35

While Lee's cherry tree quilt was on my mind, I decided to give her a call. When she answered, we began chatting about Anna's open house.

"It was nice to meet your husband today."

"Yes, he has little time to get to know my friends, but he's very supportive of my quilting."

"Your quilting is actually what I'm calling about. I've never seen your cherry tree quilt, but I hear it's spectacular."

"I'm partial to it. I made it quite a while back and did win some awards with it."

"When Cher and I decided that this year's theme for our show would be cherries, we wondered if you would let us display your quilt somehow."

Lee paused. "Claire, you're talking about displaying it outdoors, right?"

"Yes. It would be somewhere special so we could keep an eye on it."

"I'll have to think about it. I just can't risk something happening to that one."

"I understand. We'll keep thinking of a way to keep it protected."

"I would appreciate that before I agree to it. In the meantime, I'll email you a photo of it."

"Thank you. That would be great. If we find a spot, would you mind spending the day with your quilt?"

She chuckled. "I suppose I could. I'll attach the ribbons I won with it."

"Sounds great. Thanks for considering this."

When I hung up, I felt 99 percent sure of getting Lee's quilt. It would have to be outdoors, or we'd get requests from many others to have their quilts inside somewhere also.

My day had been full and I was tired, so I went on up to bed. My mind was not only on Anna's big day, but now the addition of the cherry tree quilt for the show.

I had just come out of the shower when my phone rang. I was disappointed to see it was Foster, not Grayson.

"How was your day?" he asked cheerfully.

"It was good. I attended my friend's bake shop opening in Baileys Harbor."

"How nice. That's actually where I am right now. I'll have to check it out."

"You're in Baileys Harbor?"

"Yes. I frequently stay at the Blacksmith Inn. Are you familiar with it?"

"No, but they're members of the chamber of commerce."

"Well, it's a lovely establishment on the lake. I've known the owners for some time. I like spending a weekend here to paint on the beach behind my room."

"To paint?"

"Yes, there's a nice private spot I love, just feet away from my room."

"So, it's a B&B?"

"Yes, but I rarely take advantage of their breakfast. It's located among other businesses, so food isn't an issue. I did have one of their banana muffins once, and it was wonderful."

"What more could a man want?"

"Oh, plenty," he chuckled. "There's a time when companionship is nice to have."

I didn't know how to respond to that. "Well, I'll check out the place on Google."

"That's not the response I was looking for."

"I'm sure it wasn't," I said, blushing to myself.

"I'd like to see you this week if you're free, Claire."

"Oh, Foster, I'm so busy with things right now."

"Everyone is, but think about it. You're a joy to be with, and I want to see you again before I go back to Green Bay next weekend."

"Check back with me. I've started a list of things I have to think about today."

"Now, I refuse to take this as a no. You'll have to come up with another reason."

I chuckled. "Okay, I will. I'm flattered you called and are thinking of me. In the meantime, I'll Google the Blacksmith Inn."

"I guess that's better than nothing. Have a good night, my dear."

"You too, Foster."

I was flattered, but that's all I felt. There was nothing wrong with him that I could find, so why wasn't I jumping at his offer? I think Grayson had everything to do with it.

I pulled up the covers and decided to put my energy into figuring out how I was going to handle Lee's cherry tree quilt for the show.

Chapter 36

The next morning, I was about to go get my mail when Ava called.

"Oh, hi, Ava. How's Frances?"

"I wanted to let you know that she's home now and getting good care. I'm trying to help her with her speech, and I've seen some progress."

"Wonderful! Please give her my love."

"The flowers from the club are beautiful. She was really touched."

"And how are you? Have you had any thoughts about going back home?"

"I can't leave Frances. I feel safe and happy here. I can only hope my husband is traveling and forgetting about me."

"You both are such a worry to me."

"I don't mean to worry you, Claire. How was Anna's open house?" she asked, getting off the current subject.

"It was very well attended. I sure hope you can go soon to see it. When do you think you'll be back to quilt club?"

"I can't say. Remember, Claire, when you give others an update on Frances, it didn't come from me."

I was glad to get a good report, and I headed off to the post office. I had thoughts about stopping by the Blue Horse, but I hadn't put on makeup, and with my luck, Grayson would see me.

I retrieved my mail and the latest *Pulse*. A cinnamon bagel and the coffee I could smell were calling my name louder than my inclination to shy away because I wasn't spruced up.

I walked into the cafe and was happy to see there was no line. I got my order to go and saw no sign of Grayson. I exited the building while sipping the delicious coffee, and there was my old flame coming toward me.

"Good morning," Grayson said without a smile. I knew he was as surprised as I was.

"Good morning," I responded with a smile as he passed by.

Well, that was that. I didn't turn around to look back at him. Instead, I headed to my car and tried to tell myself it hadn't happened. At least we were speaking, but what a disappointment that we couldn't be more than civil to each other.

I found myself still sitting there in the car, too preoccupied to drive away. My heart was breaking, and it was my doing. Once again, I started blaming myself that Grayson and I no longer had a relationship. I had to get it in my head that Mr. Wills was now just another citizen of Fish Creek, not my boyfriend. I finally took a deep breath and drove away.

When I got back to the cabin, I saw Tom approaching me.

"Hey, Miss Stewart," he called out. "I'm doing my usual spring cleanup next door and wondered if you wanted me to do the same this year as last. You can also call me when you're ready. I noticed that some of those bulbs you planted in the fall are starting to come up."

"Yes, I'll be ready right after the snow. I'm so excited about the bulbs. I hope they'll be okay."

"Snow doesn't hurt them. It's a hard freeze that's dangerous, but I think we're past that. If you want more landscaping done, like you mentioned a while back, I have the name of someone."

"That's great, Tom. I really want to get a garage built, but every time I bring it up with anyone, I get pushback."

He burst into laughter. "Yeah, for sure. You'd better want that garage enough to go through all the hassle of getting it."

"Well, thanks for all you do. I don't know what I'd do without you. I'll be giving you a call."

"No problem. Keep me in mind for your quilt show this year. I'm sorry I had to back out last year."

"I sure could use you!" He nodded and walked away.

I went inside and started preparing to take the Noble Park painting to the museum. I'd have to see when they'd be open. I needed to stay busy to help me forget about Grayson's behavior this morning.

A text appeared, and it was my buddy and boss, Rachael.

Chapter 37

[Rachael]
Wedding update! The location of our ceremony will now be our farm. Where, you may ask? Kent and Harry decided we need a gazebo so we can have the ceremony here along with our reception. What do you think? What would Charlie say???

Before I answered, I had to think about how I really felt. Having the wedding on the farm was truly creative and perfect for them.

[Claire]
Good news! Where on the property will the gazebo be built? Your wedding will be perfect, even if it decides to rain. This is the beginning of a new life for you and Harry, and Charlie loved you both. Go with your hearts.

[Rachael]
Thank you, maid of honor! The gazebo will be on the side of the barn where we had booths for the

Tannenbaum party. Now we'll have something new
to put Christmas lights on. The fellas will have more
work to do, but oh well!

[Claire]
Now that the location is settled, think about what I
should wear for it.

[Rachael]
That's another discussion.

[Claire]
I'm going to place some orders this evening, so I
hope I make the right choices.

[Rachael]
You will, girl! You're a natural!

[Claire]
Thanks for trusting me. Tell Harry that I like the
gazebo idea.

[Rachael]
I will. I'll see you at club!

I was glad Rachael reminded me about the quilt club
meeting coming up. I sure hoped Ava would surprise us and
show up. I was so glad we had Amy and Anna in the club
now. Cher and I stirring things up opened the door for them.

I got back to wrapping up the Noble Park painting. It felt
odd to be giving it to them unframed, but Carl had offered

to do it for free if they came to him. I wasn't sure if they'd even want to hang it. I called the museum in the park, and someone did answer.

"Oh, Miss Stewart, hello. Yes, we'll be open until three o'clock today."

"Great. I just want to drop something off for you."

The day was sunny and comfortably warm, so I decided to walk with the wrapped painting under my arm. I signed the painting and also noted the "Door-to-Door Quilt Show" on the back.

I ventured out with just a jacket on, passing many more tourists than I'd seen for a while. I also noticed that a few of the shops were now open again after the winter season. They were popping back up, just like the spring flowers in the yard.

I passed Carl's gallery and decided I'd stop there on the way home.

When I entered the museum, I had to call out to see if anyone was there. Finally, someone came downstairs.

"My name is Claire Stewart. I called about your hours so I could bring you a gift from our Door-to-Door Quilt Show we had in July and will have again this summer. You're so gracious to let us use your park, so I thought you might enjoy this painting from our exhibit here on the grounds last year."

"Oh, is that what you have in that package?"

"Yes," I said, unwrapping the paper. "It's a very colorful scene. I hope you like it."

"Oh, it's very nice, Miss Stewart! I remember seeing the ladies' Amish quilt collection. Thank you very much."

"I'm glad you approve. Thank you again for letting us use the park. If you need the painting framed, we can help you with that." The woman walked back upstairs as if receiving gifts was an everyday occurrence for the museum.

I left feeling good about giving away my labor. I had a little extra time, so I decided to stop at a shop or two before heading home. I saw a navy-striped cotton sweater and pants in a window and decided I could use something like that in my wardrobe. In just moments, I found what I needed in my size. I then went to the shop downstairs, where they had great shoes. A pair of navy sandals caught my eye. I tried them on and was happy that they were not only cute, but comfortable. My next stop was the Fish Creek Market next door to pick up some turkey slices and a variety of cheeses.

As I went on my way, I observed the buildings along the street to see where and how we could hang the quilts this year.

Chapter 38

Approaching Carl's gallery, I saw he was about to close.

"Hey, what's up, Claire? You just saved me a phone call to you."

"Oh yeah? About what?"

"This weekend I sold the sample of your *Quilted Sun* wall hanging. The buyer loved it so much. I hope you don't mind making another."

"Not at all! That's great! Maybe I can get one started later today since I just delivered the Noble Park painting to the museum. They liked it very much, so if they want it framed, I hope you don't mind doing it."

"No problem. I wish I could have seen it before you delivered it."

"I haven't decided on the next building yet, so maybe I'll take a break and do some quilting for a spell."

"Good idea. By the way, how did your dinner date go with Foster? Cher didn't say anything."

"Well, he's a charmer. It was nice, but now I'm a little bothered about how determined he is to see me again. I'm not looking for that kind of relationship."

"It's because there's another man attached to your heart, isn't that right?"

I smiled. "Carl, you may be on to something. I just don't want more complications in case Grayson decides to come back around."

"I understand. Grayson was a good fit for you. Someone needs to sit him down and tell him a thing or two."

"It may be too late for that. Even if he decided to move forward, his daughter would be a problem."

"Well, you said something to me one night when the two of us were at Bayside. You gave me some advice regarding Cher, so now I'm going to give it to you."

"I did?"

"Yes. You told me to clarify what I wanted and then go after it. While you digest that, here's another check for you."

"Thanks, Carl. You're the best!"

"Now get busy on another *Quilted Sun*!"

Dragging all my packages, I proceeded to the cabin. I thought about Carl's advice, but I wasn't sure it would work with Grayson. He didn't like aggressive women because he was from the old school of dating. He mentioned to me once it was a turnoff for him when a woman asked him out. I'd already sent him a card. Now it was his move.

I put all my purchases away before I made a turkey sandwich for dinner. It was just chilly enough to build a fire for the evening.

Puff waited patiently to feel the warmth. I was really beginning to count on her company. After I finished my sandwich, I thought about beginning another *Quilted Sun* as I'd promised Carl. But I had to be in a certain mood for special orders. Artists want the security and income that come with those orders, but they also want to create what they want to and when they want to. Michael felt the same way about his writing. I wondered about my brother and what he was up to tonight. It was a shame we didn't live closer to each other. Was it too late to call him? Our lives were flying by, and we both relied on Mom to keep us updated on what the other was doing. One day we'd look back and wonder where the time went.

Chapter 39

On a whim, I tapped Michael's number on my phone.

"Hey, Claire. Getting a phone call from you at this hour can't be good."

I laughed. "Relax, Michael. It's just a catch-up call. I'm sitting here in front of what may be the last fire in my fireplace for this year. Is this a bad time?"

"No. I'm just mindlessly scrolling on my phone. Are you calling about Mom's birthday?"

"Oh, gosh. Mom's birthday. That's right. It's coming up."

"She's going to be eighty-five. We haven't done anything since her eightieth."

"I simply can't believe she's that old. Her health has really been remarkable. So, did you have something in mind to mark the occasion?"

"Well, you won't believe this, but I've taken up cooking. Still, it's probably best if we take her out somewhere fancy for a change."

"I think she would enjoy your cooking."

"In her kitchen? I really doubt it." I laughed, knowing Michael was right. We knew to get out of her way.

"With the nicer weather, perhaps you'd like to make the drive home for her birthday."

"I may. I certainly have the right vehicle to do so. I'm very busy working on the quilt show, but Cher could handle that for a bit, I suppose. Hey, did I tell you I'm going to be the maid of honor in my friend Rachael's wedding?"

"No, but why are you always a bridesmaid and never a bride?" he teased.

"Hey, look who's talking! I don't see a ring around your finger either."

He chuckled. "Point taken, Sis. So, what happened to that great guy you were dating?"

"He actually did propose, if you can believe it, but I refused."

"That's a shocker. I'm going to have to hear more about that at some point."

"I'm so glad you reminded me about Mom's birthday. I have no idea what to give her."

"I wanted to update her TV and a few other things around there, and she wouldn't have it. I think you making the trip will be the biggest present for her."

"I'll try to bring some things from Door County that she enjoyed when she came to visit."

"Does that mean you're coming?"

"Yes, I'll be there."

"Love you, Sis."

"Love you, too, Michael."

I smiled. Michael was becoming sensitive in a way that I'd never seen. I was always the one to say I love you, and then he'd awkwardly respond. This was a nice change in him. Now I just needed to plan my trip for my sweet, sweet mama.

I went to bed that night with many thoughts swirling around in my head. If I stayed in Perryville just a few days, I wouldn't miss the quilt club meeting. There would be much to take care of regarding the show. I could pack my *Quilted Sun* piece in the car and quilt on it at night at Mom's house. I'd planned to go to the chamber breakfast meeting in the morning, but now with planning the trip to Mom's, I felt I should skip attending the breakfast. I certainly wasn't up for more rejection from Grayson, but I also wasn't going to quit the chamber. In the morning, I'd have to let Carole and Linda know I'd have time for a short visit.

The next morning, I felt refreshed, knowing I had something to look forward to. I was eating a pastry from the Fish Creek Market when my cell phone rang. It was Brenda.

"Long time, no see," I responded.

"I know. Every time I go by your place on the way to work, I say to myself that I need to stop by."

"So, what's up?"

"I had the day off today and wondered if you had time to go to lunch."

"Oh, Brenda, I'd love to, but I really shouldn't. I just committed to going home for my mom's birthday, and I have a lot to do before then."

"I figured you'd be busy, so I have a plan B."

"Really? What's that?"

"Plan B is that I'll bring lunch over to you. I won't stay long, and you have to eat at some point anyway."

I chuckled. "Oh, Brenda, that's so sweet of you. Sure, plan B it is!"

"I have some things from the restaurant you'd like. I hate always eating alone."

"I know what you mean. Well, come on by anytime."

Chapter 40

When I hung up, I became the Energizer Bunny to make the cabin presentable. Puff watched me and knew something was up. I also marked another *Quilted Sun* wall quilt and made a pitcher of sweet tea for us to drink.

When Brenda arrived, I noticed her new haircut. It was cute and becoming to her round face.

"I almost didn't recognize you," I noted as she stepped inside.

"Do you like it?"

"I do. It's really cute on you. Let me help you with all that food. My goodness, you know there's just the two of us, right?" She chuckled. "I have my little table set for us on the porch."

"What a sweet setup. I bet you use this porch a lot. It's perfect for this milder weather we're having."

"Yes, spring's a comin'!" I cheered.

Lo and behold, Brenda brought us white fish chowder from the inn. She had two pieces of cranberry bread, two wedge salads, and two slices of cherry pie. It was like having the restaurant serve us tonight's dinner.

As I arranged our food, Brenda wanted an update on Ericka. She wasn't at all surprised she'd refused more treatment.

"I'm hearing this refusal more and more," I noted sadly. "I just hope she doesn't regret it. We never truly know what we'd do in a situation until we're in it ourselves. You know, Frances from our club had a stroke, but we think she'll be fine again in time. Hey, off topic, but I want you to fill me in about you and Kent before we finish this meal."

"Oh, it's fine," she blushed. "I don't expect too much, and that's okay. You know he's helping build that gazebo for the wedding."

"I know. It's a great idea, I think. Rachael's a bit concerned about what Charlie would think about the wedding, but he'd want them both to be happy, I'm sure."

"Yeah, Kent said he's never seen his dad so happy."

"I'm glad to hear that. I've been wondering what I should wear as her maid of honor."

"It will be hot, rest assured. What about some kind of pretty sundress?"

"It's extra hard because Rachael hasn't had time to even think about what she's going to wear, let alone what I should."

We continued chatting as we enjoyed the delicious food. I was pleased she didn't bring up Grayson's name. I guess everyone but me knew the relationship was done for. I decided to bring him up.

"So, do you see Grayson still coming in the restaurant like he used to?"

She nodded. "Yes, but it always appears to be about business. Do you know if he's dating anyone?"

"I have no idea. I suppose if he was, I wouldn't want to know it."

"You miss him, don't you?"

"More than I thought I would. I had a date recently, and the contrast made me more aware of how much I loved having Grayson around."

"A date? Lucky you! With anyone I know?" I shook my head.

"This has all been so delicious. Thank you so much, Brenda. I'm stuffed, but I want you to know this cherry pie isn't leaving my house." Brenda burst into laughter.

Chapter 41

After Brenda left, I wanted to take a nap, but instead I got back to my *Quilted Sun*. The repetitive stitches almost put me to sleep. I had a way of hashing over the things on my mind while quilting. I mostly worried about Ericka when my mind would let me. I needed to get her out of the house so she'd feel the need to keep on living.

I fell asleep with the needle still in my hand as I lay back on the couch. After an hour had passed, Puff saw the opportunity and walked across my body. I jumped up to finish cleaning some things in the kitchen from lunch. I thought I'd better call Cher to tell her she'd be in charge of the show while I went home to see Mom for her birthday.

When she answered, she said she was just thinking of my mom this morning.

"Well, she's the reason I'm calling, actually. Michael reminded me that Mom's about to have her eighty-fifth birthday. Can you believe it? He wanted to know if I could make it home for a little celebration. I guess I should be excited about going, but there's so much quilt show stuff going on, I was hesitant to say for sure."

"For heaven's sake, Claire. You're not going to let that stop you, are you? Do you want some company?"

"You can't be serious!"

"I am! We're actually in good shape with the quilt show. I assume you're driving this time?"

"Do we have enough quilts as of now?"

"I'm still getting responses, but Kathy's quilt guild has really responded well, so I'm not worried in the least. I haven't heard back from the club in Green Bay yet. I'll visit the shops on top of the hill and make sure they really want to be included. Anything else you're worried about? Now, if you don't want me to go with you for your mom's birthday, that's a different thing entirely."

I chuckled. "Girl, I'd love for you to go. You know you're like family, and Mom has always been your second mother. I hope Michael isn't making this a surprise. Mom doesn't handle things well when she's not prepared."

"You're right. I'll get right on everything. How long are you staying?"

"Just a few days with travel. Does that suit you?"

"Absolutely!"

I hung up feeling like I'd just been given a bonus. Having Cher with me would be so helpful. Driving through Milwaukee always made me a nervous wreck.

I opened my quilt show folder and made the updates that Cher had shared with me. I really needed to firm things up with Marta or we'd be in trouble. I decided to call her immediately just to get that checked off my list.

"Good morning, Claire," she answered, out of breath.

"Am I calling at a bad time?"

"No, not at all. I just came in from the bake shop. Anna had an early order I had to help her with."

"She's so lucky to have you."

"I feel responsible for making sure her business is a success. But I also made her promise not to give up the quilt club because that's another of her strong talents."

"Yes, she's very talented at both quilting and baking. So, will she be with you tomorrow at club?"

"Yes, she will. Now, what's on your mind, dear? I'm sure you didn't call to talk about Anna. How can I help you?"

"As you can imagine, Cher and I have been going over everything for the next quilt show, and we wondered if you would be so kind as to help us again. You were invaluable for the first one."

"I'm sure I can. But Anna has decided there's no way she can be a vendor for you now. That girl has more business than she knows what to do with. She was going to tell you tomorrow at club. I hope she won't be letting you down."

"Not at all. But I'm so pleased you can help us again, Marta. We'll be emailing out a notice soon on our first meeting. By the way, we're including the shops up on the hill this year."

"I hope you have enough quilts and help."

"I think we do. Thanks again, Marta. I appreciate it."

When I hung up, I wanted to do a happy dance. Marta's organizational skills during the hectic day were irreplaceable for our debut quilt show. I crossed off Anna's name as a vendor.

Chapter 42

The next morning, I was more than ready to see my quilt club friends again. I could only hope Ava would show up. I thought about stopping at the Blue Horse, but the thought of running into Grayson again kept me away.

Amy and I were the first to arrive at the library and caught up while getting ourselves coffee. She had a lot of questions about the quilt show and how many quilts she should bring to sell. We talked about rain showers and other things she was concerned about. She had the idea of bringing an open tent, which was what I had in mind for Lee's cherry tree quilt as well.

In the door came Marta and Anna with a nice platter full of cherry oatmeal cookies. These cookies were favorites all over Door County. I snatched one right away to have with my coffee.

Marta said she had talked to Frances, but she wasn't up for club just yet. She didn't mention Ava.

Marta informed us that Olivia would be telling us about quilt storage and care today, but that I should first give an update on the quilt show for everyone.

I tried to be upbeat and said we were doing most things like our first show, but this year the show would include the shops on the hill in Fish Creek. I encouraged them to be a part of the Quilted Cherries challenge and mentioned that we hoped to have good prizes. My first question was from Ginger.

"Are you having any problems getting more quilts for the additional buildings?" she asked.

"We're getting more response from the guilds this year, so it's not a problem so far," I replied.

"One of these times, it's going to rain, and then what?" asked Greta with her usual negative attitude.

"That is our biggest concern every year, Greta," I confessed. "We make the decision at six in the morning whether we have to postpone to the next day. If it's just a pop-up shower, everyone has a plastic drop cloth to use."

"I sure hope quilt owners know this because there's a huge liability involved, not to mention the bad publicity if someone's quilts are ruined," she went on to complain.

"They're aware," I noted. "Are there any more questions?" I could hear Greta sighing in the background.

"I'm thrilled to be a vendor this year," voiced Amy.

"We're thrilled as well," I responded. "The vendors are all from Door County to be fair."

"I'll be there representing Barn Door Quilts," voiced Olivia. "I'm excited!"

"Now that we're talking vendors, I'll be there selling our barn quilts," Rachael said proudly.

"Some of you know that Lee has an award-winning quilt that is of a cherry tree," I added. "She has given us permission to show the quilt since the theme is Quilted Cherries." Lee blushed but remained silent.

"Outdoors for folks to touch?" Greta said, looking harshly at Lee.

"I hope not," Lee chuckled. "I'll be there the whole time."

"And that's a bonus," I added. "Folks like to talk to the maker and ask questions."

"Well, it sounds like everything is under control," assured Marta.

"Everything but the weather," Greta said softly.

Why did she always have to be so hateful? I wondered.

Marta continued. "Olivia is learning a lot about quilt care while working at the quilt shop, so I asked her to share some things with us today. Tell us a few things we may not be aware of."

"Sure, I'm happy to," she began. "We get a lot of the same questions at the shop, so I noted some of them for today. Some people have cedar chests. I have a beautiful one I inherited from my grandmother. People wonder if the chests are really safe for storing their quilts."

"I've wondered that as well," voiced Ginger.

"The best way to protect your quilt in a cedar chest is to line the chest with acid-free tissue paper or an old, white cotton sheet," she noted. "You then want to enclose your quilts in a white cotton pillowcase or a white sheet. Some people wrap them in tissue paper, including in the folds. I hope you all know by now that you should not put any textile in an airtight container. A textile has to breathe. It's also advised that you refold your quilts at least once a year. If you have a spare bedroom, laying a quilt flat is ideal, but there are precautions to take. Watch where the light in the room is coming from. Sun coming through a window can fade a quilt quite quickly. A dark room is much safer."

Everyone whispered their reactions to her advice.

Chapter 43

"We now have various products at the shop to help you clean your quilts," Olivia continued. "If you don't want to tackle washing your quilts, we have someone who will do that for you. Be sure you rinse your quilts well and then let them dry flat. This helps block their shape again. Don't dry in the sun, of course. Some people cover the drying quilt with another sheet in case there are any bird droppings." A few in the group chuckled at that.

"What if I just have a little spot on a quilt?" Amy asked. "I encounter this at the shop quite frequently."

"Always try to treat the spot first instead of washing the whole quilt," Olivia advised. "Start out with water, and then slowly get stronger with your soap. Keep in mind that you can do this more safely on white fabric, but if it's a color, be very cautious if you even want to try it."

"What do you tell your customers about hanging a quilt?" Rachael asked.

"There are many ways to hang a quilt, of course, but common sense will tell you not to hang it in direct sunlight," Olivia warned. "Next, try to hang the quilt on an inside wall for the best temperature control. Change the position if your quilt design allows it. Now, if you need a sleeve for the back of the quilt for hanging, we actually sell that by the foot if you don't want to make it."

"Okay, we'll take one more question before we have to move on," Marta announced.

"You didn't mention anything about dry cleaning," Rachael noted.

"No dry cleaning at any time!" Olivia strongly stated. "The chemicals aren't good for your quilts. I know there are fabrics you can't wash, but airing them out is the best alternative."

"Thank you, Olivia," Marta said graciously. "It never hurts for us to be reminded of these things."

"Marta, if I may, I'd like to address the fact that Ava has missed many of our meetings, without an excuse, so I make a motion that she be dropped from the club's membership," Greta suggested in a harsh tone. The room went silent.

"Does anyone know if Ava is okay?" Marta asked kindly.

"Yes, I've seen Ava," I finally said. "She has some personal issues going on, but I think she fully intends to come back to the club."

"Well, that's not much of a reason," Greta responded. "I have a motion on the floor."

Marta sighed. "Very well," she conceded. "Is there a second to Greta's motion?"

Silence followed, and no second motion came.

"The motion failed."

Greta got up and headed out the door. We all just looked at each other in sadness. A motion was made to adjourn the meeting, with a second. That was the end of our meeting.

Cher and I looked at each other and rolled our eyes.

"Lunch, Claire Bear?"

"Sure!" I said quickly. "Should I ask anyone else?"

"Let's just the two of us go to discuss some show things," Cher advised.

"How about the Wild Tomato?" I suggested. "We can split a pizza and a salad."

"That works for me!" she said with excitement.

We said our goodbyes, and I could tell folks were buzzing about Greta's bold request.

When we arrived for lunch, the weather was mild enough to eat outside. After we placed our order, Cher was the first to mention Ava.

"I'm sure glad Ava didn't have to hear Greta today," Cher said, shaking her head.

"You'd think we all had to sign a contract to be a member. Greta just can't be happy about anything, plus she has it in for both of us since we changed the club's rules."

"Are you going to tell Ava?"

"Yes, I am. I'm also going to tell her she has to be at the next meeting, even if I have to drag her." Cher giggled. "I mean it!"

Chapter 44

"Do you think Greta's going to continue to make trouble for our show?" I wondered.

"She isn't going to make it pleasant, that's for sure."

"I know. Let's give her a job to do. That way she'll feel included and maybe it will even shut her up."

"I doubt she'd agree to volunteer, but we could try."

"She's got eagle eyes looking for anything wrong, so she might make a good monitor. We sure can't put her with Marta, or she'll mess up the whole process."

"What if we asked her to monitor the shops on the hill? She'd be away from us with her territory." Cher paused while I chuckled. "It's worth a try. Tell her we're shorthanded on monitors since we added more shops. She can even bring her husband since he's never far behind her anyway."

"What's the worst thing that can happen?"

We enjoyed our lunch immensely in between our chatter. Cher shared that Carl would have her working more hours soon.

"I hope he doesn't mind that you're going to Perryville with me."

"Of course not. His birthday is next week. I'd like to do something special for him, but he doesn't like a fuss."

"No party?"

"Absolutely not! Something much lower key. Hey, you haven't mentioned Foster lately. Has he called you?"

"Yes, but I'm giving him the message that I really don't want a relationship."

"You've got to be kidding me, Claire. Why don't you at least date him for a while? What's not to like about him?"

"He's not Grayson, for one thing, and I'm not sure I can trust him."

"What's not trustworthy about him?"

"I just think I'd always wonder who he was with as he traveled about. And I guess I don't trust his feelings toward me since he's come on pretty strong so quickly. Even Puff doesn't trust him."

"Now I've heard everything!" Cher burst into laughter. "He's a good contact for you professionally. I'd be careful before you send him away."

"I know. I will. Now, getting back to the quilt show, we need that first meeting to happen soon. I'd feel more comfortable about things."

"Agreed. Carl said he knows one or two guys to replace Grayson, so that's helpful."

"Great! I suppose if I were really bold, I could call Grayson about the meeting and pretend our break-up didn't happen."

"He may surprise you, Claire Bear. We could use help with PR now that Ava isn't helping. Maybe someone else from quilt club could do it. Or what about Brenda? Is she still seeing Kent?"

"I think so, but nothing serious is going on. Did I tell you Kent and Harry are building a gazebo for the wedding?"

"What a great idea! I can't wait for the day. I love weddings."

"That's because it's not you who's getting married."

She chuckled and nodded. "Hey, one of us needs to tell Carole and Linda we're coming for a visit."

"Yeah, I've been meaning to call them," I agreed.

We looked at our watches and realized the afternoon was gone. On the way home, I thought about asking Greta for monitoring help and how best to approach her. Once I reached the cabin and had settled in beside Puff, I decided to make the call.

"Greta, it's Claire," I greeted.

"Claire?"

"I wanted to call and let you know that I took your concerns about our quilt show to heart."

"How so?"

"Well, I told Cher that it's a shame we don't have your knowledge and expertise involved in our show. Since we've added the shops on the hill this year, we sure could use someone like you to keep an eye on things. It's a great way to see the quilts, and your husband may enjoy coming with you. The time goes by quickly, and we would sure appreciate it." Silence was the only response. "Of course, you can take some time to think about it."

"Okay, I'll think about it, but you know I'm not a fan of you all hanging those quilts outdoors."

"I understand, Greta. That's why we're trying to be so careful. My friends from Perryville come to help monitor because they enjoy it so much."

"Well, I'll let you know."

"Great! We'll be having our first meeting very soon."

It was an awkward goodbye, but my gut feeling told me I'd scored. Appealing to her ego just might have worked.

Chapter 45

Cher and I had plenty to wrap up before our trip. She was concerned about leaving Ericka, but I assured her the trip would be quick, and it would be good to touch base in our hometown. Cher had managed to reach Carole and Linda, and they were happy we'd be back for a short visit.

I had two voice mails from Foster, who was trying his best to see me again. I told him that when I returned, I'd agree to see him. With his life of travel, he understood my reasoning this time.

After a good car wash and a fill-up on gas, we were ready to go. It was fun watching Cher's excitement to be going home again.

"I haven't been anywhere in ages, it seems," Cher claimed.

"You haven't been back since your mother died?" She shook her head in response. "Well, you're free to see whomever you like when we're there. You can even take my car if necessary."

"We'll see. I'd like to drive by the old house and see if the new owner has made any changes since I sold it. Of course, we'll see Carole and Linda at some point. Carole offered to have us over for lunch."

"We don't want to miss that. She sure loves to cook and still goes to cooking classes in Cape. I hate that I don't have a gift for Mom to open on her birthday, but I did arrange for flowers to be sent."

"I wonder what Bill will give her?"

"Good question. He seems taken with her. Oh, I almost forgot, Cher! I don't think I told you that Greta's thinking about our offer to be a monitor."

"No way! She didn't give a nasty no thank you?"

"No, I buttered her up first. But I had to hear all over again about her objections to the show. I told her we'd be having a meeting soon but gave her a little time to think it over."

"She'll likely decline, but it didn't hurt to ask her." I nodded.

We stopped to get fast food after driving through Milwaukee. It's a wonder my grip on the steering wheel didn't stick. It was always the worst part of the trip.

Cher took time to check on Ericka while I was in the restroom. She was smiling when I got back to the car.

"I promised her that when I returned, we'd take that drive out to the Whitefish Dunes."

"Oh, I haven't been, but it sounds so interesting."

"You can come with us if you'd like."

"I might, depending on when you go. Getting Ericka in the fresh air with new things to look at will be so good for her."

We arrived in Perryville around five o'clock. Mom was eagerly waiting for us and held the front door open as we brought our bags in. The heavenly smells from the kitchen told us she'd been busy preparing something delicious this afternoon.

Mom hugged Cher like one of her own kids. She had tears in her eyes, remembering Cher's mother, Hilda. I'm sure this was an emotional moment for Cher as well.

Mom's three-bedroom house seemed smaller to me as time went on. It was fully occupied now with me and Cher in my old room and Michael in the guest room.

As we were sitting around the lovely dinner setting, our mouths watered for the pot roast Mom had lovingly made. She explained a bit of what Michael had arranged for her birthday dinner.

"I didn't want a fuss, but he made dinner reservations at Audubon's in Ste. Genevieve."

"Oh, how nice," I responded. "I've never been there."

"He insisted on a white tablecloth dinner for me and, as you know, we don't have such a place here in town," Mom explained. "I agreed to it as long as it was just the immediate family, of which you're included, dear Cher."

"I feel honored," Cher smiled.

"Bill will join us, of course," she said like it was obvious.

We were about to enjoy Mom's chocolate cake when the phone rang.

"I'll get it, Mom," I said, jumping out of my chair.

"Hello, Claire speaking," I answered.

"Claire, it's Austen."

Chapter 46

"Oh. Hi, Austen," I said as I watched the curious looks on Mom's and Cher's faces. "How are you?"

"Fine," he stated. "I hear there's a birthday girl being celebrated this weekend. Tell her happy birthday for me."

"I'll do that. We just finished having dinner."

"I heard you were coming to town and wondered if we could have a drink together, like old friends?"

I paused. "I don't know, Austen. It's going to be a couple of busy days. We leave the day after her birthday dinner."

"We?"

"Cher came with me. I drove this time."

"I see. Well, how about nine o'clock this evening?"

"Well, okay, I suppose that could work. I should come to your house?"

"Yes, if you don't mind."

"Okay, I'll see you then."

"You've got to be kidding me," Cher said in disbelief after I hung up. "That's a lot of nerve, don't you think?"

"Yes, but I sense this is different somehow," I noted. "You don't mind, do you, Mom?"

"Of course not," she said, wiping her mouth with her napkin. "I feel sorry for him."

"Just remember what a manipulator that man is, Claire Bear," Cher warned.

"I know, I know. He said to tell you happy birthday, Mom."

"That's nice," Mom smiled.

I tried not to think too hard about what I'd just done as I finished up my dessert. I could tell Cher didn't approve.

"Is it okay to set up a lunch with Carole and Linda tomorrow?" Cher asked as she got up to help clear the table.

"Sure. Anything you all decide is fine," I said.

"Dinner is set for six o'clock, so you all have plenty of time to be together," Mom noted.

We finished helping her clear the table, and I went to freshen up. Cher said she was going to call some folks while I was gone.

I easily made my way back to the house where I'd lived with Austen for five years. It looked as grand as it always had, but I wouldn't go back to living there with him for anything.

Austen must have been watching me pull into the driveway. He was at the front door in his wheelchair waiting for me.

"Well, hello there!" I said with a smile.

"Come in! Come in," he said as he wheeled himself into the living room. "Thanks for taking the time. I remember we gave your mom a birthday dinner at the country club one year. How's she doing?"

"Yes, I remember. She's doing well. She's happy to have me home for a few days."

"The nights still have been chilly, so I made a little fire in the den for us. Shall we?"

"Oh, it looks a bit different," I noted. He ignored my comment.

"Are you still drinking merlot? I opened one of your favorites."

"Merlot sounds great. Did you manage to build this fire?"

"I'm not an invalid, Claire. I just lost good use of my legs."

"I'm sorry. I didn't mean anything …"

He cut me off. "I know. I'm just still pretty sensitive about it all."

I took the glass of wine from him, and the first swallow brought back memories in the house.

"Here, sit by me," he said as he suddenly lifted himself out of the chair onto the couch.

I was amazed he was able to do that. "It's surreal being here, I have to admit."

"I'm sure. I've had to make some changes to adjust to this damn chair."

"I'm sure you have."

"So, tell me about your artwork and, oh, your quilts," he said with sarcasm.

I knew he really didn't care about my art, but I went ahead and described the quilt buildings I was painting. I told him how pleased I was with sales at Carl's gallery.

"By the way, I ended up purchasing Cher's cabin. I told her I wanted to live there a year before deciding. I just couldn't live without it."

"It's very small," he reminded me.

"I know, but now I plan to make some changes."

"And your man friend? I think you called him Grayson."

"We're no longer a couple," I said quietly.

His face perked up. "Oh, really!"

"He asked to marry me, and I told him no. He took it quite personally."

"Well, if the sun doesn't rise," he chuckled. "I thought marriage was one of your goals in life."

Chapter 47

I rose from my seat, realizing this visit may not have been a good idea. His comment didn't sit well with me.

"Marriage was never one of my goals," I stated firmly. "I wanted a commitment that lasted, that's all."

"You had that with me, if you recall."

"Austen, all I really had after five years was a housemate who was never here."

"Now, wait a minute," he countered, raising his voice.

"Look, I didn't come here to debate our relationship."

"I don't get it, Claire. Why didn't you marry this guy?"

"I don't feel the need to share that with you, Austen. So, have you regretted retirement?"

"Heavens, no. I'm actually doing some traveling that isn't related to work, and I enjoy that. I occasionally consult, but I sure don't miss the office hours."

It may have been the wine, but he was starting to relax, which was something I rarely saw. He described some of his trips, one of which included his dad.

"You know, to this day, Dad still asks about you. He's going to be eighty-three and is still as sharp as ever."

"That's great."

"He sure loved you, as did Mom. I may have mentioned to you that I think I may write a book in my spare time."

"I think you did. How wonderful."

"It's lovely having this conversation with you, Claire," he said, touching my hand. "Every nook and cranny in this house reminds me of you in some way. I was fascinated by your creativity, although I may not have shown it."

I pulled away and decided it was time to go. "I should probably get back to Cher and Mom."

"Are you really that uncomfortable around me?"

"If I was, I wouldn't have accepted your invitation."

He smiled. "Is it okay if I call you now and then? What's the harm if you're not seeing anyone? Or is there someone new in your life?" I grinned. "You're blushing. I know that look."

"I think I've said enough. How about you, Dr. Page? I'm sure many of your female friends would love to date you."

He chuckled. "A retired man in a wheelchair. I doubt that very much."

"For some, it's about the man, not his bank account or physical condition."

"Just so you know, in those five years we were together, I never cheated on you."

I was surprised at his need to tell me that. "I never believed you did, Austen. My competition was your work and the social life it created, not another woman. I was included if necessary."

"I gave you everything you wanted to try to make up for my absence."

I shook my head. "It's getting late, and time has marched on for both of us."

He sat there staring at me in silence.

"Come here. Let me kiss you goodbye on the cheek like an old friend."

I took a deep breath and walked toward him with a smile.

He took my hand and pulled me forward, but the kiss landed on my lips instead of my cheek. It took me by surprise, and I didn't retreat as quickly as I should have.

I stood up, and he shook my hand with a grin.

"I couldn't help myself, Claire. Thanks for coming over. You've moved on quicker than I have, but if you ever need anything, please let me know."

"Thanks."

"Don't party too much tomorrow, and give Michael and Cher my best."

"I will. Please don't see me out. Thanks for the wine. I still like it." I grinned.

I waved goodbye and went out the door.

As I left the house, everything seemed odd again. Cher was right. Austen still had the ability to manipulate. I'm glad I didn't make a fuss over his kiss. Somehow, I think it made him feel more like his old self in some way, and that was okay with me.

Chapter 48

Mom was in bed and Cher was reading when I returned.

"So, Claire Bear, spill it," Cher immediately demanded. I had to chuckle.

I briefly told her it was all pretty harmless, and the fact that he was traveling told me he was moving on with life.

"I think my being in town made him wonder if he should see if anything had changed with us. I think he knows now that nothing has. I would much rather have this civil relationship than what it was before."

"Did he want to know if you were seeing someone?"

"Well, he sure got excited when I told him Grayson and I were no longer a couple."

"Oh, I bet."

"He asked to kiss me goodbye on the cheek when I left, so I agreed. However, when I got close to him, he kissed me on the lips."

"Oh, Claire. How did you handle it?"

"I didn't give a knee-jerk reaction. I think he was testing me, just like he used to. He's dealing with a lot, and we both need to move on."

"I guess you know what you're doing."

The next morning, Mom insisted we have a good breakfast. Cher was thrilled since she rarely indulges in anything more than coffee and maybe a slice of toast. I nibbled on scrambled eggs and some coffee cake from the local bakery.

"We have to let the girls know if we're going to lunch today," Cher reminded me.

"It sounds good to me, but let's make it later so we're not rushed. Maybe one o'clock? It'll be a treat to see what Carole comes up with!"

"You should probably be back here by four o'clock to get ready for this evening," Mom cautioned.

After reassuring Mom that we'd be back in plenty of time, Cher and I made a quick stop at Karen's Hallmark on the town square to pick up a couple cards for the birthday girl. With that out of the way, we headed to Carole's. We enjoyed the drive, pointing out all that had changed from our childhood in the small town of Perryville.

Carole's house had belonged to her mother before she died, but Carole and her husband, Richard, had completely renovated it when they made it their own. A home built in the 1920s, it was a nice mix of old charm and modern updates.

After a round of hugs, we all started talking at once. With these old friends, that's always the way it was. Carole showed me how her knee was healing, and then Austen's name surfaced. When Linda and Carole heard that I saw him last night, they wanted to know all the details. They loved gossip like that. I gave them the quick rundown.

We finally got around to talking about their trip to Door County for the quilt show.

"I designed some cherry earrings for your cherry theme!" Linda announced. "I'm wearing a pair now. Did you notice?"

"Oh, they're darling, Linda. I know they'll sell well," I complimented.

"I have a pair for each of you, so just let anyone who asks know where to buy them." Cher and I were delighted with the surprise.

"I would like to order quite a few," I requested. "I want all the female volunteers to have a pair."

"What about the guys?" Cher teased.

"I'll think of something."

Carole then brought out a tray of iced sugar cookies that were decorated like cherries.

"My goodness, girl! How do you do this?" I asked in wonder.

"I have a few secrets," she teased.

"I have no interest in selling any, but I thought I'd bring a box for the workers the day of the show."

"Oh, they'll love that! Great idea!" I praised.

"Here's a little birthday gift from Linda and me to pass on to your mom at dinner tonight," Carole said as she handed me a gift.

We enjoyed a wonderful lunch of beer cheese soup and chicken salad with fruit. Carole then brought out a lovely apple pie for us to eat. I was full by then, but who was I to pass up homemade pie? Carole reminded us that she wanted to bring back some apples from Door County so she could make apple crisp.

When it was time to leave, we took our usual selfies to remember our visit. Cher wanted to drive by our old alma mater, PHS, before we returned to Mom's. I teased her about being homesick. Though the school looked very different, our memories remained.

Chapter 49

We freshened up and changed clothes for Mom's big birthday dinner. Michael had just arrived from running a couple of errands.

"Claire, these flowers are so beautiful," Mom said, kissing me on the cheek. "Thank you so much."

"You're welcome," I said with a smile. "The florist did a great job."

"You will have a bouquet from me tonight at the dinner table, Mom," Michael added, not to be outdone.

"Michael, you look so handsome," I complimented. "I haven't seen you in a suit in a long time."

"You girls look fabulous, too, and what about our young mother?" he teased.

"Now, don't start teasing me, young man," she scolded.

"Is your dress new, Mom?" I asked. "I don't remember seeing it before."

"I just bought it last week for the occasion. Do I look okay?" she asked as she turned around. "I hated to buy something new at my age."

"Oh, Mom, stop it," I countered. "You should spend whatever you like, whenever you like."

ANN HAZELWOOD

Bill arrived before I could ask any more about the dress.

"Good to see you, Bill," I greeted him with a hug. "Do you remember my friend, Cher Clampton?"

"A pleasure, Cher," he said, shaking her hand. "I knew your mother, Hilda, who was a fine lady."

"She certainly was. It's nice to meet you, Bill," Cher answered.

"I'll ride with Bill," Mom announced. "All you kiddos can drive together."

We looked at each other and chuckled at her kiddo remark.

Bill was a perfect gentleman and helped Mom with her coat. The sweet gesture made me smile, and I couldn't help but think of Grayson.

We all arrived at the restaurant at the same time. Driving through Ste. Genevieve brought back memories. Ste. Gen, as we called it, was founded in the 1730s and was the oldest town in Missouri. The restaurant was located in the heart of the city amidst antique and gift shops.

A large round table with a nice white tablecloth was ready for us when we arrived. A gorgeous centerpiece of yellow roses adorned the center of the table, and there was a yellow rose corsage for Mom to wear.

Michael deserved credit for arranging such a nice dinner, buying Mom such beautiful flowers, and being such an interesting conversationalist this evening. I felt bad for not having a gift for Mom to open, but Cher gave her a beautiful pin that she'd given her mother many years ago. Mom nearly started crying. Linda and Carole had given her a box of candy and a loaf of banana bread that they knew she loved. Michael's card to her mentioned various things he

164

was going to have done around the house for her. Mom had complained for years about the gumball tree in her backyard and wanted it taken down. Michael said he'd arranged for that to happen. She beamed with love when she read his note.

Bill announced that he wanted to make a toast to the birthday girl.

"Your mother and I reconnected in a new way after we lost our wonderful spouses," he began. "Our friendship has grown as if we were man and wife." We all looked at each other as if he were going to announce their marriage. "I like to spoil her when I can because she deserves it. I would buy her anything she wanted, but I asked her if she would like a special ring to show our friendship. We chose this together, and I hope she never feels alone."

We all looked at her hand to admire the lovely silver band with diamonds all around it. How did we not notice this on her sooner? It was gorgeous.

"Happy birthday, Mary," he said, giving her a kiss on the cheek. She blushed in her delight.

"To Mary," we all repeated as we clinked our glasses. The moment was so touching we were all nearly in tears.

After dinner came a beautiful birthday cake decorated with icing of yellow roses. Mom had no trouble blowing out the eight candles with one breath. We all wondered what her wish was.

When Cher and Michael and I climbed in our car to head home, we all wanted to share our feelings about the evening.

Chapter 50

"I think your mother is in a pretty classy relationship," noted Cher.

"I agree," I nodded. "I'm so happy she doesn't have to experience loneliness anymore. Bill's a sweet man who takes good care of her. Thanks, Michael, for arranging to have that awful gumball tree removed. I think that paying Lois Bohnert to check on her for errands is also worthwhile."

"Happy to do it," Michael replied. "If we wait for Mom to ask for help, it won't happen."

When we arrived home, Bill said goodbye to Mom at the door, and then we all settled in the living room for a nightcap.

"This has been a wonderful birthday," Mom said with a big smile on her face. "Cher, having you with us has made it even better. It was almost as good as having my Hilda with us." Cher grinned.

"I wasn't going to miss the birthday of my second mom," Cher claimed. "I spent many sleepover nights in this house, remember?"

"Now kiddos, don't get started telling stories about things I'm not supposed to know because it makes me crazy!" We laughed.

"Good idea," Michael agreed. "What Mom doesn't know can't hurt her."

The nightcap did its job, and we were all ready to turn in. Leaving the next morning would be difficult. With Mom's age and the miles between us, I'm always afraid that the current visit with her might be my last.

The next morning, Mom insisted on making us some pancakes. With full tummies, we hugged goodbye. I had to admit that having this time with Michael worked out quite well. He'd really gone out of his way to make Mom feel loved and appreciated. I let him know that and gave him a hug.

The first part of the drive back to Wisconsin, Cher and I remained silent. We were in our own worlds and sleepy from the heavy pancake breakfast. I thought about the past couple of days. Austen's kiss stuck out in my memory.

After a few hours, we stopped at a rest stop to stretch our legs. Cher thought she'd better check on Ericka since it had been a few days. I watched Cher nodding intently and finally saying goodbye to her. I could tell what she'd been told wasn't good.

"How is she?" I asked nervously.

"The oncologist wants to redo some tests. He's concerned about what he's found."

"Good heavens. Why doesn't he just say he wants to make sure about something instead of scaring her like that? How long will she have to wait?"

"Don't blame the doctor. He didn't cause her cancer. Besides, Ericka knows how to push for information."

"Is she feeling okay?"

"Right now, she is. She wants to start back to work, but I can't imagine she's ready for that."

"She needs normalcy in her life, though. She probably wants to feel needed and have everything go back to the way it was before she was diagnosed with cancer. I can relate to that. If someone said I had to wait to paint, I'd be devastated."

"Well, I hope it works for her. Speaking of painting, did you decide which quilt building you're going to do next?"

"I was thinking about the Whistling Swan since it has so much history. The white building would really make a quilt stand out. Last year we could only hang one quilt in front."

"Oh yes, good idea. What about a pretty red-and-white quilt?"

We were now approaching Green Bay, so Cher brought up Foster's name.

"You know you're crazy if you don't see Foster again, don't you?" Cher cautioned.

"Is that right?" I chuckled. "I probably will if he doesn't give up on me first. When someone is aggressive like that, I always want to resist."

"I see your point."

Chapter 51

After I dropped off Cher, I was relieved to get back to my little cabin in the woods.

It was six thirty, and I was too tired to eat much. Puff was happy to have me home again, so I held on to her longer than usual. Still holding her on my lap, I decided to give Mom a call to let her know I'd arrived safely.

"Oh, I'm so glad you called to tell me that. I always worry about you, no matter your age. I sure had a wonderful birthday. Bill says I'm lucky to have such a good family."

"How about that gorgeous ring he gave you! Can you believe it?"

"He loves to spend money on me. His kids don't need it. We had a lot of fun picking it out. Is everything okay back in Door County?"

"Puff is glad I'm here and is sitting on my lap."

"It's nice to be loved. Thanks for letting me know you're home, and thanks again for making the trip. That was the best present you could have given me, honey."

The next day I felt energized after such a nice visit back home. I needed to get back to painting and stitching. I was just setting up my easel when Foster called.

"Hi, Claire. Welcome home. Did you have a nice trip to your mom's?"

"Good. Very good."

"You weren't gone very long."

"I know, but Cher and I have too much to do back here with the upcoming show."

"Do you have time for me today? I'm staying at the Blacksmith Inn, and I wondered if we could have dinner. I could show you my private beach where I like to paint."

I paused, considering what to say. "It's a bit chilly for the beach, don't you think?" I joked.

"I didn't ask you to bring your bathing suit. Not that I would object, of course," he said with a chuckle.

"Not to worry about that. I really do have a list of things to get done around here, though."

"And I'm not on that list, I suppose."

"I didn't say that exactly, now did I?"

"So, I am?"

"You might be."

"Why don't you stay home and get some things done today, Claire. I know you just got back and have to play catch-up now. Tomorrow I'm going to the gallery to see Carl. Is there any chance I could see you then for lunch?"

"You're making this very difficult," I countered. "How about just coffee at the Blue Horse around ten when I retrieve my mail?"

"Perfect. I shall look forward to it. I'll meet you there."

I knew when I hung up that Foster wasn't pleased with my compromise, but dinner or lunch would be too time consuming and too difficult to handle emotionally.

The rest of the afternoon I concentrated on sketching the Whistling Swan and was happy about the progress I was making. I could only sketch in one quilt for the front of the building, but the side had room for at least four to hang. I was covering up my easel thinking of something to eat when Ava called.

"Hey, what's up?" I asked quickly.

"I took Frances to the cemetery so she could visit with her husband today," she began with concern. "She hadn't been out there in some time because of her stroke."

"Well, that's nice. So, what's the problem?"

"We were sitting at a stoplight near the graveyard, and there was my ex in his white pickup truck. I'm certain he had to have seen me."

"Were you in your car?"

"Yes, of course."

"Do you think he might have followed you? Otherwise, he wouldn't have been looking for you there and likely didn't see you. I don't suppose he could have had a change of heart by now, do you?"

"Never. I get spooked just thinking about what he'd do if he found me."

"I understand. How's Frances?"

"Doing just fine. I know my situation is stressful for her. It was so good to see her at peace when we spent time at the cemetery. She introduced me to her husband, just as if he were there. Other regulars at the cemetery had missed her and came over to say hello. Isn't that something?"

"It really is. Now, listen. I'll pick you up for the next quilt club if that helps you, okay?"

"You're a dear, Claire Stewart."

Chapter 52

The next morning, I ventured outside for some fresh air and to see what was starting to come up out of the ground. The Bittners' place looked manicured and ready to go for the upcoming summer. Tulips were emerging, as well as other plants I couldn't identify. My wooden lawn chairs could use a coat of paint, which Tom could easily do. My cell rang.

"You're not going to believe this," Cher began before I could even say hello. "Are you sitting down?"

"No, I'm outdoors, but I could sit in one of my lawn chairs," I joked. "Shoot."

"I got a call from a Mr. Samson at Seaquist Orchards, and he said he'd like to have a cherry pie contest during our show!"

"Wow, that's wonderful! We'd talked about Anna doing something like that, but now she's out because of the bakery."

"He's looking at this as a great advertising opportunity. He has a connection to the town board, so that's no problem, and he thinks there's room near the museum on the side street for hosting it."

"This is so exciting, Cher. I hope you told him we'd love to do this."

"I did. I hope you don't mind that I answered without asking you first. He said they were thinking $500 for first place, $300 for second, and $100 for third."

"Hey, that's worth making a pie for sure!"

"Thank goodness you agree. The flyers aren't printed yet, but Mr. Samson's emailing me a few rules to list."

"It sure is about who you know around here."

"He said he'd come to our meetings. Also, he invited the two of us out to tour the orchards that are about to bloom and then watch a video in the production house on how they process and sell the cherries."

"Wonderful! I'd love to hear more about their process. I guess I'd better send out a reminder about the meeting. You've made my day, Cher Bear."

I went back inside and headed straight to my quilt folder on the kitchen table. I entered a line about the pie contest, which would make this year's show a big hit indeed.

I thought of Greta. I had to know if she would be on board so I could invite her to our first meeting. She could be trouble either way, but we needed to know. I punched in her number.

"Good morning, Greta. It's Claire."

"Good morning."

"I was about to send out a reminder about our first quilt show meeting and wanted to know your answer about helping us."

"I did think it over. I would like to be a monitor, but only at the park. I'm a member of the Historical Society and have a special interest in protecting what goes on there. I'd hate to see anything get out of hand, and I think the park setting would be most enjoyable for me."

"I see. Well, the vendors are pretty good about taking care of themselves. The Quilted Cherries exhibit will be hanging there, so I suppose that could use some protection. Lee will be there protecting her own quilt."

"It's the public you should be concerned about," she warned sternly.

"Sure, we'll be careful about that, just as we were the first time. Are you thinking about entering the challenge?"

"I'm considering it. So, are you in agreement on me monitoring the park area?"

"That would be fine, Greta. We appreciate any help you can give us. I think you'll enjoy it." No response.

We hung up, and I had to digest the conversation. She was still pulling the strings to do it her way. Now she'd be in the mix of things, and I sure hoped Cher and I wouldn't regret it. I made the changes in my quilt folder.

I checked the map and layout of the park, and it looked like the pie contest would work nicely where Cher described. There should be plenty of room, and it would be a nice space apart from the quilts.

I wanted Lee's quilt to be a special feature, so her tent would be closest to the Noble House. I hoped we'd see a lot of participation in the cherry quilt challenge.

Chapter 53

This morning I would be seeing Foster. I had mixed feelings for sure, but a coffee date would be harmless. Our meeting time of ten o'clock reassured me that I wouldn't run into Grayson.

I took extra time with my makeup, and instead of wearing my normal everyday jeans, I put on a pair of khakis that had a matching jacket, perfect for the weather.

By the time I left, Puff had settled into her chair for a midmorning nap.

The Blue Horse appeared to be very busy judging from all the cars. I had no idea what Foster would be driving, so I went ahead inside and got in line.

"Claire! Claire, I'm over here," I heard Foster say from the porch. I smiled.

"Your order is paid for, ma'am," the new employee said with a smile.

"Very well," I said as I headed Foster's way.

"Good morning, beautiful," he greeted.

"Good morning!" I blushed.

"Do you always look this good in the morning?"

"No. Just when I take time to comb my hair," I joked.

"I rarely come here. I had no idea it was this popular."

"I actually come here a lot since my mailbox is at the library next door."

"Well, now I know where to find you."

"So, you're seeing Carl this morning?"

"Yes. I have a buyer for one of my paintings at his gallery. Of course, I'll still give him a commission. I'm going to switch it out with another painting."

"That's nice," I said, taking another sip of coffee.

"Grayson!" Foster suddenly yelled out.

In shock, I saw Grayson headed our way with his coffee and bagel in hand.

"Good morning, Foster," Grayson responded without looking at me. "I think they'll be calling you on your paint job very shortly."

"That's great!" Foster responded. "I think you know Miss Stewart."

"I do. Good morning, Claire," he said with a serious look on his face.

"How have you been, Grayson?" I asked boldly.

"Fine," he answered shortly.

"Please join us," Foster said without thinking. "You haven't been in the office when I've been there lately."

"No thanks," Grayson said with ease. "I have emails to attend to when I come here. I hope you'll be pleased with the new paint job."

"I'm sure I will," Foster replied. "I'll see you soon."

Grayson walked away as if I wasn't there. I wanted to crawl under the table.

Foster looked at me as if he could see right through me.

"I'm sorry, Claire. I wasn't thinking. I can tell this was not a good encounter for you."

I paused before answering. "Did you notice how angry he still is with me?"

He nodded. "Are you bothered that he saw the two of us together?"

I didn't have to answer, but I did. "I wish you would have just ignored him. I think I need to leave."

"Claire, please don't," he said, putting his hand on mine, which made it worse.

"I'm not going to be good company, I'm afraid," I said, getting up to leave. "I'm pleased the two of you have a friendship. You're a delight to be with, Foster, but I must go. Thanks for the coffee."

"At least sit down and finish your bagel."

I shook my head. "No, I hope you understand." I turned around and headed toward the door, not looking back at either of them.

I got in my car feeling embarrassed. I should have acted more mature about the encounter, but I was caught off guard. Poor Grayson had to speak to his friend, who was also a good customer. Not only did I irritate Grayson, but Foster would write me off for sure.

Heading toward home, I was glad Grayson saw me leave alone so he wouldn't think Foster and I had come together. I would never forget the disappointed look on Grayson's face.

Chapter 54

I had to focus on the quilt show meeting coming up to get my mind off of Foster and Grayson. There was too much I needed to accomplish to wallow in this morning's awkwardness and disappointment.

I finished my *Quilted Sun* wall quilt and wanted to get it to Carl right away. I decided to walk to the gallery. The days were getting milder even though the nights were still much cooler.

"Good morning!" Carl greeted, as he stood helping some customers. "How are you, Claire?"

"Good! I have something for you!"

"Wonderful! I left the space open in case you brought in another Quilted Sun."

I looked up to see my *Quilted Snow, Quilted Blossoms*, the empty spot for *Quilted Sun*, and finally, *Quilted Leaves*. Carl and I hoped folks would collect all of them.

I looked around to see if Cher might be there.

"Thanks so much," Carl said as he took my quilt. "I guess I'll see you tonight. I have two more guys who said they would help hang quilts. One's from The Cookery, and the other's from Fish Creek Market. I'm not sure if they'll be at the meeting, however."

"That's okay, as long as you can instruct them."

When we were alone, Carl looked at me seriously.

"Foster is quite bothered by what happened at the Blue Horse earlier. He had no idea that things were still that tense between you and Grayson."

"I guess I didn't either."

"He really likes you, Claire. I wouldn't run him off so easily."

"You're sure giving me a lot of advice lately!" I joked. "By the way, I chose the Whistling Swan for my next quilt building to paint. I'm trying to get as many pieces done as I can before the quilt show."

"That's great. Hey, maybe you and Cher can join me for a drink after the meeting tonight," Carl suggested with a wink.

"Three's a crowd, so probably not. I'm glad I was able to deliver this. I want to pick up lunch at the Fish Creek Market and then get on home."

Back at the cabin, I ate my lunch while reading over all my notes for the meeting. Would Greta actually come? I was worried about a lot these days. Perhaps I'd feel more confident after getting to the Community Church, where our meetings were held.

Marta was there early, just like last time, and already had the coffee made. She was a member of this church, which meant she had permission to use the space and a key to get in. I was pleased to see Billy, her grandson, who had been such a help last year.

"Anna sent some cookies," Marta reported happily. "She hoped there would be enough."

"I have no idea how many will come," I said quietly. "I must remember to mention her bake shop tonight. Billy, don't eat all of them, okay?"

He laughed. "Claire, is that girl named Kelly going to help again this year? We had a good time pairing up for the last one."

"I know you did, but her dad isn't helping this year, so I doubt it." Marta gave me a sad look.

Folks started arriving, and they were all in good cheer. This was looking good. When Cher finally arrived, I felt better.

Lee, Ginger, Olivia, and Greta were there from quilt club. Greta was staying to herself, and I hoped she behaved.

It didn't take long for everyone to help themselves to cookies and coffee. I made a mental note to have cookies and coffee at all the meetings.

The clock showed six thirty on the dot, so I clinked a vase nearby to get everyone's attention. Greta's first thought, I'm sure, was how I could run a meeting without a real gavel.

"Welcome, everyone!" I began. "We're happy to see you back if you helped with the first quilt show, and for those who are new, we're truly thankful for your assistance. Everything will be set up like last year, except we've expanded to include the shops on the hill." A few people clapped. "Marta has once again agreed to be in charge of admissions and pickups. That's a huge responsibility, so please give her a round of applause." Everyone did. Marta blushed at the attention, and Greta looked the other way.

Chapter 55

"You all probably remember Carl from the Art of Door County gallery," I introduced. "He's in charge of the men who will be hanging the quilts." Carl waved his hand. "If anyone wants to help Carl with that, please let him know. The men did a fine job last year."

"Thanks, Claire," Carl yelled.

"Now, just a reminder: Quilts go up at six in the morning and come down at four," I stated. "Cher, my partner in crime, is in charge of PR and getting us enough quilts. Do you have anything to add, Cher?"

"I really could use more help, especially getting out flyers and such. We do have a fun addition this year. There will be a cherry pie contest held by Seaquist Orchards on the side of Noble Park. This will draw a lot of people by itself when they see the prize money involved." Many people clapped at this news.

"Thanks, Cher," I said graciously. "We're pleased to have the following vendors this year: Barn Door Quilts, Rachael's Barn Quilts, and Jacksonport Cottage. Wave your hands, ladies. We hope to have quite a few entries in the Quilted Cherries challenge that will be hung in the park, as well as the award-winning cherry tree quilt by Lee Sue Chan. Thank you, Lee!" She blushed and smiled.

When I concluded the meeting and reminded everyone that the cookies came from Anna's Bake Shop in Baileys Harbor, many of them crowded around to ask questions. Marta, especially, was overwhelmed. Many of them also stayed to enjoy the refreshments.

"You girls have got this!" complimented Rachael. "I wish I could be more help, but I'm swamped with the wedding and all. By the way, boxes of merchandise have been coming in that you ordered for the gift shop. I hope you realize that after the wedding we have to do some serious rearranging for all your ideas." I nodded and laughed. "Of course, Harry and Kent can help with that as well."

"I sure hope so!" I said, feeling relieved.

"Hey, Claire, are you going to Bayside with us?" Carl asked, standing next to Cher.

"Thanks, Carl, but I need to tie some things up with Marta and head home."

"Okay, then. Good meeting," Carl said as the two turned away to leave.

I waited until Marta was free to discuss some things with her.

"So, Marta, were you surprised to see Greta here tonight?"

"I was! I really don't know how you talked her into it. I just hope she doesn't start telling me what to do."

"Don't be nervous about that. I gave her a monitoring job, so she should stay out of your hair. I just hope she isn't terribly rude to anyone. Do you need anything to do your job?"

"No, not right now. We're in good shape with last year's supplies."

"That's good to hear. We could use more sponsors, but Cher's working on that. Be sure to thank Anna for the cookies. They were a big hit!"

We both looked at our watches and saw it was ten o'clock. Time to go home. Since she had the key, Marta's job was to turn out the lights and lock up.

I went home exhausted and envious of Carl and Cher having a good time at Bayside. I poured myself some wine and took it upstairs to my bedroom.

I turned on my favorite movie channel, TMC, and the movie *Love in the Afternoon* was just starting. It was one of my favorites, starring Gary Cooper and Audrey Hepburn. Their chemistry could be felt outside the screen. It was nice to get my mind on something else. Puff snuggled up to me as if she thought I needed attention instead of her. I think we fell asleep before the movie ended.

Chapter 56

I slept a bit later the next morning but was awakened by my cell going off.

"Aren't you up?" Cher's voice asked.

"Well, I'm awake now. Puff and I watched a late movie last night. How was Bayside?"

"Good, but that's not why I'm calling."

"Oh?"

"It's Ericka. Her tests showed more signs of what they think may be more cancer, but no biopsies have been done. She wouldn't say where the new tumors are, but I'm guessing her lungs. She'll find out more soon."

"Do you think this will change her mind on further treatment?"

"I doubt it. She's always been so stubborn and seems to have her mind made up."

"Call me as soon as you know something."

Poor Ericka. Somehow, we needed to think of a way to give her hope. I checked my emails and texts, hoping there would be something from Grayson. Nothing. There wasn't even a peep from Foster.

I went out on the porch to try to get inspired to continue the painting of the Whistling Swan. Puff claimed her spot in her chair while I painted. I guess she felt secure, knowing I wasn't going anywhere.

Out the porch window, I saw a white pickup truck pull into my place. I didn't recognize the man driving, but he took his time coming to the door. He was fairly good looking but had a sizable gut and a demeanor that suggested he was a good ol' boy. He could see me come to the door.

"Claire Stewart?" he asked bluntly.

"Yes."

"My name is Eric Chandler. I'm Ava Chandler's husband."

"Oh, nice to meet you," I said reluctantly.

"Ava hasn't been around lately, and I'm concerned about her. I think you belong to the same quilt club, and I was told you were the last one who saw her. Is that true?"

"It's been quite a while. Why?"

"Why?" he repeated loudly. "She's my wife, and I need to know where she is."

"Look, I sense something is going on here, and I don't think I want to get involved with it. I suspect she'll come home when she's ready. She looked just fine when I saw her last."

His frustration was evident. And he looked evil, as Ava had described him.

"She's in trouble with the law, and if you're trying to protect her, you're making a big mistake."

"That doesn't sound like Ava to me. I'm sorry, Mr. Chandler, but I can't help you." I closed the door in his face and went into my living room.

I waited a bit and then peered out my kitchen window to see if he was gone. Once he'd disappeared, I found my cell to call Ava. It rang and rang, so I had to leave a message.

"Ava, it's Claire. I just got an unexpected visit from your husband. I didn't tell him anything, but he said someone in the guild mentioned I was the last person to see you. I hope you're okay. Call me."

I asked myself if I should be doing anything else. Ava really needed to fess up to her situation instead of running away. I could see why she was so afraid of her husband.

Seconds later, Ava returned my call.

"Sorry I missed your call. I was at the store buying groceries. So now this idiot is going door to door to find me?"

"Look, Ava, it's only going to get worse. Why don't you take someone with you and go home to confront him? You have to think of your own life, and you can't keep running. There are people who can help you. I'm sure you could get a restraining order if he's threatened to harm you."

She was silent for a minute. "I know you're right, but I can't leave Frances right now. She needs me."

"There are others who can help her. Promise me you'll think about it."

"Okay. I promise."

"Will you promise me you'll come back to quilt club the next time?"

"I can't promise, but I'll try."

With that, I hung up, feeling frustrated. I hope I got through to her. I was determined to get that woman back to quilt club.

My painting looked like someone had deserted it. I wasn't in the mood to paint, so I covered it back up. I needed to get out of the house on this pretty day. It wasn't too soon to buy plants, so perhaps I could do that. I could always get Tom to help me plant things if I needed him to.

I remembered seeing a nursery on the way to Rachael's house. If I went that direction, I could also pop in on Rachael and see what merchandise had arrived.

With a new plan to escape my thoughts of Ericka, Ava, Foster, and Grayson, I jumped in my Subaru and took off for Rachael's.

Chapter 57

Rachael was painting on one of her barn quilts when I arrived. I was shocked to see the place in such disarray, especially in the gift shop area. I gave her a quick hug.

"I'm sorry about all the mess. We have a lot going on, and when I'm not expecting anyone to stop by, I just take over the place."

"I understand. This one you're working on is pretty and patriotic."

"Yes, I like it. It's for a neighbor down the road. His wife passed away recently, and she always wanted a barn quilt, so he decided to get one in her honor."

"How nice! So, do you want to point me in the right direction for the boxes that have come in?"

"Sure. They're in the corner over there," she pointed. "It appears to me to be mostly fall merchandise, so you may just as well keep it all in the boxes until this wedding is over."

"Of course. By the way, that gazebo is looking much bigger than I was imagining. It's beautiful!"

"Well, you know Harry. He does nothing small. The whole wedding party will fit nicely in there."

"By the way, I brought a sketch of how we can display more merchandise," I said, walking over to the area in mind. "It includes more shelves and some middle-of-the-room pieces, like furniture."

Rachael came over to look closer at my sketch.

"You've really thought this out! I like it. You know, I've got some old antiques in the back shed at the top of the hill. I bet some would work for what you have in mind. You can take a look sometime."

"I will. We'll need somewhat of a traffic pattern. We just can't line things along the wall."

"I'm excited, but for now, Harry has to clear out of here as much as he can for the reception. Those shelves you want will be no problem for Harry to make."

"I'd be happy to take these boxes off your hands, but I have no room at all."

"It's no problem. I just talked to the florist in Sturgeon Bay before you came. There will be flowers not only on the gazebo, but in here as well. I love daisies, and it's perfect timing for them. You'll carry daisies as well."

"They're one of my favorites, too. Speaking of flowers, I'm headed to the nursery to pick up some things. I'm ready to go crazy with planting since I'm now the official owner of the cabin."

"I bet you are. I just have no time this year. Kent will help us with some things, but I just can't with these orders."

"Rachael, do you have any clue what you're wearing for the wedding? I think I need to know that before I decide on a dress."

"I think I found *the* dress. Let me show you a picture of it. It's nothing fancy, but it's white and the right length. It's okay if I wear white, isn't it?" We both laughed.

Her choice was so sweet and very simple, and I gave her my approval. Then I asked about what color she thought I should wear.

"With your beautiful blue eyes and blondish gray hair, I think light blue would be lovely, but I trust that whatever you choose will be good."

"Thanks. That helps."

"Did I tell you that Anna is going to make the wedding cake? She seemed thrilled to do it."

"Oh my! How perfect! You're on the ball."

"I wouldn't be where I am on the planning except Harry keeps on me. I'm sorry I haven't been as communicative with you as I should be, but I'm so darned busy. Harry and Kent tell me to say what I want, and they'll make it happen."

"You're so lucky. I guess Kent is still seeing Brenda?"

"Yes, but he doesn't share much of that with us. I want to include Brenda in some small way in the wedding, I think. Kent is beginning to feel like a real son."

Soon after, I left the farm so Rachael could get some things done. By four o'clock that afternoon, the back of my Subaru was loaded with plants of every kind. Besides the two new bushes I chose, my flower palette focused on reds and yellows. Red geraniums were a must for my two flowerpots by the steps, and I went heavy on marigolds because of all the rabbits and squirrels that came around. I also purchased sweet potato vines to fill in the rest of the space.

I was too exhausted to begin any work after I unloaded the car, but I placed some of the plants where I thought they should go. The vibrant colors made my happy place even happier.

Chapter 58

Cher woke me up the following morning with her call.

"What's going on?" I asked with a yawn. "Don't you ever sleep?"

"I couldn't last night after I heard more bad news regarding Ericka. They found more spots on her lungs, as I suspected, that are most likely more cancer."

"Oh no!"

"She has to go in for more scanning on other areas."

"How's she handling it?"

"She acts like she's not surprised. It's like she's already decided her destiny is to die soon. With her medical background, she knows enough to be dangerous. She claims she's not in any pain and she wants to try to go back to work soon."

"Well, maybe she should."

"That's what I told myself. Now, I don't know if you've noticed, but the cherry trees are starting to bloom in some of the orchards. If you're free today or tomorrow, Mr. Samson from Seaquist Orchards wants us to come out to see the video and market."

"Today won't work. I just unloaded a lot of plants yesterday afternoon, and they need to get into the ground. Tomorrow should be fine. I'm eager to know more about Seaquist. What can I do for Ericka?"

"I'll let you know when we take our drive out to the Whitefish Dunes. Ericka mentioned it was on her bucket list, so I said we would go. I think it's too soon for her to go back to work, but that's her decision alone to make. Have fun planning your landscape. You're doing such cool things to the cabin."

When I hung up, I changed into some grungy clothes to begin my day. I left a message for Tom to check in with me and then grabbed a frozen bagel to eat before I headed outdoors. There was Tom in the distance, over at the Bittners', working away. I waved and motioned for him to come my way.

"Need some help here?" he asked nicely.

"I just left you a voice mail about helping me with the bushes when you have time. They're going to take some serious hole digging."

He nodded. "Sure. Tomorrow should work."

I described my mission for the day and where I wanted things to be planted. He always seemed to know without my saying much.

"Say, do you know someone in a white pickup truck?" he asked. Not thinking, I shook my head. "I've been over at the Bittners' house a lot this week getting the place ready for them to return from Florida, and I keep seeing this white pickup slowly driving by. The driver appears focused on your place. I thought you ought to know."

"Thanks, Tom. I think I know who it might be. It's a long story, but I'm not concerned."

"Okay, then," he said, starting to walk away.

Tom's news certainly gave me pause. It definitely was Ava's husband, Eric. I guess he thought I was lying and trying to hide her. I went inside trying to decide if I should talk to Ava again. Was he also keeping tabs on her other friends?

"Ava, this is Claire," I greeted. "I thought I'd better call and tell you that your husband is stalking my area in hopes of catching you here. My next-door neighbor's handyman was the one who noticed it."

"I'm not surprised. He doesn't stop if he gets something in his head. I'm sorry. I don't think he would actually hurt anyone."

"I'm not worried. How's Frances?"

"Good. I took her for her therapy session this morning, and they're pleased with her progress. I can't believe none of her family ever checks on her. It's so sad."

"Yes, it is. Now don't forget, I'm going to make sure you get to the next quilt club meeting."

She chuckled. "I'd really like to, Claire."

I felt better after I hung up. I finished up a few things outdoors and then went up to shower.

Chapter 59

I felt like a new person when I came downstairs. It was too warm to start a fire, so I poured myself a glass of wine and sat on the porch. I couldn't believe my eyes when I saw Foster drive up in his yellow SUV. Had I forgotten some plans I'd made with him? He had to have seen me on the porch, so I shook my wet hair and reluctantly went to the door to greet him.

"Well, this is a surprise!" I noted. "A few minutes sooner, and I'd have just been coming out of the shower."

"Oh, my timing was off," he teased. "May I come in?"

"Excuse my appearance. I spent the day planting, so if you look around, you'll see all my hard work."

"It's all charming and beautiful, as I would expect it to be. So, do you have any more of that wine to share?"

"Of course!" I said as he came inside.

Puff quickly jumped off her chair, snarled at Foster, and ran up the stairs like a streak of lightning. I had to laugh at her consistent dislike for him.

"Well, I guess I just don't have the magic touch with her," Foster joked.

"Maybe she knows something I don't," I teased, pouring him a glass of wine. "Let's go sit on the porch. There's a nice breeze coming through."

"I wasn't so sure about stopping by, Claire, but you promised after your trip we could get together. Did your mom have a good birthday party?"

"She did. It was lovely, and I'm so happy I was able to be there for it. Since my return, I've been trying to catch up here with everything."

"So, what's on the easel?"

"Oh, my next quilt building painting of the Whistling Swan. Don't ask to see it. It's just in the beginning stages."

"I would never ask an artist to do such a thing. I never allow anyone to see my work until it's done. I do want to ask, though, if you're still upset about the encounter with Grayson at the cafe."

I shook my head. "It was silly of me to react that way, I guess. Both of you know so many people."

"I know you don't know me very well, Claire, but I would never interfere in anyone's relationship. I was convinced from what Carl had told me that you and Grayson were no longer a couple."

"He's right," I said, looking into the distance.

"They say the best way to get over someone is to occupy that space with someone else." He grinned at his own offer.

"You're probably right, but why me?"

"Why not you?" he teased with a grin. "You seem to challenge me, and I like that. You're an attractive woman who is mature and doesn't play games. Should I continue?" I smiled and shook my head. "Now, you may not have such a long list of feelings for me, but I've found some chemistry with you, and that's rare for me."

"I have to admit, I was eager to get to know you, Foster. I've admired your work for a long time. And I have to admit that you're quite charming and interesting."

"By golly, I think we have a match!" he shouted as we both laughed.

"Have you had dinner?" I asked boldly.

"No, and I'm rather famished."

"Well, I make a rather wonderful omelet, but I rarely go to the trouble for myself because it takes some time."

"It sounds perfect, but I hate for you to bother. We can go to a restaurant nearby if you'd like."

"I know we can, but I think you might be worth the trouble."

He grinned at the compliment. "I can help!"

"I'll take you up on that. It takes a lot of chopping with a really sharp knife."

"I'm a great chopper!"

"I'll just bet you are!"

We walked into the kitchen, where I grabbed my cherry-print apron. I gave Foster a plain one that Grayson had worn when he grilled here. Foster smiled when I got close behind him to tie it. My kitchen was just the size of a large closet, so it was tight working conditions. He didn't seem to mind.

As we chatted through the process, I learned that Foster rather liked to cook and had certain specialties that he occasionally made. He'd never used an omelet pan before, so I showed him some tricks I'd learned while we sipped our wine.

Foster suggested we eat right there in the messy kitchen, which I'm sure was a rare and homey treat for him. He complimented the touches of cherries in the decor. I felt like the two if us were playing house.

Chapter 60

I set the table while I waited for our omelets to cook. This experience reminded me of Grayson and I eating spaghetti together. It was interesting seeing this side of Foster.

"This is delicious!" Foster said as he put the first bite in his mouth. "You put something in here to give it a kick, and I like it."

"Too much of a kick?" I teased.

"No, not at all. I think my chopping made this just about perfect."

"Hey, I diced the tomatoes, so don't take all the credit."

"You're right. I think the two of us make a perfect combination," he added with a wink.

We had some great conversation, and I got the impression he was slowing down his art production so that he could spend some time boating.

When we finished our food, we went out to the porch, despite him wanting to help me clean up the very messy kitchen.

"When I create a mess, I need to clean it up. It goes with the territory, as they say."

"Maybe so, but not in my tiny kitchen."

He chuckled. "How about we walk over to the beach and see the sunset together?"

"It's a beautiful night, isn't it? We may catch the sunset."

"We need to walk off some of these calories."

I chuckled. "I'm game."

We donned our light jackets and headed toward the nearby beach. Each night, Sunset Beach drew folks who wanted to experience the romance of the sun's final moments. I wondered if Puff would return to her favorite spot downstairs with us gone.

When we crossed the street to get closer to the view, a car came too close for comfort. Foster grabbed my hand to pull me away. The driver's eyes were already on the sunset, most likely. Foster continued to hold my hand as we arrived at the rock-lined edge of the water.

"Do you ever come down here to paint?" Foster asked with interest.

"No, I haven't yet. It's a spot I take for granted, I'm afraid. There are so many lovely locations in Door County. Do you have a favorite?"

"Yes. Where I stay at the Blacksmith Inn is my favorite. The spot I told you about right outside my room has everything I could want. I was hoping after our cup of coffee together at the Blue Horse, I could talk you into seeing it. I do hope you let me share that with you sometime."

"Sure, it sounds wonderful."

With that response, Foster brought my hand to his mouth and kissed it.

It truly was a lovely night, and it drew lovers out of the woodwork. I was happy to have let my guard down a little with Foster.

In silence, we watched the sun disappear into the water. Then we looked at each other and turned toward the cabin.

"I don't want to wear out my welcome, Claire, so I'll walk you to the door and say good night. Thanks for a delicious, healthy dinner, not to mention such wonderful company."

I smiled, kissed him on the cheek, and said goodbye. Did I just have a pleasant evening with Foster, the man I'd been avoiding? I had to remind myself that it wasn't Grayson who was responsible for my current smile.

I walked into my kitchen, which looked like a bomb had gone off, and began cleaning up. Maybe I should have let Foster help with cleanup after all. Puff kept me company, though. She had snuck down the stairs and joined me to rub her fur against my ankles as a sign of affection.

I finally went upstairs, feeling satisfaction about the day. When I looked in the mirror, I laughed out loud at how unkempt I looked. I wondered what Foster had thought.

Puff found her spot on the quilt as I undressed. Before I crawled under the covers, I checked my phone. There was a text from Foster.

[Foster]
Greatest evening ever! Thank you!

I thought about whether I should even respond. If I did, he would take it as a sign of encouragement. If I didn't, it would be rude. I stared at the text, wondering if he was waiting for a response. I finally decided a smiley face would be sufficient.

Chapter 61

When I woke the next morning, happy after my evening with Foster, I remembered this was the day Cher and I were going to visit Seaquist Orchards. I checked my phone for any messages. There was one from Cher regarding our leave time, but nothing more from Foster.

While eating a pastry I reheated from the freezer, I looked outside to find a perfectly beautiful, sunny day. That gave me another reason to smile. My phone rang. It was Cher.

"So, will eleven o'clock work for you? We could stop at Wilson's on the way for a hamburger and ice cream. Are you up for that?"

"You're like a little kid. Sure, I like the idea, Cher."

"Okay. See you at eleven. I'll drive."

Cher was on a mission that she'd arranged, so I wanted to cooperate. I had time to water some of my plants before we left, so I headed outside and grabbed the hose. Out of the corner of my eye, I was sure I spotted a white pickup truck slowly driving by. Was Ava's husband desperate enough to think she was staying with me, of all people?

I was ready at eleven, and Cher arrived three minutes after. I always had so much to tell Cher even though we talked almost every day. I took a notebook to make any notes regarding the cherries.

"I got the car washed for you," Cher said cheerfully when she pulled up.

"It does look shiny!"

"Someday I want to get a Subaru like yours."

"Did you tell Mr. Samson a certain time we'd be there today?"

"No. He told me he'd be around all day."

Wilson's was quite the tourist spot in Door County, so it was good we arrived early. Their history on the menu said they'd been in business since 1906, serving home-brewed root beer, hand-dipped ice cream, and burgers. The red-and-white awning on the corner was a signature piece in Ephraim. The flower boxes in front had red-and-white geraniums to complement the building. In my opinion, Ephraim was the most scenic village in Door County.

"I already know what I want," Cher immediately told the waitress, who looked to be all of sixteen. "I want a hamburger, medium rare, with everything on it. Naturally, I need fries and a strawberry ice cream soda, too."

I had to laugh. "Oh my. Well, I want one of your root beers in the iced mug and a well-done hamburger with everything on it," I ordered. "No fries." Cher looked shocked I'd do without. "And what's this I hear about your having blue ice cream?"

"Blue ice cream?" Cher repeated.

"Yes, we have blue ice cream," the waitress said with a smile. "We only serve it seasonally, but we have some now."

"What does it taste like?" Cher asked with a funny look on her face.

"Some say it tastes like a fruity cereal," the waitress said. "I've heard it called Smurf Blue."

"I don't know about blue food," Cher said with a sour face.

"I'd like to try it after my burger," I told the waitress.

"That settles it. I'll have a bit of yours," Cher nodded.

"So, Cher, how's Ericka?"

"I'm not sure. George was taking her out for dinner for the first time last night. I hope she enjoyed it after being so sick."

"I'm happy to hear she left the house. By the way, did you notice all the new flowers I planted when you drove up to the cabin?"

"Actually, I did. It looks great, Claire. You just might be a natural gardener. They do all the planting for us at the condo. I have to admit, I miss doing a bit of that. But I can put things in pots like the best of them."

"I had a visitor last night, Cher Bear," I teased.

"Go on," Cher grinned.

"Foster came by uninvited. I had just gotten out of the shower and looked horrid."

"Go on," she repeated.

Cher hung on to every word as I told her how I boldly asked him to stay for an omelet and then agreed to a walk to Sunset Beach.

"Girl, if this is your plan for getting rid of him, you're failing."

"Maybe I really didn't want to get rid of him. I just didn't want to start a relationship."

"Well, it's too late now, Claire Bear. What you described sounds like a relationship to me."

Our food arrived, and it was sinfully good. The cold root beer hit the spot, and our burgers were juicy and flavorful. When the waitress brought out the blue ice cream, Cher motioned for me to try it first.

"I think it tastes like marshmallows," I decided.

Cher took a bite and decided it was too sweet. It was no wonder, after her strawberry ice cream soda.

We left and headed through Sister Bay, reluctantly passing the Tannenbaum Christmas shop.

When we arrived in the parking lot at the orchard, we noticed the cherry trees blooming in white to the left of us. It was a sight to behold. Some trees were fuller than others. Cher said some orchards were not as far along with their blooms.

Before we entered the market, we snapped a few pictures.

"I read that the wind and rain predicted for tonight could take a lot of these blooms away," Cher lamented.

"Oh, that would be such a shame," I frowned.

Chapter 62

We finally stepped inside the market, and, of course, deciding where to start was overwhelming. I loved that they offered a sample counter to taste some of their offerings. Cher was not as interested in shopping as she was in the visit with Mr. Samson.

I started loading my cart with goodies from the cherry department. My first selection was cherry applesauce, which I'd never tried. Then I grabbed pie filling, vinaigrette, preserves, and a bag of cherry scone mix.

The ready-made cherry pies lined the shelves, ready to go home with each and every customer. Next to those was the bakery counter filled with yummy cookies, rolls, and pastries. Cherry oatmeal cookies were a favorite of mine, so I decided one of those would make for a healthy breakfast. I also grabbed some extras for later.

The coffee section proudly sold Door County coffee, just like many stores in the county. I picked up another bag of cherry crème, which was my favorite.

Further down the aisle was more of a gift section offering cherry-themed dishes, towels, coasters, cookbooks, place mats, and even sweatshirts and t-shirts. Before I knew it, two towels had landed in my cart. Suddenly Cher came toward me.

"Look who I ran into, Claire!" Cher said with excitement. It was Kelly.

"Oh, hello, Kelly! It's great to see you! How are you?"

She was grinning from ear to ear. "I'm good! I'm here with a neighbor who wanted some help with her kids today. They're playing outside, and they love the rope maze the orchard has."

"I'd noticed they have some fun things out there for kids to do," I added.

"When I saw Cher, I ran over to ask if you guys needed my help again this year with the quilt show," Kelly explained.

"I told her absolutely!" Cher interjected.

"Well, we'd love to have you if it's okay with your dad," I noted. She shrugged her shoulders like it didn't matter if he approved or not.

"Of course, it is," she said with certainty. "I told Dad that I wanted to help again. Billy and I had a lot of fun last year."

"I'm happy to hear that. Billy asked about you, by the way." I reported.

"Aww, sweet!" she grinned. "I guess I'd better get back to Mrs. Wilcox. She might be ready to move on to something else with the kids."

"Tell your dad I said hello," I said impulsively.

"Oh, sure!" she said, running off.

"Well, if that isn't something. Maybe Kelly's growing up," Cher stated.

"I'm shocked," I said, shaking my head.

"I talked to Mr. Samson, and he said when we're done shopping to come over to the production facility."

We got in line and checked out all our goodies we'd combined into one basket and then headed out the door.

Mr. Samson was immediately likable, and he got a kick out of our excitement about the market. We joined him in his office, which had glass windows allowing him to see most of the facility. He began by showing us an informative video that he said the public can watch when they enter the facility. Their generations of cherry growers went back to the 1900s. Anders Seaquist planted the first cherry trees then, and the rest is history.

I'd always wondered who picked all the cherries. The days of handpicking are long gone, but the new harvesting system is fascinating. It's quite the process: In just 3 seconds, a machine harvester shakes all the cherries from the tree at the fruit's prime ripeness. Then, the cherries are captured in a frame and stored in cold water tanks before being sent to a processing plant that de-stems, sorts, pits, and packs them into multiple container sizes. Frozen cherries are for sale by request.

The orchard currently has about 1,000 acres of tart cherry trees and over 50 acres of apple trees and sweet cherry trees. In an average year, Seaquist produces 6 million pounds of cherries, but tart cherries have been its focus since 1983.

Mr. Samson also noted that the Montmorency cherries have great health benefits for heart disease, arthritis, gout, and, even better, sleep. When Cher asked to hear more about their apples, he said they produced thirty different varieties, but the most popular was the Honeycrisp.

The video showed how the orchard produces its pies. Each pie crust has die-cut dough to ensure that every pie is the same. It's quite a remarkable assembly line. To our delight, Mr. Samson told us to help ourselves to a cherry pie when we left. He didn't have to twist my arm!

"How generous!" I responded. "This was so informative today, Mr. Samson. Thank you for inviting us. And the cherry pie contest will be a huge asset to our quilt show, especially this year with our theme of Quilted Cherries."

Our visit to the orchard was sweet, to be sure. Not only did we get a free cherry pie and learn all about the production process for the tasty fruit that's a signature of Door County, but I got to see Kelly, who offered to be part of our show again this year. Would she tell her dad I said hello?

Chapter 63

For the next two weeks, I concentrated on finishing the Whistling Swan painting and another *Quilted Sun* for Carl's gallery. The quilt show was falling into place nicely with unexpected volunteers.

Foster was traveling, so I didn't have him pestering me. A text now and then was all I received. He'd say something cute like, "Hey good lookin', what ya got cookin'?" I would just reply with a smiley face.

Cher was preoccupied with Ericka most of the time when she wasn't working on the show's promotion. Ericka was determined to get back to work, so the hospital agreed to take her part time. Cher said even part-time work was draining on Ericka, but it helped her spirits. Ericka was still putting off coming over to my place or joining me for dinner because she was exhausted. I couldn't imagine what she was going through.

My birthday was this week, and for some reason I felt more emotional about it than in years past. I wondered if it was because I'd been watching Ericka, who's younger than I am, go through so much just trying to live. Ericka never seemed to care whether she had a man in her life, and I wondered if it was because she and her brother George were so close. As for me, I felt off-balance without a love interest. I was a Gemini with the typical two personalities. I was definitely a romantic, enjoying someone making decisions for me now and then, but I also had a strong independent side that wouldn't let someone else call the shots. A fortune-teller years ago confirmed that without a man in my life, I was like a wild woman in the streets. I've never forgotten that, and it always makes me laugh to think about it.

I wondered if Grayson would remember my birthday. I didn't want Foster to know, or he'd make a big deal of it. Last year, Cher and I decided to go to Bayside Tavern to celebrate. She ended up telling a few friends who surprised me, and the evening ended up being quite fun. I knew if I didn't plan something for my birthday, Cher would.

The outside of my cabin was looking quite lovely with all my new plants and flowers. They really did cheer up the outside, and I was hoping that with my morning watering, they'd stick around awhile. I'd originally considered painting my white wooden lawn chairs, but I scrapped that idea and scrubbed them to look like new. Tourist traffic was increasing with the better weather, and some people drove slowly by to admire my place.

After my birthday, I had Rachael and Harry's wedding to look forward to. I ordered a pale blue dress at Rachael's suggestion and hoped it would fit when I got around to trying it on. It certainly would look pretty with the yellow daisies she told me I'd carry. It would be a perfect summer wedding at a lovely farm with lovely people. I asked Rachael if her friend and I could give her a wedding shower, but she refused. She wanted no such thing since it was a second marriage for both of them. Besides, Harry gave her the financial security she'd lacked with Charlie, so there wasn't a single thing they needed.

I was puzzled as to what to give the two of them for a wedding present. I knew Rachael would love a white cotton nightgown, but Harry was another matter. He could buy anything he wanted, so what could I contribute?

Rachael said she'd asked Brenda to attend to the guest book and help serve the wedding cake, so it appeared that Brenda was becoming part of the family now that she was dating Kent.

Our next quilt club meeting was coming up, and I needed to make a point to bring Ava to end all the rumors. I felt for her in her situation. I guess I could relate to her running away from a man because, in a sense, it was what I'd done when I left Austen in Perryville. Sometimes you just know when it's time to go and never look back.

Chapter 64

I was sitting on the porch, enjoying a breeze with the windows open, as I watched Tom mow my yard. The smell of freshly mown grass always took me back to my childhood. Dad's tradition was to mow our lawn every Saturday morning. Once he was done, Mom would make a pitcher of lemonade for the four of us, and we'd sit outside sipping it and talking about the upcoming week. Looking out at my firepit, I was reminded of a pleasant barbeque that Grayson, Kelly, and I had in the fall. The food tasted so good outdoors. And just like that, I had an idea about how I wanted to spend my birthday.

"Me? Grill outdoors?" Cher responded when I told her my plan. "Do you know who you're talking to? I haven't done that since I left home."

"I did most of it when I lived with Austen. If I actually let him near the grill, he burned everything."

"So, you want me to do this with you for your birthday?"

"I don't like drawing attention to my birthday, but I thought this would be fun."

"I don't know why you always want to keep your birthday so secretive. Look at Ericka. I bet she wishes she could celebrate with a party every year."

"To each her own. I don't want you to bring a thing, okay? I saw a new Weber grill for sale at Nelson's the other day, and I'm going to buy it. It's like the one I used to have at home. Do you trust me with some steaks?"

Cher chuckled. "Steaks? Well, it's *your* birthday. I can certainly bring some wine. Goodness knows, I still have plenty from my welcome home party."

"I do remember. I teased you about adding a little wine cellar somewhere."

"I can also bring some shrimp for shrimp cocktail."

"Now you're talking!"

"Okay, so I'll see you tomorrow at quilt club. Are you still bringing Ava?"

"She agreed to it, so I'm holding her to it. She wanted to meet me there, but I was afraid she'd back out."

"Say, Claire, will you let me buy that grill for you as my birthday gift? I've been knocking myself out on what to give you. I'll call Nelson's and give them my credit card number."

"Really? Well, I'd love it if that's what you want to do. I think once I have one, I'll use it often."

I hung up excited about having a simple yet fun way to celebrate my birthday.

The next morning, I called Ava, knowing I'd probably wake her up.

"Get dressed, girlfriend! It's going to be a good day," I encouraged. "There will be so many folks who will be happy to see you."

"Even Greta?"

"Hmm. Let me think about that!" We laughed.

I dressed and hopped in my car, knowing it would take me about forty-five minutes to get to Frances's place. If I was successful with this, I hoped to talk Ava into going back to her house.

When I arrived at Frances's, Ava opened the door before I had a chance to knock. Her face was all made up, and she wore a sequined turquoise V-neck, a hot pink pair of pants, and gold dangly earrings that brushed her bare shoulders. Ava had a flare for her wardrobe, no matter where she was going or how early in the day it was. She informed me she was trying to be quiet because Frances was still in bed.

"You look great, Ava! Do you have a show-and-tell to bring today?"

"Nothing to show. Just a tell."

I didn't pay much attention to what she said. I just wanted to get her in the car and be on our way. As we drove, I tried to bring her up to date on the quilt show.

"Cher says she misses your help from last year."

"I enjoyed helping her, but I just can't take any time away from Frances right now. Maybe next year."

We arrived at the library at the same time as Marta. She had a big grin when she saw Ava.

"It's so good to see you again, Ava," she said, giving her a little hug.

When we got back to the meeting room, everyone was tickled to see Ava and came over to say hello. That had to make her feel good. Greta, to no one's surprise, was silent and remained seated.

Anna brought some small cherry crumb cakes that looked heavenly. She had a German name for the cakes, but I only caught the last name, which was kuchen.

"Welcome, everyone. Especially you, Ava. We've missed you!" Marta said to start the meeting. "We have a brief appliqué program by Lee today called Appliquéd Appliqué. Of course, there's no one better to teach this subject." Lee blushed, and everyone clapped.

"You all are too kind when it comes to my appliqué," Lee said bashfully. "I just wanted to show you the method I use to give my appliqué pieces more dimension. I basically appliqué a piece right on top of the appliqué I want to put on the quilt. Sometimes I do this before I place the piece on the background fabric. See this bird? She has many layers to her wing, so I appliqué one layer at a time until I get the dimensional look I want. I think Anna has done this method on some of her work." Anna nodded and smiled.

Lee then passed around some examples of her method. I, like many of us there, would never be doing this, but everyone loved learning her method.

Chapter 65

"Now, who brought a show-and-tell today?" Marta asked as she looked about the room. "Please don't show a Quilted Cherry challenge quilt if you're entering it in the contest."

"I have something," Ginger voiced. "I made a bunch of these small pincushions out of this old, tattered quilt I had, and they're selling well. I'd like each of you to please take one." Everyone quietly voiced their thanks.

"How nice of you, Ginger," Marta commented. "You can't have too many pin cushions."

I chose one shaped in a bow-tie pattern, which reminded me of all those ties Michael gave me to make a quilt. Olivia rose from her chair to speak next.

"I started this Tumbling Block baby quilt for one of the girls at the shop," noted Olivia. "I love it in these pastel colors, which I never, ever work with."

"It's adorable," Anna was the first to compliment.

"I have a tell!" announced Ava as she turned around to face all of us.

"I know you've been concerned about my absence, and I really appreciate it." You could hear a pin drop it was so quiet. "I'm leaving my husband after some long, unhappy years. The good news is that I've moved in with Frances permanently. I was there when she had her stroke, and I'll continue to care for her in that large house of hers. She has been a dear and has been happy to have me there. I guess we both need help in some way."

"Oh, Ava, this is all good for us to hear," Marta stated graciously. "We all want your happiness."

"The divorce will be difficult, but I feel I'm strong enough now to see it through. I also want to thank Claire for getting me back here today."

"So, will Frances be back with us soon?" Greta asked, businesslike.

"Yes, I'm sure she will," Ava nodded. "She was very bothered by her speech at first, but that's improving."

"Oh, Ava, I don't know either of you very well," Amy began, "but this sure sounds like a win-win for each of you."

"Thank you," Ava smiled. "Frances sent her best to each and every one of you. I will take her a piece of Anna's delicious cake."

"Thank you for updating us, Ava. Moving on, Claire, do you have any updates on the quilt show?" Marta asked, looking at her watch.

"Not a lot, but we want to thank all of you for helping in some way," I noted. "We even have our friend Greta helping us this year." Greta looked away, embarrassed.

"Who is judging the Quilted Cherries challenge?" Ava asked.

"We don't want to announce that until it's over," I said quickly without thinking. "It will not be Cher or me." Everyone chuckled.

"We're running a little late, so please speak with Claire or Cher if you have any other concerns about the show," instructed Marta. "Thank you, Anna, for the delicious treat, and all of you, please remember to support Anna's Bake Shop."

"Do you have time for lunch, or do you need to get Ava back?" Cher asked as she stood up.

"Ava wants to get back home because she's concerned about leaving Frances too long," I replied. "Hey, be thinking about that judge question we were just asked." Cher winked, knowing we hadn't taken care of that.

As Ava and I headed back to Sturgeon Bay, I praised her braveness for telling everyone what was happening.

"So, does your husband know you've filed for divorce?" I asked.

"He does by now," she nodded. "I just hope he hasn't changed the locks before I get my stuff."

"Please take someone with you when you go," I advised.

"I will. I have someone in mind. Thanks, Claire, for this day. I feel better already."

I smiled.

Chapter 66

When I awoke on June 17, the anniversary of my birth, I assessed my older body to see if there were any new aches or pains. Oh yes, my gardening of late had left my muscles sore. All in all, I had to consider myself quite lucky, especially when I thought of Ericka.

Mom always called me early on my birthday, so I picked up the phone by my bed to see if I'd missed her call. There was just a text from Cher.

[Cher]
Happy birthday, Claire Bear! I called Nelson's and gave them my credit card info. Get some grilling tools, too! See you tonight! Love, Cher Bear

I smiled. Cher was one of the most giving people I knew. There was nothing from Grayson, which would have been a real birthday surprise.

I climbed out of bed knowing my first order of business was going to retrieve my mail, and then picking up food for tonight's cookout. I had every hope tonight would be a success.

Puff and I ate in silence for our breakfasts. Looking out the window, I knew it was going to be a perfect day to be outdoors. I was about to head upstairs when Mom called.

"Happy birthday to my favorite daughter," she said sweetly. "Do you have plans?"

"Thanks, Mom. Tonight, Cher and I hope to grill outdoors. It's just the two of us. Cher is giving me a Weber grill like we have at home. I can't wait to try it out!"

"That sounds lovely, Claire. I hope you get my card today. I just enclosed a check. I never know what you might need."

"You didn't have to do that, Mom, but thanks so much."

"You know I can help you, if need be," Mom reminded. "Now, please tell me about dear Ericka."

"She's trying to work part time, but I know it's a struggle."

"Please give her my best, and you and Cher have a fun time tonight."

"We will. Say hello to Bill for me."

I quickly dressed and headed to the post office. After I retrieved my mail, I sat in the car to open a few cards I received from Carole, Linda, Mom, and, of all people, Austen. Austen's handwriting seemed different. He signed "I will always love you" at the bottom of the card.

I didn't know what I should make of that. But it's nice to be loved, I suppose.

I arrived at the Pig in Sister Bay, and it was crowded as always. It was hard to resist all their offerings, but I had no space to store everything. The deli helped me with my menu of thick beef filets, potato salad, fresh veggies, and strawberries.

From there, I went on to Nelson's to pick up my birthday gift. The man at the counter knew I was coming and wished me a happy birthday.

"You've got a nice friend there, Miss Stewart," he noted as he got things together for me. "I told her I'd let you have our display grill that's all put together for ya."

"Oh, that's great! Definitely saves me some time!" I responded. "Now I just need the charcoal and whatever else I need to make a fire." He chuckled.

By the time I left Nelson's, my Subaru was packed. I made the trek home and unloaded everything, which took a few trips. I was tired, but it was a fun kind of tired. It took me a while to organize all my wares. Puff knew something was up when I reorganized the porch. I suddenly remembered I hadn't thought of dessert, so I put aside a brownie mix, which was my go-to favorite.

I was in the kitchen putting things away when there was a hard knock at the front door. I figured it was probably Tom offering to help after he saw me unload the car.

When I walked to the door to see who it was, I nearly fainted. It was my brother Michael!

Chapter 67

"Happy birthday, Sis!" Michael said as he stood there with a birthday cake.

"Oh, Michael, I don't know what to say!" I smiled as I opened the door to let him inside.

"Claire, do you remember my friend Jon Gray?"

"Sure, I do!" I responded with surprise. "How are you, Jon?"

"Claire, it's so good to see you again," he said, giving me a slight hug. "When Michael asked me to come with him to Door County to see you, I couldn't resist. I've been to Wisconsin before, but not the peninsula."

"I'm overwhelmed that you're here," I said. "I just got back from running errands."

"Now look, Claire, Jon and I aren't here to interrupt any plans you may have for your birthday," Michael stated. "We'll just be here a few days to visit with you."

"There's no interruption, and I'm thrilled you're here. The only plan I have for my birthday is to grill some steaks here at the cabin with Cher, who, by the way, gave me a brand-new Weber grill for my birthday," I explained.

"Well, can we crash that party?" Michael asked with a big grin. "Jon is especially good at grilling. We can pick up a couple of extra steaks."

"Sounds great!" I said with excitement. "I think I have plenty of everything else."

"I hope you'll like this cake," Michael grinned. "I brought it all the way from Hoeckele's Bakery early this morning."

"How special," I responded. "I love their icing, and I usually don't like icing. Make yourself at home and look around. The cabin is small, but I'm in love with it. How about some iced tea?"

"Works for me," Jon answered quickly.

"So, did you have trouble finding my place?" I asked curiously.

"Not at all," Michael answered. "We loved all the little villages along the way, but you have quite the spot here in Fish Creek."

"I tried to tell you," I reminded. "Do you have a place to stay? As you can see, I'm a little short on room."

"Yes, we're good to go," Michael replied. "We tried several places, but they were all full. We're at the Water Street Inn, which is quite lovely, actually. It's right on the St. Croix River, and our room has a balcony that overlooks it."

"I've heard only good things about it," I noted.

"Your place is really charming," Jon complimented. "Michael said your cabin was reconstructed here in the 1940s from the Peninsula State Park. We definitely want to see that park while we're in town."

"Yes. Every log is numbered," I noted. "The bathroom was a recent addition. So, Jon, should I assume you're still a bachelor like my brother here?" I asked jokingly.

"Yup, I tried marriage for a short time, and it didn't work, I'm sorry to say."

"Jon has a printing company near Springfield, so our paper has been doing business with them for some time," Michael explained.

"How nice," I nodded.

"Sis, where should we go to pick up good steaks?" Michael asked.

I described the Pig, which they got a kick out of. I also mentioned that while they were in Sister Bay, where the Pig was located, they should drive through and see the progressive village.

As soon as they left, I called Cher.

"Guess who's coming to dinner?"

She chuckled. "The guy from the movie?" she joked. "Sidney Poitier, or something?"

"Even better. My brother and his friend Jon just surprised me!"

"You're kidding! Does your mom know?"

"I don't think so. She didn't say anything when she called to wish me a happy birthday."

"So, are you telling me there will be two boys and two girls at your cookout this evening?"

"I am! You'd better bring two bottles of wine now."

She chuckled. "This will be fun! See you around five."

I rushed around like crazy to prepare for tonight's big event. Poor Puff was nowhere to be found in all the excitement. I just couldn't believe Michael had taken the time to come and surprise me.

Chapter 68

Michael and Jon were gone a couple of hours. I used my time to tidy up, set the table on the porch, and fill the Weber grill with charcoal.

The guys came back in a jolly mood. I could hear them laughing all the way from their car.

"Here are some dandy steaks. Thanks for telling us about Sister Bay," Michael said. "I also love that little town of Ephraim."

"Yes, Ephraim's setting on the bay is the best," I agreed.

"I'm sorry we just missed the lighthouse festival," Jon noted. "That's right up my alley."

"Well, the eleven light houses will always be there, so maybe you can see some on your own. The one at Peninsula State Park has just been redone. You can see it when you go there tomorrow."

"Yeah, like you've been saying, there's so much to do and see," Michael recalled. "I can see why you fit in here with art galleries on every street corner."

"I know," I nodded. "I'm so lucky to have found Carl's gallery right away. I would love for you to meet him."

"Sure! That sounds great!" Michael nodded. "Now, what can we do to get this meal together for you?"

"We picked up a few munchies as well, so I'd be happy to get those out for you," Jon offered.

"Cher was bringing some shrimp and some wine. She should be here any minute."

"I don't think I've met her before, but I've certainly heard her name," Jon recalled.

"Oh, by the way, their nicknames from grade school on have been Claire Bear and Cher Bear," Michael said with a chuckle.

"Good to know!" Jon grinned. "Michael and I go back to high school days."

"Hello! Anyone here?" Cher yelled from outside the door. "Happy birthday, Claire Bear!"

The guys rolled with laughter. "See?" Michael said, making fun.

"Thanks, Cher Bear," I said, giving her a hug. "You know Michael, of course, but this is Jon Gray, his friend from high school."

"Nice to meet you, Jon," Cher responded. "It looks like the party has started, but here are some things I brought. What can I do to help?"

We took her wine and plate of shrimp. The guys opened the wine and poured us all glasses.

"I've never seen shrimp this large!" I praised.

Michael and Jon left us girls for a moment to get the fire going. Meanwhile, Cher and I fiddled around in the kitchen and remarked about what a nice surprise it was to have the two of them here.

When it was time to eat, the conversation never stopped. It appeared the four of us had plenty to joke about for the evening and knew many of the same people. I saw a side of Michael I'd never seen before. He seemed to be truly happy and relaxed. The darkness began setting in, and the breeze picked up.

"Cake!" Michael shouted out. "Don't we have a birthday cake for the birthday girl? I thought I saw one somewhere."

Cher and Michael took off to the kitchen to bring out the cake, which had one candle in the center. Cher carried the plates, and Michael brought the cake to the porch. When Michael lit the candle, they all started singing happy birthday. It was crazy to think I was here, celebrating with my brother of all people.

"I hope you made a wish," Cher reminded.

"Speech, speech, from the birthday girl!" Jon shouted.

"Oh, where do I start?" I began. "Thank you all from the bottom of my heart. I'll never forget this birthday, Michael. What a treat to have you here. I love you all!" Tears began to blur my vision.

"You're welcome, Sis," he returned, giving me a kiss on the forehead. "Now, I hope I bought the right flavor."

"You got lucky there," I noted. "It's not dessert unless it's chocolate." Everyone agreed.

In our conversation, Jon and Michael said they'd be going to a print convention in Las Vegas soon. I wondered if any business at all took place in an area known for its entertainment. In the back of my mind, I wondered why Michael had decided to pay attention to his sister now.

Chapter 69

Jon and Michael left around ten o'clock, and Cher stayed behind to help me clean up.

"That was a first in many ways," Cher noted.

"You mean this cookout?"

"No, I mean Michael coming to see you."

"Oh, I know. I think having someone to travel with him made the difference."

"He seems to be enjoying life for a change."

"Did you notice how good I was about not bringing up the fact he still hasn't found a woman in his life?"

"Maybe he's like us. We don't have to have a man in our lives to make us happy."

"Well, let's not go that far. You certainly love having Carl in your life, and I had no complaints with Grayson. Tomorrow, Michael and Jon are going into Peninsula Park, and then the next day they'll hit Washington Island."

"They'll love it. Well, the party's over, Claire Bear, so I'm heading out."

"Thanks for everything, Cher Bear. If you need to borrow a grill, I'm your girl! Thank you again for my gift."

After Cher left, Puff followed me upstairs for bed. I'd had a special birthday for sure.

The next morning, I felt renewed, knowing I was still healthy and a year older. I happened to see a box from UPS outside my door. It must be the dress I ordered for the wedding. With excitement, I tore into it, held it up, and nodded my approval. It was perfect.

I still was bothered that I hadn't thought of a wedding gift for Harry and Rachael. I looked through my phone for any photos that reminded me of them but didn't have any luck. I thought of calling Carl to see if he had anything at the gallery they would like. My thoughts of wedded bliss for my friends were interrupted by a call from Ava.

"Oh, girl!" she began.

"Ava, what is it? What's wrong?"

"I went to my house."

"Alone?"

"No, I took Bella, a neighbor of Frances's that I've gotten to know pretty well. She reminds me a lot of you."

"Okay, so what happened?"

"Well, I asked Bella to stay in the car. My plan was to get a few things from the house and be on my way quickly, but then Mr. Creep arrived. I think he was stalking the place."

"Oh no, Ava. What did he do?"

"He shouted obscenities, wondering what I was doing there. When I told him I was moving out and leaving him for good, he grabbed my wrists and pushed me hard against the wall. Thank goodness Bella had come inside when she saw him arrive because she saw firsthand what he was capable of. When Bella threatened to call the police if he didn't let me go, he just laughed. 'Go ahead,' he yelled. 'They'll just arrest her instead of me because she's the thief here.' That's when I yelled for Bella to call the police. I told Eric I was done with his threats and to let me go immediately."

"Oh, Ava!"

"He let me go, but every time I picked up something to take with me, he tore it out of my hands and told me I wasn't going anywhere but jail."

"So, did the police come?"

"Yes, and rather quickly, thankfully, so they got to see him in action. He was yelling all sorts of bad things about me, and the cops had to restrain him in handcuffs. I don't think they paid attention to anything he was saying. They told him he could calm down inside a jail cell. The two cops were very nice to me and told me what to do to get a restraining order against him. I'm just scared he really will hurt me worse if I do."

"Go as soon as you can and take Bella with you as a witness. Now's the time to break loose, Ava."

"I will. I'm ready to have him completely out of my life."

"I'm proud of you. Please thank Bella for me."

I hung up feeling grateful that Ava had taken this big step to free herself from her husband. Who knows what would happen now? I could only add her to my prayer list and hope for the best.

My cell rang again, and it was Mom asking me about my birthday. She then jokingly asked if I had any surprises for it.

"So, you knew Michael was coming?"

"He mentioned he might, but I wanted it to be a surprise for you."

"It really was! He was the last person I expected at my doorstep! He and Jon are having a wonderful time exploring Door County."

"I'm so glad. It makes me so happy when I know my two children are together."

Chapter 70

When I hung up the phone, Michael sent a text.

[Michael]
Can you meet us at the White Gull Inn at six o'clock for dinner? We loved the park.

[Claire]
Yes! With bells on!

I loved going to the inn every chance I got and was pleased Michael and Jon were going to have the experience while they were here. I was hoping Brenda would be working so she could meet them.

As soon as I put my phone away, another text came in, this one from Rachael.

[Rachael]
I should have asked you first, but we invited Grayson to the wedding. Alert! Alert!

[Claire]
I understand. I hope he comes, but don't be

disappointed if he doesn't. By the way, my dress arrived, and I love it. I just hope it fits.

[Rachael]
Mine had to have an adjustment, but Harry approves.

[Claire]
My dear, don't you know the groom isn't supposed to see the bride's dress until she walks down the aisle?

[Rachael]
We're too old for that nonsense. Oh, the gazebo is finished, and it's gorgeous!

[Claire]
Wonderful! I can't wait to see it! Hey, is there going to be a honeymoon?

[Rachael]
Sore subject! Not sure.

[Claire]
How early should I come to the house Saturday?

[Rachael]
An hour or two ahead.

[Claire]
Got it. Can't wait!

Rachael had to be under a lot of stress this close to the wedding. Knowing Harry, I had a feeling their wedding would be like no other. Without a doubt, it would be a lot of fun. I wondered if Grayson would really show.

As dinnertime arrived, I decided to wear a skirt and blouse for a change. I rarely went out in anything other than jeans.

I was the first to arrive, and I was pleased that someone was playing the harp tonight. I agreed to be seated and went ahead and ordered a glass of wine. I didn't see Brenda anywhere.

"Hey, Sis!" Michael greeted when they saw me.

"This place is quite quaint," added Jon.

"I love it here," I expressed. "See, I even got a little dressed up tonight." They both chuckled. "I was hoping my friend Brenda would be working tonight, but I don't see her. She was so sweet when I first moved to town."

"That definitely helps in making you feel at home," Michael noted.

"So, you loved the park?"

They both nodded. "The lighthouse is amazing, and we even walked a bit of the trail. I would be there every day if I lived here," Michael claimed.

"Yeah, it made me realize how out of shape I am," Jon joked.

"The next time we come, we're staying at the Evergreen Condos so we're right by the park," Michael noted.

"I'm happy you're already talking about a next time. And hey, you'd be closer to my cabin if you stayed there."

We all enjoyed our drinks and food as we continued to visit. Michael and Jon particularly liked hearing the harp music throughout dinner, which added to the ambiance of the beautiful inn. As we shared some cherry cobbler for dessert, I invited them to come back to the cabin afterward. They declined, which reminded me that I was the third wheel more and more these days. Most likely they were going to have a nightcap somewhere. It was only nine o'clock.

When I arrived home, the cabin seemed extra quiet and lonely. Puff was already curled up asleep, so I didn't disturb her. I decided to sit on the porch and enjoy the cool breeze. Of course, my mind was on Grayson. I wondered how he would respond if I sent him a text telling him I missed him. I picked up the phone and then put it back down on the end table just as quickly. I couldn't risk the letdown. If he didn't answer, I'd be humiliated. For all I knew, he could be with someone else tonight.

Chapter 71

I turned over in the morning to the bright sunshine and reached for my phone. Did I do something foolish last night, or had I been dreaming?

The only text of significance was one from Michael, who said he and Jon were about to board the ferry to see Washington Island. They were certainly in their comfort zone here.

Cher called while I was at the breakfast table eating some cinnamon toast. It was my favorite breakfast growing up, and I still enjoyed it as comfort food now.

"I just wanted to report that I purchased a real dress to wear to Rachael's wedding, if you can believe it. I found a cute aqua one at Kim's Boutique here in town."

"You'll look lovely in that color, Cher. I've always wanted to stop in that shop."

"Question: Do you think it would be okay if I asked Carl to accompany me to the wedding?"

"Why sure! Rachael and Harry have met Carl before, and I know they wouldn't mind."

"Good! Now I just need to get him to agree to go. Who else from quilt club is coming, I wonder?"

"The only two in doubt are Frances and, of course, Greta, who refuses to be part of anything happy."

"You're terrible, Claire!"

"Listen to this. I got a call from Rachael yesterday, and she warned me that Grayson was invited."

"How do you feel about that? Do you think he'll come?"

"I hope he does. They've been so gracious to him."

"You two can't avoid each other forever, you know. I'm trying to finish a Fourth of July quilt to sell in the gallery. I just need to bind it."

"Good timing. I'm trying to finish the Whistling Swan piece. By the way, do you think there's anything in the gallery that Rachael and Harry would like for a wedding gift?"

"I'm not sure. I took some photos at their Tannenbaum party I'll send to you. I'm sure they have everything they could possibly need."

"I don't want to give them anything that would remind Rachael of Charlie. Thanks in advance for the pictures. I'll talk to you later, Cher Bear."

I finished my work on the Whistling Swan by three o'clock that afternoon. I had to admit, it wasn't my favorite. As I stood back to observe it one more time, I noticed Cotsy Bittner from next door coming my way.

"Welcome home!" I greeted.

"Well, we got back last week, but I haven't had time to pop over until now. I like what you've done to the yard. The new flowers look amazing, Claire."

"Thanks. Tom helped me some, but they can't compare to all the beauty in your yard."

"Tom said I should be cautious about a white pickup truck that seems to be stalking the area."

"I haven't seen it lately. It's a long story, but I think the driver was looking for a friend of mine in a domestic dispute situation."

"I see. Well, I also wanted to invite you to a Fourth of July gathering we're going to have on our patio. It's early enough in the day so folks can still get to their fireworks displays."

"I'll be happy to come. Can I bring anything?"

"The food's being catered, so you don't have to bother with anything. I'm glad all is well with you." She smiled and walked back to her house.

It was comforting to know the Bittners were back for the summer. I loved the idea of going to a Fourth of July party.

I called Carl to see if he would still be at the gallery if I left the house right away. He said he'd be leaving in the next half hour, so I checked my face in the mirror, and off I went.

I couldn't believe all the tourists I was passing by on the sidewalk. Carl had quite a few people in his gallery. I had to wait until the last one left before he could look at my latest work.

"This is so different from the rest," Carl noticed. "I guess because it features just one quilt on that large white building. I like it. A lot of folks stay there, and this will be a good remembrance."

"I hope so. Now, would you prefer I paint or quilt something before the quilt show?"

"A painting. I think you're on to something here. I know the paintings take longer, but displaying a quilt on the building makes these renditions unique."

"Okay. I'll see what I can come up with next."

"I should probably lock the door before anyone else comes in. I have to be at a dinner party very soon. Actually, it's at Foster's. He's having a group of gallery owners for dinner."

"That sounds great. Tell him hello for me."

Chapter 72

"I can, if you're serious."

"Well, maybe not, then. I don't want him to think I'm after his attention."

"Women!" Carl exaggerated. "I'll never understand them in a million years!"

I laughed. "We act in mysterious ways on purpose," I teased. "You have a great evening, Carl. By the way, with all these tourists, you need to hire some extra help."

He chuckled, knowing who I meant. "Cher will be in tomorrow. You know, she asked me to go to the wedding with her."

"Can you?"

"If my sister will agree to watch the shop, I'd love to."

"Great! Well, I may see you then, I suppose."

Off I went to head home, where I needed to decide on another painting. My cell rang.

"Hey, Michael!" I answered.

"Hey, Sis. We're just getting off the ferry, and we're exhausted. Is it okay to skip seeing you tonight?"

"Yeah, that's fine. I'm so glad you enjoyed the day."

"Jon's a great photographer, so he captured some amazing shots. Is everything okay with you?"

"Yep. I just turned in another painting, and my next-door neighbors have returned from Florida, so it's been a good day."

So that was that. Michael and Jon were having their own wonderful time in Door County. I suppose it was just as well. I was perfectly happy to have my evening free. I had lots of odds and ends I'd been putting off. Now I just had to focus.

I fixed a salad for dinner that had everything in it but the kitchen sink, as they say. I sat on the porch and sipped some wine as I crunched away on my salad. There sure was a lot of traffic going by. I was guessing that the crowds were forming for the sunset. I began wishing Grayson were here to watch it with me.

By eight o'clock, I was ready to turn in and watch a good movie. As I undressed, Michael called.

"Hey. What's going on?" I asked curiously.

"Change of plans, I'm sorry to say. Jon just got a call that his mother is in the hospital from a possible stroke. He's very upset, so we're leaving right away. I'm sorry we can't say a proper goodbye to you, but we need to go."

"Of course. I'm so sorry. Please tell Jon his mother will be in my prayers. I hope you're not too tired for that long drive. Be safe, okay?"

"We'll be fine. We'll take turns driving. Thank you so much for your hospitality, Sis."

"Michael, I truly loved having you here and can't wait until you can come back."

"I think you made a wise choice moving here, and yes, we'll return. Love you."

"Love you, too!" I said with sadness.

Michael's visit was short and sweet, but I would never forget the effort he made for my birthday. It meant the world to me that he cared where I lived and what I was doing in my life. Jon was fortunate to have such a good friend as well in his time of need.

I was just surfing the channels on the TV when a text came in from Rachael.

[Rachael]
Do you really think I'm doing the right thing here by getting married? What If this doesn't work?

[Claire]
Relax, my friend. You're just getting the normal premarital jitters. You're doing the right thing.

[Rachael]
But Charlie!

[Claire]
Charlie's smiling on both of you.

[Rachael]
I keep getting signals that he may not be.

[Claire]
Stop, Rachael. Now, is everything checked off your to-do list?

[Rachael]
Yes, I think so.

[Claire]
Tomorrow's going to be one of the best days of your life. Harry adores you. Everyone can see that. You have absolutely nothing to worry about.

[Rachael]
Nothing? I'm marrying Harry, for God's sake.

[Claire]
You've got this, girlfriend. I'll see you at the house. I'll be right there with you.

Chapter 73

The next morning, I heard church bells. I was searching for a wedding, but there were no bride and groom in the church. I slowly came to reality from my sleep and realized it was Rachael and Harry's wedding day. It was going to be great fun, even if something went wrong. I was hoping Grayson would show up and we could get past our awkwardness from the past six months.

After breakfast, I took my time showering and dressing. I decided to wear my hair pulled back to show off the pearl jewelry I had in mind to wear with my new blue dress. I got lucky with the dress I'd ordered. It fit me perfectly.

It was a cloudy day, but there was no chance of rain. I had to admit, I was a little nervous to be Rachael's maid of honor since I'd be on view as part of the wedding party. As I drove to the top of the hill to get to Rachael's house, I could see a lot of activity going on.

Rachael was already in her lovely wedding dress when I walked in. It had simple lines and a classic, timeless style. All she needed was the ring of daisies on her head.

"Oh, Rachael, you look so beautiful. Harry is going to pass out when he sees his gorgeous bride."

Rachael burst into laughter. "Well, if he does, he'd better snap out of it quickly! We spent too much time planning this day for him to spend it on the floor!"

"I want you to enjoy every moment of this special day, my friend. You and Harry are perfect for each other."

Rachael smiled. "Now, about our honeymoon, we're just going to be gone a few days. We can do a trip later. I certainly don't want to miss vending at the quilt show because it's a great opportunity for me." I nodded and smiled my approval.

Rachael and I walked hand in hand carefully down the hill to the barn, from which she'd later walk to the gazebo. Brenda was already there and looked sweet in a pretty yellow dress. The daisy corsage was perfect for her. Rachael gave her instructions on the guest book that was placed near the door of the barn.

I peeked out the barn window and saw the beautiful gazebo, which was all decked out in daisies and greenery. The white chairs for the guests were placed in a U-shape on one side of the gazebo. They were filling up quickly, as the wedding was about to begin. My job was to make sure Rachael had everything she needed.

Under a tent nearby, three string musicians were playing soft music to create the mood. Guests were murmuring quietly to each other in anticipation of the event. Those in attendance weren't allowed in the barn until after the wedding.

Five minutes until showtime. That meant it was time for me to place the ring of daisies on Rachael's head. I got chills. She looked so pretty, and she couldn't stop smiling.

"Can you see Harry or Kent out there?" Rachael asked nervously.

"Yes. They're standing just outside of the gazebo. Your groom and best man are ready for us, my friend. Are you ready? Brenda has sent the signal for me to start walking."

"I'm ready," Rachael said softly. I squeezed her hand as one last sign of encouragement.

I came out of the barn and slowly walked to the gazebo, careful not to trip. Kent offered his hand to help me step into the gazebo. He looked so handsome and a bit nervous, too. We took our positions and looked for the beautiful bride to make her entrance. The music suddenly changed to the traditional "Here Comes the Bride."

All eyes were on Rachael's entrance. She was beaming and looked stunning as she left the barn to meet her groom. Harry looked mighty dapper in his tux. Was that a tear I saw fall as Rachael approached him? He gently took her hand and gave her a wink as they joined us in the gazebo. We were now facing the preacher who was going to marry them. Thank goodness I didn't have to look in the crowd to see whether Grayson was there.

After a brief reminder about the importance of the marriage vows, the preacher asked them each to say their vows. They'd taken the time to write their own. Rachael had tears slowly creeping down her cheeks during hers. I was holding mine back with everything I had. I'd never seen Harry as serious or as sweet as when he pledged to be by Rachael's side until he took his last breath. He was completely in love with his bride, and it showed all over his face.

"You may kiss the bride," the preacher said, and the crowd broke into applause.

Harry, in his dramatic way, took Rachael in his arms, gave her a dip, and planted a passionate kiss on her lips. The crowd loved it and cheered their approval.

The music began again, and we followed the two of them to the reception line on the side of the barn. I hugged Rachael like she was my own sister. I was so happy for both of them. Harry grabbed me like I was part of the prize, which made me laugh.

"Thanks for helping my lovely bride today," Harry said with tears in his eyes. I grinned with pride.

Brenda gravitated next to Kent in the line, leaving me, once again, feeling like the third wheel.

Chapter 74

I knew many of the folks in the receiving line, but suddenly there was Grayson, right in front of me. I was speechless.

"You look very beautiful, Claire," Grayson told me before moving on to Harry, who was next in line. Grayson gave Harry a generous hug of congratulations. I just stood there, not knowing what to do except smile.

Grayson also hugged Rachael. For a moment, I tried to imagine his arms around me again.

After folks went through the line, they headed into the barn where there was a bar and food. The barn had been transformed into a beautiful reception hall with cheery flowers, greenery, and white table coverings. There was a nice round table set for the wedding party and Brenda. I glanced around and noticed some quilt club members. There was Lee and her husband, Marta and her husband, Ginger, and Anna, who likely came with Marta. Cher and Carl looked great together; he'd chosen an aqua tie to complement her dress. Everyone appeared to be having a merry time. Olivia and Amy, all dressed up, were starting my way. Olivia whispered in my ear that Ava and Frances would not be coming. Cher then joined us and gave her account of how romantic the ceremony was. I had to agree.

"It was perfect for the two of them," I noted. "Harry likes things short and sweet." They chuckled.

Carl joined us and invited me to sit with them. I said I would after Kent gave his toast and I gave mine.

The barn became so full then that I truly lost track of Grayson. I was pretty sure he'd left after going through the receiving line. Kent clinked his glass for our attention.

"Congratulations, Rachael and Dad," he began. "I couldn't be happier for the two of you. I love you both and wish you all the happiness in the world." Everyone clapped. Now it was my turn. I took a deep breath and stood up.

"Harry and Rachael, you started out as friends and became so much more. This is your time and your special day. You're a perfect match with so much love to offer. May God bless you both." I sat down as the guests applauded. Kent and I had both kept it short and sweet like the couple had requested.

"Thanks, Claire, for everything. You've become such a special friend to me, and I appreciate that you were here to stand up with us on our big day," Rachael said to me with watery eyes. "Now, did you get to talk to Grayson?" I shook my head.

We were served an array of entrées, including sushi, sugar-cured ham, and beef Wellington, and an array of sides to match. I had a feeling Harry chose the abundant menu. There were many toasts and clinks of champagne glasses as time went along. How fun this would have been with Grayson at my side.

The musicians continued playing soft music in the background, but no one chose to dance. A beautiful, large wedding cake was wheeled out from the kitchen. Anna was right there, orchestrating everything. The layers of fancy white icing were embellished with red raspberries. After slices were cut for folks requesting a piece, a light drizzle of chocolate topped each piece. Brenda helped serve it. I found the cake to be the best part of the reception's food offerings.

Some of the crowd began to disperse outdoors, where there was a small outside bar set up. I had to give Harry credit today. He kept his eyes on his bride instead of being the party animal I knew he was. He looked at Rachael with such adoration, as if he'd just won the biggest prize of all.

Carl, Cher, and I decided to walk outside along with the crowd.

"We got to visit a bit with Grayson before he left," Cher reported.

"Did he get a bite to eat?"

"No," Carl said, looking down. "He complimented the wedding but said he had to leave. He didn't say why."

"Well, at least he came," I replied. "It meant a lot to Rachael and Harry."

"I'm sorry it hasn't worked out for the two of you," Carl said sadly.

"It is what it is," I said, shrugging my shoulders. "In more pleasant news, wasn't that cake to die for?" They laughed.

Chapter 75

"Claire! Claire!" Kent yelled. "You're wanted at the gazebo to catch Rachael's bouquet. Brenda tried to get out of it, but I made her promise she would stay."

"Come on, girls," chimed Ginger to Cher and me. "I want to know my future." We laughed and followed her.

Rachael stepped up on the gazebo and sized up the crowd behind her.

"Beware, ladies!" she teased. "One of you could be next."

We all looked at each other and tried to hide behind Cher. In her heart, I knew she would love to catch it.

"No cheating!" Harry yelled out.

"Okay, on the count of three, I'm going to give this a whirl," Rachael warned. "One, two, three!"

Cher quickly moved away from me in front, and the bouquet landed directly in my arms. I quickly reacted by bouncing the bouquet back to Cher, but she wouldn't have it. The crowd went wild with cheers.

"Congratulations, Claire!" Rachael called out. I cringed, knowing the whole episode was on video.

Harry then took the stage and waved a garter in his hand. Very few men were there, but some young boys thought it would be fun to be in on the action. On the count of three, Harry threw the garter over his head. A young boy who didn't look any older than twelve clamored for it. Everyone cheered.

The photographer then quickly took a picture of the two of us.

"Do you want this for a keepsake?" I asked Rachael when I encouraged her to take the bouquet back.

"Sure," she reluctantly agreed. "I know it was embarrassing for you."

"I wish Grayson would have been here," Cher noted.

"I hate to ask, but it appears Anna and Brenda need some help with the wedding cake," Rachael hinted.

"Sure, we can help," I offered quickly. "Is there anything else?"

"Yes. Harry and I want to leave soon, so we'll be going up to the house to change. Kent knows everything that needs to be done. He's going to put the gifts in the back room when everyone is gone. I can't thank you enough, but we want to get away before something goes wrong!" We all burst into laughter.

Folks seemed to leave all at once after that. Cher, Carl, and I helped where we could. Kent had a plan for executing the cleanup efforts, and we just followed his lead. As we worked, Carl kept teasing me about catching the bouquet.

"Brenda lucked out," Kent teased as he was folding some chairs.

Carl and Cher decided to leave then. After saying farewell to Kent and Brenda, I walked up to Rachael's house to get my car. Harry's Hummer was still there, so they hadn't left. Funny signs saying *Just Married* were applied all over the

Hummer. My imagination refused to let me reason why they were still in the house.

As I drove away, I felt the bittersweetness of the day. Everything had gone perfectly as planned for Rachael and Harry, but my emotions were all out of whack. It would have been so nice to have had at least a brief conversation with Grayson. I hoped no one would tell him I caught the bouquet.

My cabin felt quiet and lonely tonight. I picked up Puff and hugged her as I ascended the stairs.

Chapter 76

Since July 4 was at our doorstep, I decided to pull out the flag that Cher had stored in the front closet. My next mission was preparing for tomorrow evening's quilt show meeting. When I sent out an email reminder, I made sure Kelly was on the list, too. It was nice that she was now driving, but Grayson was likely having nightmares about it. I needed to run off some copies for the meeting, so I headed to the library. When I got out of the car, Cher called.

"Hey, Claire. I'm working at the gallery today, and there's a lady looking at your quilt buildings. She's wondering which building you're doing next. Do you know?"

"I'm not sure yet. Does she have any suggestions?"

"She was asking about Julia's restaurant by the park. She stays at the Evergreen Condos a lot."

"Well, I'll check and see whether I have a photo of that. Get her name and number in case I do one. That large lawn chair is quite the signature there, so perhaps I could put a quilt on that."

"You might have something there."

On the way home, I gave Julia's corner restaurant some more thought. I'd have to look into it.

The rest of the evening, I was occupied by thoughts about the meeting and then checking my phone for photographs of Julia's. My mood wasn't the best, so it was hard to get enthused about anything. I just wanted to sleep.

Checking my phone the next morning, I was pleased to see there were many RSVPs to the meeting, including one from Kelly. When my phone rang, I was happy to see it was Carole.

"Good morning!" she greeted. "I just talked to Cher to confirm that we had a place to stay during the show."

"We can't wait to see you! We're having a meeting tonight, by the way."

"Linda and I wondered if we would have the same area as we did last year?"

"Yes, you will. We've had to add more monitors this year because of the shops on the hill being included. We also have a naysayer of the show monitoring the park area. I'm a bit nervous about that."

"Oh boy. You asked Greta?"

I chuckled. "They say to keep your enemies close. By asking her to help, I knew she couldn't complain as much."

"Smart! Hey, your mother said Michael came to see you for your birthday. How sweet is that?"

"Yes, he and his friend Jon came and had a great time. Unfortunately, they had to leave a day early because Jon's mother went into the hospital."

"Jon Gray?"

"Yes."

"I remember that handsome guy. The two of them shouldn't have any problems getting the ladies."

"I gave up on thinking that will ever happen. How was my mom when you saw her?"

"She was fine. I took her some leftover chicken and dumplings, and she was delighted. I told her that they didn't compare to hers, of course."

"Thank you. Yes, her dumplings are to die for. I don't think she cooks too much for herself anymore."

"Well, have to run, Claire. Linda said to tell you hello. We're certainly looking forward to our trip."

When we hung up, I had renewed excitement about the quilt show.

Chapter 77

When I walked into the church hall, Marta was relieved to see my brownies. Billy had been complaining that there were no refreshments.

"Gee, thanks, Miss Stewart," Billy said, helping himself.

"You're welcome," I replied. "Guess who's coming to the meeting tonight?"

"Kelly?" he asked with a grin. I nodded.

The place started filling up, which was nice to see. I didn't relax until Cher arrived.

"Carl couldn't get away tonight, but he said all is cool."

"Good. So far, Greta's a no-show. Is that good or bad?"

"It's just fine by me," Cher cheered.

"It's seven o'clock, Claire," Marta reminded. I took a deep breath.

I welcomed everyone as a way of starting the meeting. As I was speaking, Kelly arrived, which made me lose my concentration. I called on Cher first, who had the most to report. She recommended that everyone advertise the show on their own social media pages. She also noted that there were flyers for everyone to take home and pass out.

Next up was Marta, who wanted everyone to know how the pickup and delivery process would work.

"Please help remind everyone not to just help themselves to their quilt once the show is over," she said. "There's a process of accountability in place for security purposes. Other than the challenge quilts, everyone in the park is responsible for their own setup and takedown."

"I have a question!" Tom called out. "When will they announce the winner of the pie contest?" I looked at Mr. Samson, who was standing in the back, to answer.

Mr. Samson began, "We'll announce that around three o'clock since the show ends at four. We're quite pleased with all the paper entries so far. Besides our top baker at Seaquist Orchards, we've asked Anna Meyer from Anna's Bake Shop to be a judge." Anna grinned at the mention. "There are three cash awards to announce."

"Thanks!" I nodded. "I'm glad there's a lot of participation. Are there any more questions?"

"What about rain?" teased the guy from The Cookery.

"There won't be any, but if there is, you all have your instructions. Thank you all for coming and helping us again this year. If there are any brownies left, please help yourself." Everyone clapped.

I saw Kelly coming my way.

"Are Billy and I in the same area this year, Claire?"

"Yup. You're stuck with me," Billy chimed in with a smile.

"Claire, I'm so sorry Dad isn't helping this year," she said nicely.

"It's okay," I replied. "We have it covered."

"You know he's not very happy these days, and I think it has a lot to do with you." I didn't know what to say, and Billy remained silent.

"I doubt that's the case," I finally answered.

"Can't you give him a call or something?" she suggested quietly.

"Well, I think it's a little more complicated than a phone call, but thanks for trying to help," I explained. "How's Spot doing?"

"He's doing great!" she noted. "He still drives Dad nuts. How's Puff?"

"Well, recently, I saw her throw a hissy fit at someone, which I'd never seen before," I reported. "She then took off like lightning upstairs."

"They let you know how they feel, alright," Kelly nodded. "We need to get Spot and Puff together again sometime."

"Anytime," I grinned.

Marta wanted my attention, so Kelly and I said goodbye. I then visited with Marta about any loose ends after the meeting. I reassured her that all was well.

"Okay, Billy!" she called to get his attention away from Kelly. "We need to go now."

We closed up the church together, and Cher suggested we have a drink at Bayside. I was ready for a drink and more since I hadn't had dinner.

We decided to sit at the bar for a change, ordering our usual beers and Bayside burgers.

"I guess we won't see Rachael behind this bar now that she's married to Harry, huh?" Cher asked as she sipped her beer.

"Well, she certainly doesn't need the money anymore, but she did seem to enjoy it. Harry would prefer she not, though," I explained.

"See what happens once you're married?" Cher joked. "Hey, I saw you talking to Kelly. What's up there?"

I told her what Kelly had suggested I do, and Cher stared at me.

"If that isn't a signal to make a move, I don't know what is," Cher said with a grin.

Chapter 78

"Oh, please!"

"I bet she knows she had something to do with your refusal to marry him, and she's sorry for that."

"I doubt she knows he asked me. She loves her dad, and she doesn't like seeing him sad; that's all. In other news, how did you feel about tonight's meeting?"

"Good, as long as everyone follows through with their commitments. Hey, what are your plans tomorrow? Do you want to go with me to see the fireworks?"

"Thanks, but I'm invited to the Bittners' party tomorrow, remember?"

"Oh, that's right. I bet you'll be able to see a lot of the fireworks from there."

"I don't do well in those big crowds. Maybe Carl will go with you to catch the fireworks."

"I'm working tomorrow, so maybe he'll suggest we do something afterward."

"I just bet he will. I haven't heard from Foster, so I have a feeling he's getting my message."

"Well, your message hasn't always been consistent with him, Claire. I hope you don't regret blowing him off, though. Have you heard from Michael since he's been back?"

"No, and I wonder about Jon's mother. Michael also mentioned they were going to Las Vegas soon for a convention."

"What a life."

"I'm just so glad he's happy and that he helps Mom."

"Carole and Linda are excited about coming. I was hoping to have the guest room painted for them, but that's not going to happen."

'I'm sure they won't care."

"Have you started the painting of Julie's yet?"

"I've got it sketched. Hey, what time is it?"

"Not quite midnight."

"Well, I need to head home."

We hugged each other goodbye. Cher offered me a ride, but the weather was nice so I said I'd walk.

I was making my turn into Cottage Row Court when I felt like someone was following me. Maybe it was Cher wanting to make sure I got home safe. I turned around and saw the white pickup truck. I looked right at Ava's ex, Eric, in the headlights. My good sense said to keep walking and just get inside the house.

As soon as I entered my cabin, he stepped on the gas and sped down Cottage Row. It was too late to call Ava, but I wondered what he meant by it. I went up to bed and managed to fall into a deep sleep.

The next morning, I made sure to hang the flag from my porch. I could hear fireworks already at nine o'clock. I wasn't sure what the fireworks rules were in Door County.

I'd noticed there weren't nearly as many fireworks stands as we had all over the state of Missouri, though.

In no time, there seemed to be a lot of activity next door at the Bittners' with deliveries. I didn't have a view of their backyard and patio, so I wasn't able to tell what was going on.

As I ate my breakfast of fresh strawberries and yogurt, I was truly looking forward to going to the party tonight. I was surprised to get a call from Rachael.

"You're back already?" I greeted.

She chuckled. "We are! We had a great deal of fun, but we have a lot to do here at home. A few days at the Del was just fine for both of us. It truly was our first trip together as a couple, and it went well. So, how did the quilt show meeting go?"

"Good. We're all set. Cher and I went to Bayside afterward and sat at the bar. We talked about your hope to come back there and work. Also, I had a little excitement coming home. Ava's husband followed me when I walked home."

"Claire, are you okay?"

"I was pretty rattled by it, but nothing happened. For some reason, he thinks I had something to do with Ava's decision to leave him."

"You should have called the police, Claire."

"I don't want to get involved if I can help it."

"I can understand that. Just be careful, okay? You and I need to have lunch and hash over the wedding and what plans we should make out here at the shop. By the way, more merchandise has arrived."

"Yes, we need to catch up. What are you and Harry doing for the Fourth?"

"Kent is having us over for a barbeque and fireworks for the kids."

"Sounds like married life is settling in right in! I suppose Brenda will be there?"

"Yes, when she gets off work."

"I'm going to a party next door tonight. I'm hoping they've invited Grayson even though he blew me off at your wedding."

"We were pleased he came."

"Yeah, it was nice to see him. Well, happy Fourth!"

Chapter 79

The day was getting away from me, and I had accomplished very little painting. It was hard getting motivated these days.

After lunch, I went upstairs to decide what to wear to the party tonight. I had a pink floral sundress I'd only worn once. If I could find a scarf or a pashmina to go with it, it could work. I finally paired my dress with a pink polka-dot scarf that belonged with another outfit and set it on the bed. I jumped in the shower and then made myself presentable. I pulled my hair into a bun, which looked better with my drop earrings.

I peeked out the side of the porch and saw cars beginning to arrive. It appeared the party was much bigger than just a few folks dropping by. I grabbed a spare bottle of champagne as a hostess gift. I wouldn't wear my scarf until later but tucked it into the side of my purse. When I thought enough folks had arrived, I went to join them. I had on high heels for a change, so it was more of a challenge walking across the yard.

Dan greeted me graciously at the front door and was more than happy to accept my hostess gift. He said Cotsy was in the dining room, where one bar and a food table were set up.

Gorgeous wasn't an adequate description of how everything looked. This couple really knew how to throw a party. No wonder Tom was working over here every day. The patio was lined with flowers and lovely greenery that must take a lot of maintenance.

I recognized some faces from the Bittners' previous parties I'd gone to. I ventured out to the patio, where a sweet couple was standing at the bar. I looked around to see if there were any single folks and, of course, there weren't.

The couple introduced themselves and said they were relatives of Dan's from Branson, Missouri. They said they came to get away from the heat and all the tourists this time of year. When I told them I lived next door in the cabin, they went nuts with excitement.

"If you ever want to sell your place, would you notify us immediately?" they requested. "We would love a place here in Door County, and next door to Aunt Cotsy and Uncle Dan would be incredible!"

"Well, I just purchased the place myself," I explained.

I briefly told them the story about how I managed to be there.

"Oh, Claire, I'm so glad you got to meet these lovely folks," Cotsy said as she joined us. "I told them all about you. Now, please start helping yourself to some of this food or we'll be eating leftovers for days!"

"Everything looks fabulous as usual, Cotsy," I admired.

"Thank you, Claire, but you know who does most of the work around here." We chuckled and I nodded.

I left the young couple to fill my plate with some of the fruit, sushi, and shrimp. I went to sit in an empty spot at a table nearby. A lady was sitting there alone, so I thought we might share a nice conversation. It was then I heard a voice that was all too familiar. Grayson.

His back was toward me, and he had his arm around the shoulders of a young, blonde woman he was introducing to another couple. He'd brought a date! My heart sank. How could he? I knew I had to get out of there immediately while he was distracted. I was pretty sure he hadn't seen me on the patio. I tried to observe the woman, who couldn't be over thirty. The lady seated next to me kept talking, but I didn't hear a word she said.

"I'm sorry, but I'm going to refresh my drink," I said as I got up to leave. She looked puzzled.

I managed to walk through the sea of people until I arrived in the living room, where I set down my glass. I knew I could get out the door rather quickly now. Thank goodness neither Cotsy nor Dan were in the room when I went flying out the door. I felt bad not saying goodbye, but that apology would have to come at another time.

Chapter 80

I never looked back once I was out the door. When I reached the cabin, I didn't turn on any lights because I didn't want to draw any attention. I had no idea where Puff was. She was likely on the bed waiting for me to return. In the darkness, I threw myself on the couch. The shock of Grayson bringing a date gutted me. Yes, he had seen me having coffee with Foster, but I had left alone, so he knew it wasn't a date. Who would have thought Grayson would be attracted to a woman so young? Maybe she was older than she looked. The Grayson I knew was not one to show his affection in public.

Tears were running down my face from grave disappointment. I also felt humiliation about leaving the Bittners' house without saying goodbye. Would they ever invite me again?

I hated being this emotional, especially because of a man I'd stopped seeing six months ago. If I'd just handled Grayson's proposal differently, things could be different now. Why didn't I just say I needed time to think about it? Instead, I had said the harsh words, "I can't possibly marry you," which must have been devastating to him.

I buried my head in the couch pillow to create more darkness to fall asleep.

Puff was the first to get my attention at eight the next morning. She brushed against me, reminding me I was still wearing the now-crumpled dress. I sat up to get my bearings as I watched Puff walk back and forth from the couch to the kitchen. I'm sure she wondered what on earth was wrong with me.

I reluctantly rose to feed her. I didn't want to look outdoors, so I went directly upstairs to shower. I wadded up the dress in hopes I'd never see it again.

I let the water pour over my skin and hair as if I could wash away my pain.

I put on a t-shirt and jeans, letting my wet hair hang in disarray. I needed coffee badly, so I went downstairs to make some. I sat at the kitchen table wondering what I would say to Dan and Cotsy. Should I just admit what happened or tell them that I'd become terribly sick?

I had no desire to paint or do anything other than have a pity party for myself. I could burden Cher with my story, but I knew she'd just tell me how foolish I was being. She'd most likely had a great evening with Carl after work.

I looked out my kitchen window at what appeared to be a very nice day. My flag was waving in the breeze, so I decided to bring it in. It was just a reminder that my Fourth of July ended poorly.

When I stepped outdoors to retrieve the flag, I saw Cotsy coming my way. *Uh-oh.*

"Claire, are you okay?" she asked with concern.

"I am."

"Did you become ill last night? All of a sudden you were gone, and Dan and I didn't get to say goodbye." I looked to the ground in shame.

"I'm so, so sorry, Cotsy. The party was lovely, and I really enjoyed visiting with your family from Missouri."

"Aren't they the sweetest?"

"They are. I just don't know how to put into words what upset me."

"Upset you? Did someone upset you?"

I paused. "I wasn't expecting to see Grayson. It threw me off."

"Oh dear. I apologize for that discomfort you felt. I'd asked Dan if we still should invite the two of you since you broke up, and he thought it wouldn't be an issue."

"Dan's right, but seeing Grayson with another woman was more than I could take. I was shocked and just didn't want to face him."

"Another woman? Are you referring to the young lady who came with him? She is his late wife's niece, who was in town visiting him. He had called us to ask whether it was okay to bring her."

"A niece? Well, that explains her age. I feel so foolish about how I handled myself, especially knowing that."

"Well, I think your reaction says a lot about how much you still love him. Am I right?"

"I suppose. He broke it off with me when I turned down his marriage proposal."

"Is that what happened?"

"His daughter was becoming an issue, and I felt her feelings had to come first. He'd never brought up marriage until he proposed, so I was caught off guard."

"I see. Well, it sounds like you may have had a good reason to do what you did, but telling a man no can have unintended consequences. When Dan and I started dating, I turned him down a lot. Then he began to date another woman, and I was terribly sorry I'd rejected him. This is a second marriage for both of us, and we didn't want to make another mistake. Being with him has been no mistake at all, though. We've been married twenty-two years now and have no regrets."

"That's a long time."

"Dan and I both had baggage. It's just something you have to work through."

"Cotsy, can you possibly forgive my foolishness?"

"Of course, Claire," she said, giving me a hug. "Love does crazy things at any age. They say that even in nursing homes, folks can act just like foolish teenagers when they fall in love." I chuckled.

Chapter 81

Throughout the rest of the day, I kept thinking about the big mistake I'd made last night. I'm sure Grayson would have introduced me to his niece, and that could have broken the ice between us. I wondered if he'd seen me and knew I left. I'd likely never know.

I painted until about three o'clock when I received a text from Cher. She was going to be out picking up quilts, and if I was home, she might stop by. I told her I wasn't going anywhere.

I managed to tidy up some things before she arrived at five o'clock. I greeted her outdoors.

"Hey, Claire Bear," she said. "Here's a list of the quilts we'll be adding to the inventory. I'm hearing great things from everyone about the show, but now they're worried about the forecast."

"The show must go on somehow. The businesses are finding out that this event puts money in their coffers."

"Hey, how was the Bittners' party last night? Carl had planned to visit his sister, so I just stayed home and watched all the fireworks in the neighborhood."

"I wasn't going to tell you about my night because it didn't go well."

"Oh boy. I bet this has to do with Grayson."

We sat down on my front steps, and I began telling her everything. There wasn't much I could keep from Cher. As she listened, she kept shaking her head as if she knew this wouldn't end well.

"You're going to have to confront this beast one way or another, Claire. Either go to him and tell him how you feel, or call Foster and let him know you're interested in getting on with your life. You're making yourself and everyone else crazy!"

"I know, I know. Last night was the last straw, I think."

"Isn't it cocktail hour around here?" Cher joked.

"I believe so! I guess we'd better find some wine."

"The girls arrive next week. I was hoping to do more than just buy some new linens for my guest room, but that'll have to suffice. It will really help that they were here last year. They'll know their way around."

"Yes, I'm glad they'll be on their own, so to speak."

"Have you heard from Ava lately?"

"No, and I'm taking that as good news."

"How's the painting of Julie's coming along?"

I sighed. "Slowly. I just haven't been in the mood to paint lately. I like taking breaks to work outside, but with all the landscaping I've done, Julie's piece needs more attention. I did hear from Rachael. She and Harry had a short but sweet honeymoon at the Del. I need to get out to the barn after the show and start rearranging their gift shop."

"You will love that new role at the shop, and what fun to have the freedom to order what you want!"

"It's also just a joy to be out there. I'm adding Halloween and fall items to their inventory."

"At a Christmas tree farm?"

I chuckled. "Yep! We can do fall events like a pumpkin fest. There's a guy down the road who sells pumpkins wholesale."

"I know you're a Christmas person, but I love Halloween."

I left Cher for the kitchen and made us a platter of cheese, crackers, and fresh strawberries from the Pig.

"You know, Cher, I haven't been back to the chamber since Grayson became president."

"What are you saying?"

"Well, I think it's time I return. Why should I stay away because of him?"

"Attagirl. You shouldn't. The next one is over in Sturgeon Bay, just so you know."

"Yes, I know. Why don't the two of us go and then visit Frances while we're over there?"

"Oof! It's a breakfast meeting, which means leaving really early," Cher complained.

"Do you work that day?"

"I'm not sure, but I could just go in for the afternoon, like I do many days."

"Okay, then. I'll pick you up."

At nine that evening, Cher finally left. I was talked out and went on up to bed. Before I fell asleep, I thought about the chamber meeting. It was a great opportunity for me to promote the quilt show. I was nearly asleep when Cher called.

Chapter 82

"Did you forget something?"

"No, but I wanted to tell you something that concerns me. When I left your place, a white pickup truck was parked by the curve near your house. There was a man in it. Do you think that was Ava's husband?"

"Good heavens, it sounds like it. Why would he still be watching me?"

"I don't know. Are you sure he's harmless?"

"No, I'm not really sure. Maybe when he saw your car here, he thought Ava might be here as well."

"Look out your window and see if he's still there."

"Okay."

I turned out my bedroom light, and when I looked out the window, I didn't see his truck.

"No, he's gone. Your leaving meant his jollies for the night were over."

Cher laughed. "Okay then, Claire Bear. Good night."

"Good night, Cher Bear."

I lay there for a while wondering if Ava's husband really was harmless or whether I needed to be worried about him stalking my cabin. Thankfully, the two glasses of wine

I drank with Cher put me to sleep within about fifteen minutes.

The next morning, I woke up in a good mood for a reason I couldn't pinpoint. I needed to accomplish a lot today, so I dressed for the day before going down to breakfast. After I made my coffee, I decided to check my phone for any messages. It rang just as I picked it up, which startled me. It was Brenda.

"I didn't wake you, did I?" she asked softly.

"Not at all. I'm just having my breakfast. What's up?"

"I know it's a last-minute invite, but there's a concert in Ephraim tonight. The weather's great today, and I thought about going. Would you be free to join me?"

"Yes! That sounds like fun."

"I'm glad! Kent would never be interested in something like this, and he's been so busy with the girls lately."

"Well, I'm your date, and I'm happy about it!"

"Great. I'll pick you up about seven o'clock."

It was nice to have plans for the evening. That should get me moving quicker around here. I uncovered my easel and began working, thinking about how long it had been since I'd been to a concert. I knew with the cooler weather in the evening I would need to bring a jacket or sweater. I'd have a quick bite to eat before Brenda picked me up and then suggest we go somewhere afterward.

I made the mistake of checking on the weather again for the days and weeks ahead. It showed a 40 percent chance of rain for the day of the quilt show. I knew the weather could change on a dime, but I couldn't ignore the forecast. Of course, if it wasn't raining at six o'clock, the show would go on.

When Brenda came by, I was ready to escape my work for the day.

"I have our lawn chairs and something for us to drink," she noted.

"How thoughtful! I hadn't even considered that."

"I've been to these concerts several times before. It's hard to get in nearby restaurants like Wilson's when this is going on, so I just brought our own refreshments. I have no idea what kind of music there will be tonight, but I've never been disappointed."

"I like most any kind. This was a great idea, Brenda. Thanks for inviting me."

Parking wasn't easy, but we didn't mind the walk along the bay. We finally found a good spot to set up our chairs. The view was grand.

"I heard your brother was in town recently," Brenda recalled.

"Yes, he was, and he brought a friend with him. Unfortunately, his friend's mother was sent to the hospital, and they had to leave a day early. We had dinner at the inn one night, but you weren't working. I would have liked for you to have met him."

"I'm sorry I missed them."

The music started out with a peppy tune that grabbed our attention. Families were all around us enjoying every note as children ran around and even danced. They were so cute.

"Do you ever think you'll regret not having any children?" Brenda asked me.

"I'll don't really know, I suppose," I responded. "Time goes so quickly, and before you know it, it's too late. I try not to look back. How about you?"

"Watching Kent and the girls has its good points and bad points." I laughed and nodded. "I love their hugs and silliness, but then there are times I'm glad to walk away."

Chapter 83

Brenda's liquid sustenance had a tad of cherry vodka in it. It was cold and refreshing on this pleasant evening. I asked if I could treat her to something after the concert, but she explained she had to work the breakfast shift tomorrow at the inn and was used to turning in by ten o'clock.

The music was still playing in my head when I arrived home. I grabbed Puff and took her upstairs for the night. Cher sure knew what she was doing when she left me her cat to take care of. Puff was the only company I had most days of late.

Tomorrow morning was an early riser because of the chamber meeting. I had to get my mind off of the what-ifs regarding Grayson and just focus on the fact that I could make a push for the quilt show.

The sound of the early alarm wasn't my preferred way of waking up on a Saturday, but we couldn't be late. I had serious thoughts about canceling, but I couldn't do that to Cher.

I had to look my best today whether Grayson spoke to me or not at the meeting. It was a chilly morning, so I wore a tan pantsuit and pulled my hair back in a low bun.

I told Cher all about last night's concert, and she said she'd always heard good things about the concerts but had never gone.

We arrived at Cedar Crossing a few minutes early. It was just down the street from the quilt shop and Novel Bay Booksellers. We walked in like we belonged there. The food line was in progress and, so far, I saw no sign of Grayson. We parked ourselves in line and said hello to some familiar faces. Cher had actually gotten to know many more businesspeople than I had because she'd worked with them on last year's show. We took our places at the rear of the building, far from Grayson's podium.

He finally appeared before everyone, looking more handsome than ever. He welcomed everyone without laying eyes on Cher and me. Then he announced there would be a short program from the Veteran's Association before we discussed current events. The Veteran's Association was a new member of the chamber, and Grayson was interested in how they could be part of the business community.

We ate a delicious serving of French toast and fruit while we listened. The coffee was extra good, and we drank it with abandon. When Grayson was finished with the formal part of the meeting, he asked those who wanted to speak to get in line for their announcements. That included me.

The first to take the podium was a representative from the farm near Sturgeon Bay. He said they were now open and had many new things to see this year. Next was Mr. Samson from Seaquist Orchards. He announced he was a sponsor for our quilt show, and the orchard would be doing a cherry pie contest in Noble Park. Everyone showed their support by clapping. Next was a representative from the Skyway Drive-In Theatre, which was between Ephraim and Fish Creek. The rep was proud to share that the drive-in had been around since 1950 and was the longest continually running drive-in in the state. Another round of applause followed. The last person to speak before it was my turn was a woman from the Lavender Spa, located in the Settlement Courtyard in Fish Creek. She was handing out brochures stating all their new services.

I was up. I stood at the microphone while Grayson stared at me rather coldly. That didn't help my nerves, but I couldn't let him fluster me.

"The second annual Door-to-Door Quilt Show is next weekend, I'm delighted to say. We'll be having all new quilts, vendors, and exhibits. I'm also pleased to tell you that we've included the shops at the top of the hill in Fish Creek. I hope to see all of you there. We have flyers here with all the details."

That wasn't so bad. I walked back to my seat without looking at Grayson. I bet some people in the room were wondering about our relationship. Cher said his expression hadn't changed.

When Cher and I left the building, Grayson was nowhere to be found.

"I think your observation of Grayson is correct, Claire," Cher said as we walked to the bookshop. "The best thing for you to do is just forget about him. He has a problem. Go have fun with Foster, and call it a day." I smiled in disbelief.

We did a quick walk-through of the bookshop and picked up a list of new releases. I love the owners, as they're always fun to visit with. I told them someday I'd join one of their book clubs.

When we arrived at the quilt shop, we asked for Olivia, but she wasn't working. Cher quickly fell in love with a multicolored polka-dot fabric, so she had to purchase it. I mostly worked with solid fabric for my wholecloths, so it was easier for me to walk out without opening my purse.

Chapter 84

"Claire, did I tell you I took the liberty of booking two judges for the challenge quilts?"

"No, but I'm glad you did."

"Amy told me about this incredible Amish quiltmaker, Ethel Yoder. She said she's a real perfectionist and would be a very qualified judge. Well, I called her, and she accepted. Then I thought we needed someone from the art perspective, so I asked Carl. I hope you don't mind."

"No, Cher. That's perfect. Thank you. I'm sorry I've been so distracted. We've had more details this year to think about, and your load has been heavier. You're doing a great job."

Cher grinned at the compliment. "Look at the time. I guess we'd better get to Frances's house."

Not far from the quilt shop was Frances's large, Victorian house. Ava answered the door and seemed quite happy to see us.

"Come in, ladies," she greeted. "Frances is in the parlor."

There Frances sat in a pretty pink floral dress, with a walking cane beside her.

"How nice of you to come, ladies," Frances calmly said. "Please sit and have a spot of tea. Ava has baked some shortbread cookies. We're both thrilled to visit with you."

"We've missed the two of you," Cher noted as Ava presented her tray of cookies.

"This is a treat," I complimented.

"Ava keeps quite busy spoiling me," Frances claimed. "She's always cooking or baking something. I have to say, it's been a delight to have her here."

"It's a win for both of you," I said with a smile. "How many years have you lived alone here, Frances?"

"Clarence left this world ten years ago," she reported sadly. "I was seeing him most every day at the cemetery until the stroke set me back, but Ava has been nice enough to get me there recently. I should be able to drive again soon."

"I'm glad you're doing better," I expressed.

"Now, tell me all about the show," Frances requested. "Ava filled me in on the last quilt club meeting. I would have loved to have entered the Quilted Cherries challenge, but I wasn't able. I hear you even have Greta helping you out this year."

"Well, we'll see how it works out," I said with hesitation.

"That woman can be so ornery," Frances said boldly. "I don't think I've ever seen her smile."

"Well, if it hadn't been for her starting our club many years ago, I never would have met you ladies," I reminded. They smiled.

"We're going to try to make the show," Frances stated.

"Oh, good," I responded. "It's a fun day for everyone, and it goes so quickly for everyone who helps."

"Are things getting settled for you, Ava?" Cher asked.

"It will be ugly for some time, I'm afraid," Ava said, shaking her head. "I don't know when the man works. I know he's stalking me, and I could get him in real trouble, but I don't want to make the situation worse. I did get most everything out of the house that I wanted. The house was a complete mess when I finally saw it again. Living here, I needed very little furniture. I made sure I got all my sewing things out, and I'm sure he was grateful for that." We chuckled. "I also took a few family photos, but most everything else I left because I don't care about it. I just don't have pleasant memories from there."

"I told her they're just things," Frances chimed in. "She needs a fresh start. Speaking of fresh starts, Ava tells me that you're no longer seeing that Mr. Wills."

"That's right," I nodded. "I've had to move on once again." Only Cher knew what I meant.

"Well, you're never alone when they're still in your heart," Frances said with emotion. "I still go to sleep each night with Clarence holding my hand, and when I wake up in the morning, I can still hear him say, 'Frances, honey, it's time to get up.'"

"That's so sweet," I responded. "You were lucky to have each other."

"Now, ladies, before you go, I want to give the two of you a little gift," Frances said as she took an envelope off the table next to her. "I have more money than I will be able to spend. I want to do my little part for your wonderful show, so I have a $1,000 check for you to cover some of your expenses."

"Oh, Frances, we're in good shape, really," I countered. "You don't have to do this."

"I want to," she insisted. "You and Cher have shaken up our fuddy-duddy quilt club, and with your energy and creativity, you have brought quilt awareness to our beautiful Door County."

Cher and I looked at each other in disbelief.

"She means it, y'all," Ava confirmed with a big smile.

"Thank you, Frances," Cher said with gratitude. "We'll make sure it's spent wisely in your name."

"Thank you, Frances," I said, getting up to hug her.

Chapter 85

A half hour later, we left feeling overwhelmed with gratitude.

"I haven't asked lately, but just how is our money situation for the show?" Cher asked frankly.

"We're good, I think, but all the bills aren't in yet. We shouldn't need her check. We'll have to figure out something else to use it for."

"We need to do something special with it in her name," Cher stated.

"I like the idea. We need to think this over. Frances's words were so endearing."

"She and Ava seem happy together."

I nodded. "So, speaking of our show, I guess I'll be brave and ask Greta to bring all the challenge quilts back to the church at four o'clock."

"Well, it's part of her job at the park, where she insisted on being."

"Not to bring up a scary topic, but have you been checking the weather like I have?"

"Yes, unfortunately. And the weather's even worse the next day, so we're stuck. I hope we have plenty of the drop cloths."

"Let's just hope they use them, or we'll be needing Frances's check to pay damages."

I dropped Cher off after a very full day. As soon as I stepped foot inside my cabin, I called Greta with high hopes.

"Hello, Greta, it's Claire. I have an additional favor to ask you since you will be working in the park."

"Another favor? What is it?"

"It would be very helpful if you could bring all the challenge quilts up to the church at four o'clock." There was a pause.

"How many would that be?"

"I know for sure there will be ten."

"I think it's best you find someone else, Claire. I know those quilts are small, but that is more than I can manage."

"Okay. You may be right."

"You know we're likely to be rained on that day, like I warned. Do you know what a mess that will be?"

"We'll just have to hope for the best. Thanks for your help."

I hung up, realizing that asking her was a huge mistake. I'll take the quilts to the church myself if I have to. *Oh, please God, do not let it rain.*

I poured myself a glass of wine, feeling the exhaustion from my day. My cell rang just as I was starting to go over my quilt papers. I answered abruptly.

"Is that a yes?" Foster joked after I answered.

"Sorry, Foster. I was in the middle of something."

"So, are we experiencing showtime jitters?"

"I suppose. I'm not happy with the forecast, for one thing."

"There's not much you can do about that, I'm afraid. I'm calling to see if you are free for dinner tomorrow night. I think you could use some R & R."

I paused and thought about Cher's advice to me. "Sure, that would be great."

"Wonderful! I'll plan something special on the beach, so dress casual. It should be a beautiful evening."

"You're determined, aren't you? I'd love to see it."

"I'll pick you up at five o'clock. Or is that too early?"

"It's perfect."

I hung up wondering how I managed to have a change of heart. But I had to move on, like Cher said. I've been a fool, thinking Grayson would come back into my life. Clearly, he wouldn't if he hadn't by now.

As I lay in bed that night, many things were tumbling through my mind. Now I had to include Foster in that mix. Tomorrow was the deadline for the challenge quilts. Cher was in charge of getting them judged. I thought about everything that could go wrong.

Sleep took me to a dark place where it was pouring rain and I was the only one to rescue all the quilts on Main Street. When I woke up the next morning, Puff wasn't on my bed, and my covers and pillow were in disarray. It had been a long night indeed.

Chapter 86

"There you are, Puffy," I said, picking her up from the kitchen floor. "I'm sorry if I disturbed you last night. Let's get you something to eat." She purred in agreement.

I made myself some cinnamon toast and remembered I had a big date with Foster tonight. Why wasn't I excited about it? Would I be happier here, alone in my cabin, with a good Turner Classic movie? I might be.

Carole and Linda were traveling today and would probably arrive at Cher's around six o'clock. I would have to think about when I could see them.

Before lunch, I managed to get a little further on my painting even though I was having a hard time concentrating on it. Perhaps I should be doing a quilt project such as getting out the bag of ties that Michael gave me.

After a quick sandwich for lunch, I went upstairs to visit the ties from the past. I sat down and started sorting them by color and style. All of a sudden, I had a brilliant idea on what to do with them. If I was making this quilt for Michael, I could make him a bookshelf quilt. The long, narrow strips would be much better to work with than trying to do a bow-tie quilt, which had been my first thought. I'd seen this idea done many times before and loved it. Since I was doing a wall quilt, I could create two or three rows of books on a shelf using a black background. It would be the perfect gift for a book and newspaper guy like my brother.

The afternoon flew by as I chose which ties would work. I eventually pulled myself away. I had an early date tonight, so I needed to shower and make myself presentable.

I dressed in white slacks and a blue-and-white pin-striped shirt. I had a white shell underneath in case it became too hot. I was hoping that dressing would get me more excited about the evening, but it didn't happen.

At ten minutes before five, Foster showed up, looking quite dapper. He had more of a suntan than the last time I'd seen him, and I liked the straw hat he was wearing.

"It's so good to see you again, Claire," he said as he gave me a kiss on the cheek. "Are you ready, or am I too early?"

"I'm ready to go."

Riding in his fancy yellow SUV was itself a different experience. I'd wager there wasn't another SUV like it anywhere within a hundred miles. Foster never stopped talking. He appeared to be much more excited about this date than I was.

"I have everything arranged on the beach, but first I'd like to show you my room at the inn," he said with a grin. "Now, don't get the wrong idea, but the place is quite nice and has unique decor."

"Sure, I'd like to see what the rooms look like there," I said without concern.

Baileys Harbor on the Michigan side of the peninsula is so different from the Green Bay side. It's known as a haven for nature lovers because of its wildflowers, natural sanctuaries, sandy beaches, and waters for kiteboarding, kayaking, salmon fishing, and more. It's also not as populated as the bay side, making it a quieter getaway. The Blacksmith Inn, on the shore of Lake Michigan and in the heart of Baileys Harbor, is a B&B with a New England look to it.

Foster and I parked in a lovely bricked lot and headed to his room for a better view of the beach. I learned that the B&B actually had three separate houses: the Zahn House, the Harbor House, and the Orchard House. Foster mentioned that his room in the Zahn House was rarely rented to anyone else unless the owners knew Foster would be gone for a good length of time.

The decor was stellar. I'm no expert on decorating styles, but I'd describe it as New England primitive. Unusual artwork was placed all about, which I'm sure was an attraction for Foster. The hardwood floors, fireplace, and expansive bath were all to be admired, but my favorite part was the hammock on the balcony overlooking the harbor.

"Very, very nice, Foster."

Chapter 87

"The food they serve here is amazing, though I rarely partake with my schedule. They have good snacks whenever I need something, and a lunch basket is also available for me. I guess you could say they spoil me. See what a single man like me has to put up with?"

"Yes. You're spoiled alright."

"The owners were nice enough to help me prepare some things I needed for the beach tonight, so let's get on out there."

Once we were outside, we walked on a boarded bridge for about fifty feet until we hit the beach. The view was breathtaking.

"Oh, Foster, this is amazing." He grinned with delight. "It's like a secret, private beach."

He had a tent set up for shade. It was decked out with a minibar and two comfy lounge chairs that had side tables for drinks or whatever. A small grill and a cooler sitting next to it held our dinner contents, most likely.

"Are we expecting guests?" I asked with humor.

"It's for just the two of us, silly. So, what can I get you to drink?"

"Whatever you seem to be mixing there looks pretty refreshing," I replied.

"Well, I call it my fruity-tooty, for lack of a better name," he said, laughing.

"I can't wait to taste it," I said, trying to please.

Foster had plenty to talk about during our date. He explained how he sets up his easel and which time of the day or night he gets the best lighting. As he described his work, I saw the passion and love that showed through his artwork.

The drink was amazingly refreshing, and the time flew by until it was time for the sun to set. We nibbled on shrimp and avocado dip while he enticed me with the main course of halibut, which he was about to grill.

We were standing close together as the sun disappeared into the water. It was a romantic moment, and Foster's arms went around my waist.

"I've watched this moment many times at this same spot, but it's 100 percent better sharing it with you."

I smiled. Foster kept shooting questions at me, but I was careful about how much to share with him.

"I hope to be back in Door County in time to see your show," he noted.

"And I'm hoping to finish another painting for Carl before then."

"I don't know Carl very well, but he seems a lot happier these days. Is it because of that sweet employee of his?"

I chuckled at his nod to Cher. "I hope so."

While Foster was grilling our halibut, I stared into the water. I hadn't been this relaxed in a long time. When the fish was ready, he served it with fresh slices of dilled tomatoes. It was the perfect combination, and the halibut melted in my mouth.

Foster seemed to notice how much I was enjoying myself, so I told him it would be hard to leave. That's when he shared that I really didn't have to leave, but I took his reply with humor instead of making it a big deal.

We did leave about eleven o'clock, leaving everything like it was at his insistence. The drive back to the cabin was relaxed and quiet. There was no question that the evening was perfect for both of us.

When he walked me to the door, Foster took me in his arms to kiss me. It was gentle and sweet, and I found myself kissing him back. He stopped at that point, which I thought was admirable. He left without pressuring me for another date, and I appreciated it.

Puff was sound asleep in my bedroom when I walked in. I tried not to disturb her as I undressed and slid under the covers. As I lay there in silence waiting for sleep to take over, I had time to replay the evening and fantasize in my mind, and my thoughts weren't about Grayson this time.

Chapter 88

The next morning, while I sat at my breakfast table eating yogurt, I got a text from Cher.

[Cher]
Ethel Yoder and Carl are judging the challenge quilts tonight at Carl's gallery if you want to stop by. We now have eleven of them.

[Claire]
I'll pass, if you don't mind. I think it's best I abstain.

[Cher]
Okey-dokey! I'll let you know who the winners are.

I was hoping for more entries, but the quilters didn't have very much notice. I checked the weather forecast again, and nothing had changed. Just then another text came in.

[Cher]
Forgot to tell you that Linda and Carole arrived safely last night, so they may pop over to see you.

[Cher]
Yes, please tell them to come over.

Now I really had to get going on my day to tidy up. Tom had just finished mowing the yard, so all looked good outdoors.

While I started cleaning the porch, I assessed my painting that was waiting for the next stroke of my brush. There was no way I'd have it finished by the show. I could only hope that the lady who suggested it would end up buying it.

Puff did not like the sound of the vacuum cleaner, so when I turned it on, she ran up the stairs and hid under my bed. Around eleven o'clock, Foster called.

"How is the loveliest lady in Door County today?"

"She's not looking too lovely right now. She's trying to tidy up for friends who are in town to help with the quilt show and could arrive at her cabin at any time."

"How nice for you. I suppose this means your time is well taken then."

"Yes, unfortunately I'm very busy at the moment."

"Well, I'll just have to wait my turn then."

"Until this show is over, I need to stay focused."

"I can hold my breath until then."

"I hope you make it back in time for the show."

"We shall see, but in the meantime, I wish you the best of luck with everything."

"Thanks, Foster. I appreciate that. We could certainly use some of that luck for the forecast."

Carole sent me a text announcing that they were on their way and would arrive at my place around five o'clock. I quickly mixed up my brownie recipe and put the pan in the oven. I couldn't compete with the queen baker who was arriving, but the brownies were the best I could do.

As I waited for them to arrive, I picked some of my flowers that were blooming and mixed them with some of the many wild ferns I had growing on my property. The arrangement was quite nice.

Shortly after, they arrived. We shared our usual group hug, and then they began showering me with compliments about the cabin and how much it had improved since their last visit.

"It's so good to be back, Claire," Linda grinned. "Carole got us here with lightning speed. I guess we missed you!" I nodded and laughed, remembering Carole's driving habits.

Once inside, I pulled the brownies out of the oven and paired them with the vanilla ice cream I'd recently bought at the Pig. Carole had brought some of her cookies iced with quilt motifs, but they were works of art, not something we should eat.

When we went out on the porch to enjoy our brownies, Puff jumped up on Linda's lap. That was quite unusual, as she often hid when people came over.

"All cats love me and know I love them, I suppose," Linda claimed.

I then told them about Puff's strange reaction to Foster, and Linda said I should pay attention to that.

While we enjoyed our treat, I brought my friends up to date on the quilt show and my worries about the weather and Greta. They seemed to have something else on their mind, though.

"Aren't you wanting an update on Austen?" Carole teased.

"Is there something I should know?" I asked with a chuckle.

"Well, the word at the hospital is that he was seen with a woman at the country club," Carole said suggestively.

"Oh, really? Anyone we know?" I asked with interest.

"I don't think she was a local, from what they said," Carole noted.

"Well, it appears all the men in my life have now moved on, and I suppose I'm trying to do the same thing."

I then began to tell them about Foster and our unbelievable date on the beach. They were drooling as they listened intently. They couldn't believe I hadn't fallen in love with him.

"Other than Puff having a reaction, he's a little too perfect," I admitted.

"Just go with your gut like you always have," Linda advised.

"You'll never move on until you're over Grayson," Carole claimed. "Frankly, I think the two of you will still get back together one day."

"Cher thinks he's done, and I should move on more seriously," I shared.

"Hey, there's a little something different in your brownies," Carole noted. "What is it?"

"It's a secret," I teased.

My cell rang just then. It was Ericka, so I excused myself and went into the living room to talk.

Chapter 89

"Ericka, are you okay?"

"I'm not sure," she said, sniffling. "I'm just having a bad moment, I guess. Cher and George are at work, and I guess I just needed to talk. Am I interrupting anything?"

"No, but can you hang on for just a minute? I'm on the porch where it's noisy."

I whispered to Carole and Linda that I needed to take the call. They nodded and understood.

"Okay, so what brought on those tears tonight?"

She paused. "I don't want to die, Claire," she spilled out boldly.

"Ericka, my dear friend, you will one day die like all the rest of us, but you have every reason to believe you can beat this beast." She had no response. "I think the mere fact that you have gone back to work is remarkable."

"I think that may have been a mistake. My coworkers treat me like I'm some sort of foreign object that may die on their watch."

"Please don't talk like that. They're just worried and concerned for you and don't want you working as hard as you used to."

"I didn't come back to be treated like that. I want to be like everyone else. I was always the one in charge, and now they act like I'm supposed to do as they say."

"I'm sorry you're getting that reaction from them, Ericka. I'm sure they mean well. Sometimes things have to change for all of us. You can't just pick up where you left off, but you can do what you can and be thankful for it."

"Thankful? For what should I be thankful? I have nothing to live for. I have no husband, no children, and now, no job, which I dearly loved. I'm certain the hospital is going to let me go permanently any day now."

"Ericka, honey, stop. Your cancer could be a lot worse than it is."

"But it's getting worse, Claire. My treatments aren't helping, so the heck with them."

"I'm sure it hasn't been easy, friend. Cher said you've been feeling better lately. Can you feel grateful for that?"

"What good is feeling better when I still can't do what I used to?"

"None of us can, Ericka. We're all challenged by something. Have you been able to talk to someone about accepting Christ into your heart? I really think you'd experience more peace and healing if you did."

"No. I've never been a spiritual person. I used to go to church with my parents when I was young. After I finished grade school, I never attended church again. None of my friends went."

"Going to church wasn't really what I was talking about. It's about having a purpose in this life and turning it over to a bigger power than ourselves. I can only speak for myself, but I find peace and comfort in the faith I was brought up in.

The Bible verses and hymns I learned in school come back to me as solace when I'm troubled. It's yours for the asking."

"Asking?" Ericka repeated in disbelief.

"Yes. There's something bigger in life than just being a person on this earth. Even here, we can't do it alone. We need family and friends for strength and encouragement. Community is so important."

"You've given me a lot to think about, Claire. I knew you would. You're so strong and sure of yourself. Thanks for listening to me."

"Anytime, my friend. I'm here anytime. It might help you to get out more. Maybe you could see the quilt show coming up. There's so much beauty lined up on the street. You wouldn't be sorry."

"Cher told me the same thing. George said he would take me."

"That's wonderful, Ericka. I know you'll enjoy it."

We chatted another five minutes before we hung up. I was hoping I got through to her just a little bit and helped her feel less discouraged. I went back to join the girls, feeling more somber than when I'd left them.

"Is everything okay?" Linda asked with concern.

"I'd like to think so," I reported sadly. "I'm sorry for the conversation taking so long."

I then told them more about Ericka, and they seemed to know others who'd had a hard time picking up the pieces after such a daunting diagnosis.

"I don't know what I'd do without my Catholic faith," Carole shared. "I thank my parents for leading me that direction."

"Faith in something higher is always helpful, but especially during the dark times. I know I'd be lost without mine. Off subject, it's almost nine o'clock, and we haven't had dinner," I noticed.

"I couldn't eat another bite after that brownie delight," Linda claimed. "I'm ready to hit the bed. How about you, Carole? It's been a long day."

"I agree," Carole said. "It's been so pleasant sitting here on your porch in the center of Fish Creek. I'm so glad you bought this place, Claire."

"I'm thankful for it every day. It really feels like home."

Chapter 90

I finally got up at four. It was showtime for the quilt show, and my insomnia reflected my nervousness. I hoped my morning saying of *This is the day the Lord hath made, let us rejoice in it!* would ring true.

I looked out the window at the darkness. I checked my phone once again for the weather update, and the forecast still said there was a 40 percent chance of rain around noon. It was going to be a rough call because at six o'clock, there wouldn't be rain. Rules were rules, though.

I headed to the shower and wondered if Cher had gotten better sleep than I had. I hoped so. I was sure Marta was already up and about. We had agreed to meet at the church at five thirty to make our decision about whether to go ahead with the show. Marta likely had other farm chores to complete before heading to Fish Creek.

I dressed and then made my coffee. I was definitely going to need caffeine to get me through the day. I grabbed my quilt folder from the kitchen table, texted Cher that I was on my way, and headed out. My nerves wouldn't let me eat anything quite yet.

The light in the sky appeared like any normal morning. Thank goodness the church was close by my cabin. Marta's car was already there.

"Good morning!" I greeted, sounding more carefree and awake than I felt.

"As Billy always says to me, 'Grandma, are you ready to rock and roll?'"

I laughed. "Well, as ready as I can be," I responded happily. "So, what's your assessment so far, Marta? Should the show go on as planned?"

"Honey, this is your day. I'm just here to help you through it."

"It doesn't work that way, Marta. You know it takes a village."

"Well, you have to weigh and balance your pros and cons and then follow the rules. It's now six o'clock and no rain. The good news with these cloudy skies is that there isn't hot sun hitting those quilts."

"You're right about that. And canceling could cause problems as well." Cher arrived just then and apologized for being late.

"It's a go, right?" Cher asked anxiously. Marta and I looked at each other and nodded.

"It's a go!" I agreed.

"Good. I just saw Carl, and he should be here with the guys any minute now," Cher noted. "Just make sure they give out plenty of drop cloths."

As the guys started showing up, Marta lectured each one about their block assignment. I was answering texts from Amy, Rachael, and Olivia, who wanted confirmation. So far, no one objected to our decision. Then Greta arrived and cast a shadow on our decision to move forward. She started in first with Marta about how, within hours, everyone's quilts would be wet. I ignored her as I helped Marta check off quilts for the guys to take.

At eight o'clock, my quilt monitors would be arriving. Greta seemed not to be listening, and the frown on her face said everything. Carole and Linda said they were well rested and offered to help in any other way they could until nine o'clock when the show began. I suggested they grab their monitor badges and go to the park to help Lee with her tent or any of the other vendors who needed some help. Greta was heading my way by this point, and her stern look never wavered.

"You're going to regret this decision, Claire," Greta scolded. "Do you realize the liability here? The first thing folks will do is criticize the Quilters of the Door."

"No, they won't," I stated firmly. "This show isn't sponsored by our club. Cher and I have taken full responsibility here. We've followed the rules of the show, and you should, too."

"Well!" she said in a huff as she walked away. Why had I fooled myself into thinking she would be a team player?

Kelly came in the door and made a point to let me know she'd arrived.

"My dad said to tell you to 'break a leg.' I guess that means good luck."

We both laughed. "Tell him thanks!" I said with a smile.

Carl came to get the challenge quilts to hang. From what little I saw of them, they were gorgeous! I couldn't wait to find out who won.

Chapter 91

So far, everything was going as planned. The sky was even clearing, providing the hope I so desperately needed. Cher suggested at ten o'clock that we take her car and slowly drive down the street and then up to the shops on the hill.

"Is everything alright, Marta? Do you need anything?"

She chuckled. "It's going well. Having more hangers this year has made this go quicker than last year."

"That's great. Please don't let Greta get to you."

"Heaven's no. I've put up with her more years than you know. I'll stay here at the church while you girls check things out. Enjoy it while you can because if it starts raining, all hands will be on deck. Some of the guys won't pick up the quilts until four o'clock regardless of what happens, so let's hope the quilts get covered."

"Thanks so much, Marta, for all your reassurance and calm. The good news with the quilts on the hill is that they will have an overhang to protect them," I noted.

"Some on Main Street do as well, so we'll hope for the best," Cher added.

"I think Olivia will have a tent, as will Lee," I mentioned. "I wish everyone did."

"When you girls get back, I would like to go see the pie entries for the cherry pie contest," Marta requested.

"No problem," I nodded as Cher and I went out the back door where her car was parked.

When we arrived on Main Street, we looked in awe at the colorful quilts flapping in the breeze. The sight gave me chills as I felt so proud.

When we reached the top of the hill, the view was like seeing a quilt village, all on its own. It made me wish these hilltop quilts would have been included last year also.

"Can you believe this, Claire?" Cher asked in amazement. "Let's park here for just a bit to take it all in." I nodded.

We couldn't believe how many folks were already showing up. I told Cher that these shops could have done their own quilt show without us.

"Look what we did, Cher Bear. It's glorious. I guess we'd better get back so Marta can take a break," I suggested. "I'm sure most of our crowd will come early in case it rains."

On our way back to the church, we concentrated our views on the other side of the street. I was gathering ideas for which buildings would make good paintings.

Back at the church, I could tell Marta was upset about something.

"Did we stay too long?" I asked with concern.

"No, sweetie," she said, shaking her head. "I just got a call from Olivia saying that Greta demanded she move her entire tent to a different location. Olivia had just finished setting up everything."

"Why did Greta ask her to do that, for heaven's sake?" I inquired with disgust.

"I don't know, but Olivia wasn't having it until she talked with you," Marta reported.

"Okay. I'll call her right now," I said, going into the back room.

I calmed Olivia down and insisted that she stay put. I told her we'd planned everyone's spot for a reason. I'm sure Greta was going to be disappointed, but so be it.

"I'll go on, then, to see the pies," Marta announced. "I won't be long. By the way, I heard Lee won first place in the challenge contest. I can't believe I won third place!"

"Oh, Marta, that's wonderful! Congratulations!" I said as Cher and I cheered. "I can't wait to see the winners."

As Marta left, a lady came through the door with two small boys. She had one in each hand, and she didn't look very happy.

"Are you in charge of this quilt show?" she asked, looking straight into my eyes.

"Yes, Cher and I are cochairs. How can we help you?" I asked with concern.

"We were just in the park, admiring all the quilts, one of which was made by my mother. Suddenly, a very rude lady came our direction, yelling at us quite loudly about touching the quilt. I told her it was my mother's quilt, and we meant no harm. I then got a lecture about bringing my young boys to such an event. The woman claimed my boys were out of control, running around. I was so embarrassed. I thought you should know. When I tell my mother, I'm sure she'll never enter a quilt again."

"Oh no. I'm so sorry," I immediately said.

"I'm sorry, too, that the monitor reacted as she did," Cher added. "We have these monitors placed about to make sure none of the quilts are harmed. We take that responsibility very seriously, but it sounds like it backfired in your case."

"Well, I'm sure the woman turned a lot of people off, and you'll likely be hearing from them as well," she said as she pulled her boys out the door. Our mouths were open in disbelief.

Chapter 92

"Oh, Cher! What do we do about Greta?" I asked in disbelief.

"Calm down," Cher insisted. "I'll go over and reprimand her the best I can."

"We'd be better off without anyone at all, the way she's behaving!"

Cher flew out the door and I poured myself a cup of coffee, wishing it was something stronger. I then called Olivia to see if everything was okay with her booth.

"Well, I just flat told Greta I wasn't moving!" Olivia stated. "She then told me I wouldn't be invited back. I brushed off her comment, but she'll probably yell at you next."

"I'm so sorry, Olivia. How's the crowd?"

"Very good, and sales are good also. Now just keep that rain away."

"Great. Keep up the good work."

Cher walked in the door shaking her head.

"Well, as I expected, Greta gave me another story. To hear her tell it, the boys nearly destroyed the place. I thanked her for being cautious but told her she would have to be nicer."

"Nicer? Greta doesn't know the meaning of that word."

"You're probably right about that. Amy's booth looks great. She is prepared with many drop cloths. I think she's done outdoor shows before and knows what can happen. I sure hope she has good sales."

"What about Rachael and Harry's booth?"

"Well, they're taking up a bit more space than we'd planned, but they sure brought some pretty barn quilts, and some are quite large. There were a lot of people looking at them. How in the world does Rachael produce all that?"

"Harry has been helping her just like Charlie did. I sure wish I had a place to put one of her barn quilts. Someone suggested I put one on my little shed out back, but frankly, I don't want to draw attention to it."

"I know what you mean. Safety first."

"Okay, Cher, I'm going to check out the pie contest and take some photos."

"On your way back, bring some lunch, okay?"

"The restaurants will be packed, but I'll see what I can do."

As I approached the orchard's attractive red-and-white tent, I noticed all their attention to detail. The pie entries were under glass with the proper information on the ribbon winners. The pies looked so very good they were making me hungry. It seemed that the orchard's intent with its pie contest was to sell its cherry products, and judging from the line I saw, it was doing just that. I suddenly felt like I was at a county fair. This tent was really an appealing addition to our quilt show.

When I stopped by to say hello to Rachael and Harry at their booth, they were beaming. They'd just sold one of the large barn quilts they'd brought.

"We're thrilled about the sale," Rachael glowed, "but now I'm worried about those dark clouds overhead."

"I know what you mean," I nodded. "Those clouds are making me nervous, too. I really hope the rain holds off, if for no other reason than I'd have to listen to Greta say she told me so, and that would be dreadful. Well, I need to find lunch for Cher and Marta, so I'd better get a move on."

Near the Seaquist booth was a taco stand that was very popular. The line wasn't too long, so I stood there to take care of our lunch. All of a sudden, I heard a loud ambulance go by. Everyone stopped what they were doing, and my heart sank. Now what?

I rushed back to the church with a bag full of tacos and quickly asked Cher what the ambulance was all about.

"A lady fell on the sidewalk in front of the Homestead Suites," she reported. "I don't know if she became ill or what."

"Oh, that's terrible. I hope she's alright," I said, handing Cher a couple of tacos. "I've been worried that with everyone looking at the quilts, someone would get hit by a car."

"Well, this woman's fall sure stopped up traffic from what I've heard. It probably hurt the shops at the top of the hill. Claire, thanks for picking up these tacos. They'll hit the spot. Marta went to deliver some supplies to the On Deck store. They had a quilt come down, and they didn't know how to rehang it."

"How in the world did that happen? What next?"

"Who knows? I'm not sure I want to guess," Cher said as she continued to eat.

Chapter 93

Just then, a woman came in the door and announced she was a reporter from the *Pulse* newspaper. She asked if she could take a photo of Cher and me, which we agreed to.

"Now ladies, do you have a plan for the rain that is predicted?"

Cher and I looked at each other. I did what I could to explain what we had planned. I told her that our rule was to decide at six in the morning whether to have the show. She nodded.

"I just took a photo of the cherry tree quilt, which is so beautiful!" the reporter noted.

"Did the creator tell you that she won first place in our Quilted Cherries challenge as well?" I asked.

"Yes, she did, but we were told to take only two photos," she responded.

"We thank you very much," I said with a smile as she left the building.

"Well, look who's here!" Marta announced, coming in the door with Frances and Ava.

"Hey, you made it!" I cheered.

"Well, you all sure pulled off a great show," Frances praised.

"I don't know how you do it," Ava said, shaking her head. "We saw most of it from the car, but when we saw the cherry pie booth, we just had to check it out. Anna needed to be here with her cherry strudel."

"I wish she could have been here too, but now she has a business to run," Marta added.

"I don't know if you saw those black clouds that are out there now, but I figure they're going to burst any minute," Frances lamented.

"We know," I nodded. "I just hope everyone remembers what to do."

"Next year, ladies, I promise I'll be more help to you," Ava claimed. "We heard sales were going well, so that's always good. Well, we'd better go before the rain, Frances. We need to make a wine stop at the Main Street Market in Egg Harbor, don't we?" Frances chuckled.

"You can't run out of wine!" I joked. "Thank you again, Frances, for your generous donation. I promise it will be put to good use." Marta looked puzzled.

When they left, I took a moment to inform Marta about Frances giving us the $1,000 check. She couldn't believe it.

"Frances has always been a bit of an odd duck, if you ask me," Marta noted. "Her quilts are strange, but she does have great talent. When she had that séance at her house, I couldn't support it, but she truly feels connected with the supernatural, so I suppose it seemed perfectly ordinary to her. Her heart is always in the right place, though. I don't believe I've ever heard her say a bad word about anyone. This financial contribution for the quilt show is most generous of her."

"We agree, Marta," I nodded.

All of a sudden there was a loud clap of thunder and a flash of lightning. All three of us jumped.

"Oh, no!" I said, looking out the door. My cell phone rang.

"Claire, it's Carole," she announced. "Should we be telling businesses to cover the quilts?"

"Yes. Better now than later," I stated. "If they disagree, just let them handle it."

I hung up and looked at Cher, whose fear showed in her eyes. The thunder grew louder, causing the church windows to shake. It was out of our hands now. I walked to the door again and asked God for mercy. I knew He was listening.

Chapter 94

Marta, Cher, and I looked at each other with fright and knew we had to stay here for all the commotion that was about to come.

"Claire, Carl just called me and said he was taking down the challenge quilts with the wind and sprinkles picking up," Cher reported. "He just wanted us to be aware."

"It's the right thing to do," I nodded. "The quilts were shown and the winners chosen, so their job is done."

"What time is it?" Marta asked with panic in her voice.

"It's only two o'clock," I said sadly.

"I guess we were lucky the bad weather didn't start sooner," Marta noted.

"My phone says the storm is coming from the south and headed our way," I reported.

"If only it had held out two more hours," Marta said, watching by the door. In walked Foster, much to my surprise.

"Ladies, I think you're going to need some help," he offered.

"Carl's in the park, and he likely could use your assistance," I suggested. "Do you mind?"

"I'm on my way," Foster said, going out the door.

"Marta, I guess you're wondering who that was appearing out of the blue," I chuckled. "His name is Foster Collins, and he's a friend of ours."

"Well, we need all the help we can get," Marta said. "It's nice of him to volunteer."

I wasn't sure Foster would be back in town to come to the show but, apparently, he was, and thank goodness. He'd come by to help, and that meant a lot. The sprinkles were getting increasingly larger and heavier.

"I'm glad God gave us a warning," I said with gratitude. "I was worried about a sudden downpour."

We could now see Carl and Foster running across the street toward us with their arms full.

"Put them all on this table, fellas," Marta instructed. I'll start checking them off. Claire, if they're not too wet, go ahead and enclose them in their proper bag. If they're damp, lay them over the pews in the sanctuary."

"Foster and I are going back to the park to help the vendors," Carl alerted. "It's pretty crazy, and folks are running around frantically."

"Thanks, guys," I said, feeling grateful.

Cher and I got busy, trying to help Marta with the challenge quilts.

"Something's wrong," Marta said aloud. "There should be eleven quilts, and I just counted ten. The one missing happens to be mine!"

"Oh no," I said. "Let's look again."

"I'll call Carl right now and tell him to look for another quilt," Cher said in a panic. "Maybe they dropped it in the rush." We looked at Cher for Carl's response as she called to tell him.

"Carl says that's impossible," she reported. "He swears they got them all."

I couldn't look at Marta. I could only imagine what she was thinking. Suddenly another loud clap of thunder and flash of lightning made us jump. It was so black outside that it looked like midnight instead of the middle of the afternoon.

The room then began to fill with everyone from spectators of the show to quilt owners here to retrieve their quilts. *Please help us, dear God.*

"Ladies and gentlemen," I called out as loud as I could, standing on a chair. "Please be patient. Many of your quilts have been covered or put inside the shops. When they're returned and checked off, you may have them. Everyone is doing their best."

My warning didn't do much good, and the noise of the storm didn't help.

"Claire, if you and Marta are okay, I'm going to the park to look for Marta's quilt and help Carl," Cher announced.

"Sure. There are umbrellas by the door," I offered. The wind blew the door shut when she left and scared all of us.

"I worry those drop cloths have blown away by now," Marta said with concern. "Remember when last year someone took their quilt without telling us? You can bet some of that took place today with the rain."

"Oh yes. How could I forget?" I responded. "I wish you had grabbed yours, Marta. What could have happened?" Marta shook her head in disgust.

After a while, Cher came in the door, soaking wet. I gave her one of the extra tablecloths to dry off.

"I'm afraid I don't have very good news," Cher said, wiping her face dry. "I looked everywhere and asked some of the folks nearby, yet I got nowhere closer to locating your quilt, Marta. We'll find it, though. Don't worry."

"Well, maybe not," Marta said, shaking her head.

Chapter 95

"So, any more bad news?" I asked Cher with hesitation.

"Yes, actually," Cher said, looking down. "Lee said an orange drink of some kind was spilled on the corner of her quilt. She said it must have happened when she took a short break in the Noble House."

"Oh, I hate to hear that," I responded. "So, what did she do?"

"She said she took it down immediately to put some water on it. Of course, shortly thereafter, the rain came. She wasn't as upset as I would be. She mentioned that she would work some more on it when she's back home. I bet she regrets showing it."

"I bet she does, too," I agreed with sadness. "She was so nice to let us show it."

"Outdoor shows are risky, like our dear friend Greta reminded us," Marta reminded. "You have all ages running around, and most everyone has food or drink in their hands. And children have sticky fingers and love to touch."

"You know Lee was watching everyone carefully," I noted. "I almost wonder if this was intentional."

"Claire!" Cher reprimanded.

The men started arriving back with the quilts they'd hung. They looked frightfully wet and exhausted. I could only imagine what the quilts looked like. I helped take the quilts out of the bags to look them over as Cher and Marta crossed off the names. Some of the quilts were damp and needed to dry off.

"What a mess," Cher said, shaking her head as she took more quilts to lay over the church pews.

In the door came Kelly and Billy. They were a sight, soaking wet from head to toe. Unlike the others, they must have enjoyed the rain, as they were laughing up a storm. I was glad someone was having fun with this nightmare. I told Kelly there were towels in the bathroom to dry off.

I stayed with Marta to help as best I could. I could feel her frustration and worry about finding her quilt. A friend of Carl's, Alex, came in to report that all the quilts that were hung on the top of the hill had been placed inside their shops. When the rain stopped, he would retrieve them. I agreed it was the right thing do.

My cell rang, and it was Rachael.

"Hey, I just wanted to let you know that we finished loading up and are on our way home."

"Okay. Was anything damaged?"

"No, but as soon as it started sprinkling, I told Harry we were gonna pack up. We did have fun, and we had some good sales, so all was not lost."

"That's good to hear. We're still here at the church with some problems. We're missing a challenge quilt, and it happens to be Marta's."

"Oh, Claire, that's terrible! I heard about Lee's quilt being damaged. What a shame."

"Well, thanks for coming, Rachael. Were Amy and Olivia still there when you left?"

"Olivia was going nuts, but Amy seemed to not be as concerned. She had a lot of things covered in plastic."

"Thanks for the update. Well, I need to get back to work."

I returned to helping Cher and Marta, who were struggling with identifying some of the quilts. The quilts were to be taken down and put in the same bags with their names on them, but with the rain, quilts were just grabbed and brought to us.

By four thirty, the skies were starting to clear in the light rain. The show was technically over, but the damage was done. Carl and Foster came back to the church and looked totally beat. I'd never seen Foster looking that way. He always looked so put together.

Carl went to converse with Cher, and Foster came toward me, showing concern.

"Are you okay?" he asked kindly.

I shook my head. "Are all the vendors gone now?"

"Yes. We stayed to help the very last one," he answered.

"Thank you. I'm sure they were upset," I noted.

"They were stressed like everyone, I'm sure," Foster added.

"We have one missing quilt and another probably ruined. And who knows how many more," I shared, nearly in tears. Foster shook his head in sympathy.

Chapter 96

"Look, I know you have to be here for a while, but maybe I could take you for a drink afterward if that would make you feel better. I'll wait to get your call," Foster offered.

"That's sweet of you to ask, but until the last quilt comes in, we'll be here, no matter how late."

"I understand," he nodded.

"I really appreciate all your help," I said with gratitude. "It's just one of those events where you can't plan for everything."

"Of course. Just remember that none of this was your fault," he reassured me before he left.

I grabbed a cup of coffee, made early this morning, for Marta and me. It tasted as bad as we felt. I told her that the quilts should be arriving from the top of the hill anytime now since the rain had let up.

"Here's a quilt that blew to the ground somewhere," Marta said, holding it up. "It's too soiled to put on the pews, unfortunately. It belongs to Ginger, but I know she will understand. The dirt should wash out okay."

I looked closer, and it was a cute grandmother's fan made out of vintage quilt blocks. That was Ginger's work, alright.

I put it in a clean bag with her name on it. I decided to take it home and wash it for her.

"Did Carl leave?" I asked Cher.

"Yes. He said he had to get back to the shop. His sister's been working there by herself all day. I bet she was swamped with folks wanting to get out of the rain."

"I was so surprised to see Foster jump in to help like he did," Cher noted.

"Me too. Completely unexpected. I'm sure Kelly described our nightmare to her dad," I said, shaking my head. "I'm still shocked Grayson remained a sponsor for us this year."

Alex arrived with all the quilts from the hill. There were so many that it took him two trips to bring them in. Our lucky break was that these quilts were put back in their original bags. We thanked Alex for his work and then spent the next half hour checking off every one of them.

Carole and Linda finally came in the door. They told us they headed to the library when the rain started because it was close by and then decided to grab something to eat. They wanted to share many of their stories, but they could see how stressed we already were. They offered to take us to dinner, but we told them we had no idea when we would be finished and agreed to go another time.

At eight o'clock, it appeared everything was in the building that was coming back except for Marta's quilt. We offered to take Marta out for something to eat, but she wanted to go straight home. Billy was nowhere to be found, but she didn't seem concerned about him.

"We'll find your quilt, Marta," I assured her.

"I just don't know who would take it right off the clothesline," she said, disheartened.

"That's a good question for us to ask Greta, who was guarding this area, as you recall. She has a lot to answer for. I bet she went home as soon as the first drop of rain hit the ground instead of staying to be helpful."

"You're probably right, Claire," Cher agreed.

"Well, it's just a quilt, ya know," Marta replied, trying to make light of the situation as she began to tidy up the place.

"We can never let something like this happen again," I said in anger. "We have to manage this better the next time."

"We sure do!" Cher nodded.

By nine thirty, we were prepared to lock up. Marta did seem pleased with how many of the quilts were picked up. When we left the church, the sky had cleared. We hugged each other and went our separate ways. Our second quilt show was over.

My nerves were a wreck when I returned to the cabin that night. I was too angry and exhausted to call Greta. I decided to wait until morning. Right now, I just needed to relax and de-stress.

Puff jumped off her chair to greet me. I wasn't a bit hungry, but I did pour myself a much-needed glass of wine. My companion watched me as if she sensed something was wrong.

When I went out to sit on the back porch, wine in hand, Puff jumped onto my lap to keep me company. I stroked her back gently and rubbed her ears, inhaling and exhaling deeply as I did so. I focused on the breeze coming through the screens, which was gentle and pleasant. The wine and the quiet were beginning to calm the hecticness of the day that had gone nothing like we'd hoped for. My phone alerted me to a text, and I did a double take when I saw the sender. Grayson? Why would he be texting me now after all this time? Did Kelly not come home?

Chapter 97

[Grayson]
So sorry about the rain today. Kelly enjoyed the show just the same. I hope your recovery went okay.

I was stunned to hear from him. I guess he really was thinking about me in some way. How many days and weeks had it been since we exchanged words? Should I respond or not? I decided to keep it brief, like his message to me.

[Claire]
Thank you. It was a stressful and somewhat damaging day. Thanks again for your sponsorship.

Okay, that was simple enough. I pressed send and waited for a response, but there wasn't one. How could he not ask me about what was damaged?

I was so tired that I really didn't want to think of anything related to the show. Tomorrow, I would begin making calls to the vendors and to Greta, who'd been such a disappointment. I was having many regrets and thoughts about how I would do things differently next year. Actually, there might not be a next year. Perhaps this was the last show of Door-to-Door Quilts after today's disaster.

With that thought, I decided to get ready for bed. I lingered in the shower, wanting the water to wash away the bad parts of the day. I had to remind myself that half the day went as planned.

I crawled into bed, hoping I wouldn't have an extended nightmare about today's activities.

I was pleased to sleep until ten o'clock the next morning without interruption. I needed that. The show was over. Now it was time for cleanup and addressing the bad PR.

It was sunny when I went out to the porch to check the temperature. The cabin was completely covered in shade with all the surrounding trees, and that helped keep it cooler.

I sat near Puff, who was already in her favorite chair for a morning nap, to read my emails and texts.

Two emails were complaints from women about the condition of their quilts when they picked them up. One made it clear it was the last time she would let her quilt be used. Another quilter remarked how sad she felt about the weather and wished us well. My phone rang, and I cringed imagining who else was contacting me about something that hadn't gone right. It was Mr. Samson.

"Good morning, Claire! I'm just touching base about how you all made out with the rain?" I paused a bit before I answered.

"It was challenging, I'll say that."

He chuckled. "We thought we were prepared, but when you have to pack up in a hurry, it's not good. I wanted to let you know I'll be sending out the winners' checks today. I was hoping for more entries, but I think there will be more next year."

"I'm not sure there will be a next year after this experience."

"Don't talk like that. You can't control Mother Nature, and everyone knows that."

"You were a wonderful addition to the show, Mr. Samson. I can't thank you enough for participating."

"Well, if there is a next year, please contact me for a sponsorship."

"Okay. We'll be in touch."

After that bit of encouragement, I decided to bite the bullet and call Greta. Her phone rang and rang with no answer, so I had to leave a message.

"Good morning, Greta. It's Claire. We need to discuss the show, so please give me a call."

Maybe it was for the best that the call with Greta was delayed a little. I decided to touch base with Olivia and Amy, but before I could do that, my cell rang with another call.

"Good morning, Ericka," I greeted my friend.

"Good morning to you, too. I hope you're in a better mood than our friend Cher. She's really bummed out about the show, as I'm sure you are as well. I hope my call will make you feel better because I did get to see it. George took me for a ride to see all the quilts before the rain started. It was spectacular, just as you both described it would be. It truly was an art show like this town has never seen, so congratulations!"

"Thank you, Ericka. Your words are just what I needed to hear this morning. I'm so glad you were able to see it. The rain certainly caused many problems, but that was out of our hands."

"I kept thinking about what you said about it taking a village to pull off something like your show. Perhaps I can be of help next year if I'm healthy enough."

"Thank you, but that will be up for discussion. The village may not feel it's a good idea to continue based on what happened yesterday."

Chapter 98

Olivia called me before I could dial her. Phone calls were likely to take up my whole morning.

"Claire, it's Olivia. How are you?"

"Surviving. How about you? Do you still have a job at the quilt shop?"

She laughed. "Honestly, I'm not sure. We had to discount or throw away some merchandise that got wet."

"I hope they understand it was not your fault."

"Perhaps, but I chose the merchandise, and I was supposed to take care of it. I worry about Amy and her quilts."

"I'll be talking to her next. We're pretty upset about losing a challenge quilt that belonged to Marta. Did you see anyone around the display you thought was odd? We can't figure out how her quilt was removed without Greta noticing. I haven't talked to Greta yet, but she's the one who was supposed to be watching those quilts."

"Oh dear. Greta was probably so jealous of Marta winning a ribbon that she stole Marta's quilt. I wouldn't put it past her. Why is that woman so evil? I have one piece of advice for you for next year: Keep that woman out of the show completely."

"Yes, I agree. We got a lot of complaints about her. She requested that area because she belongs to the Historical Society, but I don't think they would be too pleased with her behavior."

"There will be a next year, right?"

"We'll see. This year was close to being a disaster."

"Well, no one should complain. Everything was free for vendors and attendees alike for this wonderful art show."

"Thanks, but we'll hear more at our next quilt show meeting, I'm sure."

"I was thrilled to see Ava and Frances drive by."

"Me, too. They stopped by the church to say hello. Ava seems so happy now with the divorce on the way."

"She sure is! She briefly told me that her soon-to-be ex-husband has a new love interest, so he has pressure to move on with this divorce. How about that?"

"Thank goodness for small favors. That guy is quite the lowlife. His new woman will be the next victim, I'm sure. Well, I have more calls to make, Olivia, so I'll let you go. Good luck with your boss."

When I hung up, I felt so down. It was hard not to blame myself for some of yesterday's failings. Maybe we made the wrong decision to have the show with a 40 percent chance of rain. I needed a break from the phone, so I stepped outdoors to see the blessing of the recent rain on my yard and flowers. Everything looked so pretty. The beauty helped me remember to keep things in perspective.

To my surprise, Brenda pulled into my driveway just then. She was likely on her way to work.

"Hey, girlfriend!" Brenda yelled when she got out of the car. "Did you dry out?"

"That's not funny," I joked.

"Lots of problems? Can I help?"

I shook my head to her offer. "Was it really crazy at the inn?"

"It was. But I was at Rachael and Harry's booth just as it started to rain, so I was able to be help them for a bit. I really thought we'd have a nice day the way it started out."

"Me too. We can only prepare so much. I think you may have seen our last show."

"Now, it wasn't that bad. I wish I could have been more help to you. By the way, I told Rachael if you needed assistance getting the gift shop in order, I can help."

"That's great, Brenda. I'll be happy to be working on something else for a change."

"Well, I've got to go. I may be late for work. See you later."

I sat on the steps to watch my friend leave. I thought I should try Greta again, though I wasn't looking forward to the conversation that would follow if she answered. After several rings, this time she picked up.

"Greta, we're all trying to recover from the show, so I hope you're well." Silence. "As you witnessed, there was a great deal of commotion when it started raining. Since it was your job to monitor the park, were you aware that one of our challenge quilts is missing?"

She paused. "No, I was not aware of that."

"We've looked everywhere and talked to many folks in the area without any luck. By the way, it's Marta's quilt that's missing. She won third place, and it would be a shame if we couldn't recover that quilt for her."

"I knew she won."

"Since you were so careful about who was doing what, did you see anything you thought was odd, or did you see anyone remove a challenge quilt for any reason?"

"Well, of course, I had to warn many not to touch the quilts, but no, I didn't see anyone take a quilt, or I would have alerted the police."

"Would you have told us about it?"

"Of course! What a thing to ask, Claire. You know how vocal I've been about all the bad things that can happen at an outdoor show like this. Now we have a stolen quilt, not to mention all the ones that were likely damaged. I hate to say it, but I told you so."

"I didn't say the quilt was stolen. I said it was missing. It has to be somewhere, and we're going to find it."

"Are you suggesting it was my fault or that I took it?"

"No, but that quilt was your responsibility. You asked to monitor that area, and we agreed. When did you leave? Did you bother to help anyone like Lee or the vendors when it began raining?"

"I think you've said enough, Miss Stewart. If there's anyone to blame, it's you and Cher," she said and abruptly hung up.

Chapter 99

Well, that went well, I told myself. Not for a second did she feel bad for Marta having lost her quilt. It did make me wonder how evil she could be. I wondered how much she would fight to end the show if we did decide to have it again. Why did this have to be so hard? My cell was ringing again. Now what?

"Hey, Claire!" Cher greeted. "The girls want me to set up a dinner for tonight. Do you have any suggestions?"

"I'm hardly in the mood, but that's not their fault. Sure, you pick it. I'll be there."

"Well, we owe them a nice meal for making the trip and helping us at the show."

"Yes, you're right."

"I'm sorry you're so down. What's going on that I should know about?"

"I just talked to Greta, and it didn't go well."

"I'm not surprised. You'll have to fill me in later. The girls did some shopping this morning and they're pretty tired, so we may want to have an early dinner."

"Just let me know when and where," I said reluctantly.

To get my mission of phone calling over with, I rang Amy.

"You beat me to a call," Amy said apologetically. "I guess I'm recouping from yesterday, like everyone else. Wouldn't you know that today is a perfectly beautiful day?"

"I know. Our timing was really off. I'm calling to find out if you had any damages from the rain?"

"Nothing serious, thanks to lots of drop cloths. I just couldn't take any chances when I felt the first sprinkle. I'm thrilled that we did sell one quilt. We also sold a lot of smaller items, so the event was still more profitable than a normal Saturday here in the shop even though we ended early."

"That's good to hear. Unfortunately, we have a missing challenge quilt that belongs to Marta. Did you notice anything unusual or happen to see anyone remove a quilt from the display?"

"Oh, that's awful. No, I didn't see anything unusual like that. Greta was her usual drill-sergeant self if anyone got near one of the quilts. Things got really crazy when the rain started. It was every man for himself, so what a convenient time for someone to take something without anyone noticing."

"Can you tell me if Greta remained in the park through the rain?"

"I'm not sure. To be honest, I don't remember seeing her after the rain. Of course, I knew better than to ask her for any help, like relieving me in my booth if I needed a break."

"We just have to find Marta's quilt, Amy. If word gets out on this, it would be bad. Plus, poor Marta deserves to have it back."

"Is she really upset?"

"She's not showing it if she is. She's the backbone of this show, and I hate that this has happened to her, especially. She worked so hard to make sense of what came back to her so haphazardly."

"She's amazing. Thank you again for letting my shop vend. I'm sure you had many requests."

"So, you would do it again next year if we have it?"

"Of course!"

Well, that was some relief. There were some good comments, which I had to consider.

I made myself a glass of tea and sat in front of my laptop to send an email of thanks to all the helpers for their extra efforts. I couldn't apologize for the weather, but I could certainly recognize the extra efforts they made with the weather challenge. I wasn't going to share with them about the missing quilt or other complaints. When I finished, I took a deep breath, as if it were my last step. Cher's text popped up.

[Cher]
The girls chose Alexander's restaurant. Clean up and cheer up, Claire Bear. We need to celebrate!

I had to smile. It was just like Cher to see the bright side. With Carole and Linda at her house, how could she not?

While it was still daylight, I decided to tackle the job of washing Ginger's quilt. I held it up, and it looked totally ruined with all the mud and soil. It must have lain in a puddle or something worse before anyone found it.

I looked underneath my kitchen sink to find a product I'd used for soaking quilts and linens. This quilt would have to soak at least overnight, but perhaps longer.

ANN HAZELWOOD

I dissolved the powder in the warm water in my kitchen sink. When I added the quilt, it turned the water black, so I had to start all over again. It took three times before I could see it was clean enough to soak. I felt such relief when I saw the dirt disappear, as I felt I could effectively salvage this quilt. I would check it again in the morning and hope for the best. I'd need to remember to lay the quilt flat to dry so it could block itself. One success after the many disasters of this show would be helpful.

Chapter 100

I showered and put on a white sundress for the evening's dinner. Food was sounding better and better since I hadn't taken time for lunch today. My nerves had been in no shape to let me eat anything, but tonight was about thanking Carole and Linda for their help. It was a relief to know the show was over, but there certainly were problems ahead we would have to address.

I loved going to Alexander's in Fish Creek. It was a sizable, white-tablecloth restaurant that had wonderful food and yummy bar drinks. Besides that, the owners are known to be quite charitable with donations to nonprofit arts and community organizations that need them. It's just a classy place all around. I found my friends waving at me as soon as I walked in.

We all hugged as if we hadn't seen each other in ages. I had to look twice at how nice they looked, as I was used to seeing them in casual wear.

"You all look gorgeous!" I complimented. "Linda, you must have made the jewelry you're wearing."

She nodded and blushed. "Do you like it? I ended up selling the cherry earrings instead of giving them away. I'm so glad people like them."

"Of course, they do! I don't know how you work with such little things as jewels," I answered.

After we ordered our cocktails, Cher told the girls it was our treat and they could order anything they wanted. They grinned and didn't object.

Our conversation started with them sharing their shopping experience from earlier in the day and itemizing everything they'd purchased. It was fun witnessing their excitement.

After a lot of discussion, we all ordered shrimp cocktail and the halibut special for the evening.

"So, did you call your mom and tell her about how the show went?" asked Carole.

I shook my head. "No, nor did she call me, thank goodness," I noted. "She likely knows it rained and that I had my hands full." Just that single question about the show brought me back to reality.

"Did Grayson show up?" Carole asked.

I shook my head. "Not that I know of. He did text regarding the weather and letting Kelly help us," I reported. "I thanked him for being a sponsor this year."

"That's all you said after he reached out to you like that?" Linda asked, obviously puzzled.

"I guess after what the day was like, I just wasn't in the mood to make conversation," I explained.

"Well, that was nice of him to contact you," Cher noted.

"We're ready to hear more about mean Greta who caused so many problems," Carole requested.

"Well, the first time I called her, I had to leave a message for her to call me," I reported. "Of course, she didn't, so I had to call her back."

"Oh boy. How did that go?" Cher asked with dread as she took a sip of wine.

I took my time telling the girls about the exchange with Greta, and their faces showed their shock.

"She's never going to change, and since she hung up on me, she'll have it in for Cher and me, which is nothing new. We changed the entire club that she had controlled for many years."

"I hope she's so angry that she quits the club," Cher expressed.

"Well, if there's another show, I guarantee you she won't be part of it."

"I couldn't agree more!" Cher repeated.

"Okay, enough about the quilt show. I want to hear more about this Foster guy," Carole inquired. It was just like her to want the details. "I saw him helping Carl, and what a handsome man he is. He's older, it appears, but probably rich. Am I right?"

We chuckled. "He's all of the above," Cher jumped in.

"He was a big help just when we needed him, which was totally unexpected and kind," I noted. "He's quite pleasant and famous as an artist, of course, but he's really more like a friend. I can't see a real romantic relationship evolving."

"Too bad," nodded Linda, "but I do think you know right away if there's electricity or vibes with someone. I remember hearing about Grayson early on and how you just knew there was something about him that attracted you."

"Interesting observation, Linda," I noted with a grin.

"That's why we weren't the least bit surprised that your relationship with Grayson developed," Linda explained. "I don't know how if fell apart, and it's none of our business, but it seems like such a shame. Your mother still can't believe it happened."

"From what we heard," Carole added, "he was more serious than you were about the relationship, right?"

"I guess you could say that, but we really just didn't communicate very well, and the relationship fell apart," I said sadly. "It takes two to get it back together again, and he made it clear he was no longer interested. Right, Cher?" Cher nodded sadly.

The food arrived with all sorts of great garnishes, and the conversation went in every direction as we enjoyed every bite. All through dinner, I kept thinking about that guy in the red scarf who'd changed everything for me but then disappeared from my life.

Everyone was getting pretty merry and kept ordering more wine. When we were finished with the four courses, Carole insisted that we have an after-dinner drink. She was our guest, so we went along with her idea.

"Well, I'm just glad I don't have as far to drive home as you girls," I said. "Please send me a text when you're back home, Cher Bear," I requested. "Be very careful."

"Aren't you going to leave, too?" Cher asked as she rose from her chair.

"You girls go ahead," I encouraged. "I'm going to order some coffee. I know these girls don't drink coffee, but I'm just going to sit here for a while and digest the day and sober up a bit."

Cher looked at me oddly. "Very well," she said, giving me a hug. "We did our best, didn't we, Claire Bear?"

"Yes, you did," Carole and Linda said in agreement.

"That's all we can do, I guess," I nodded.

We all hugged each other goodbye, and the three of them headed out the door.

The waiter asked if he could start clearing the table, and I said it was fine. I looked over at the bar, which had mostly emptied out, and asked the waiter to bring my coffee over there.

The hot coffee did taste good and had a way of soothing the raw edges of the day.

When I glanced to my left, I couldn't believe my eyes. Grayson and his friend John had just walked in the door. I wanted to hide, but there was nowhere to go.

Chapter 101

"Claire! Are you celebrating your quilt show alone?" John called out when he saw me. Grayson had a look of shock on his face.

"My friends just left," I said with a smile. "I felt I needed a strong cup of coffee before I drove home. We got a little too merry."

"May we join you?" Grayson asked with concern.

"Of course," I said, looking away.

"John and I just left the Rotary banquet and decided to get a nightcap," Grayson explained.

"I recommend the Amaretto shot. It was delicious," I said, staring at his handsome face that I missed so much.

"I think you were smart to have some coffee," Grayson agreed as he looked at me with worry. "Are you going to be okay?"

"Do you really want to know?" I asked with sarcasm.

"Yes, I'd like to know," he responded softly.

"I think I'll go chat with the Colliers sitting in the other room," John suggested, feeling awkward.

"I haven't been okay since you left, if you're really curious," I said with some resentment.

"I'm not the one who left," Grayson countered. I sighed, knowing he would never understand.

"How about I drive your car and take you home?" he suggested kindly.

"I'll be fine," I insisted. "The coffee helps. We just had a few too many toasts this evening. You enjoy your evening with John."

"John's okay on his own right now. I bet you and your friends had a lot to toast to, and deservingly so," he noted. "Look, you've had a lot of stress these last days, but now you can relax. Quit being so independent and let someone like me take care of you for a change."

I stared at his dark blue eyes and knew he had my best interest at heart. I suppose in some small way, he did still have some feelings for me.

"Will John mind?" I asked meekly.

"I'll go tell him we're leaving right now."

In the seconds he was gone, I questioned my decision. When Grayson returned, he was smiling, and as we walked out the door, I felt his arm go around my waist. The gesture and his smile took me by surprise. I'd certainly missed both.

"I've never driven a Subaru before," Grayson informed me as we drove away. "I can see why you like it."

I remained quiet while we drove the short distance to my cabin.

"Now, how will you get home?" I asked when we walked to the door.

"I don't know. I just may have to sleep on your couch," he said, winking.

It was terribly awkward when we walked inside. I was at a loss for words.

"Look, I'm not sure this is the time to talk because you're obviously tired and stressed," he said as he sat on the couch.

"I don't know what to say, Grayson. How about some coffee?"

"I would love some," he said, getting comfortable on the couch.

I left him and went to the kitchen. My mind was not on the task at hand, but I did manage to pour us some coffee. I said a quick prayer that was only one word: *Help!*

When I came out with a mug of coffee for him, he thanked me.

"You're welcome," I replied, sitting at the other end of the couch.

We sat in silence for a bit, sipping our drinks. I knew it was my turn to start the conversation.

"So, did you think I'd say yes on New Year's Eve?" There it was. I'd jumped right in.

Little did I know that that question would lead us into conversation until four in the morning. We sat on opposite ends of the couch until we were at a loss for words and dozed off. I was so tired of talking and explaining. I could tell he felt the same way.

At seven thirty in the morning, Puff walked across my chest and startled me. I jumped and thought of Grayson. Was this a dream? No, there he was across from me with his head back and his body in an awkward position. He was in a deep sleep, and I didn't want to disturb that. But how did this happen, and how in the world would he explain it to Kelly?

I quietly got up and went to the kitchen to feed Puff while I put on more coffee. It was surreal to still be in my clothes and to have Grayson here. This is not at all what I expected the previous night to turn into.

He then walked into the kitchen with a grin on his face.

"I'm hungry. How about you? Do pancakes and bacon sound good?"

I burst into laughter. "What do you think this is, a short-order diner?" I teased.

"Well, if you can muster up some pancakes, I can surely fry the bacon."

"Deal!" I agreed.

We began our mission, trying to stay out of each other's way in my tiny kitchen.

"So, Mr. Wills, you are without a car if you remember. How do you suppose you're going to get home?"

"I recall that. I suppose I'll have to ask this gracious host if she could give me a ride back to my house."

"You're going to have a lot of explaining to do."

"Exactly. That's why you're coming in the house with me."

"What?"

"You heard me," he insisted.

Just then my phone rang. I didn't recognize the name, so I figured it was another complaint about the show.

"Miss Stewart?"

"Yes, this is she," I answered.

"My name is Cordele Miller, and I'm a volunteer at the Noble House. Yesterday someone turned in a wall-sized quilt they found by the intersection of Highway 42 and Main."

"Oh my goodness! Really?"

Chapter 102

"Yes. It's such a shame. It must have blown away in the storm. It's in terrible shape, I'm sorry to say. When it was found, everyone was gone. I still happened to be here closing up when a gentleman brought it here. I laid it out to dry and looked up your name this morning to contact you. It does have a label of the maker. It says, 'Made with my love for cherries, Marta Bachman.'"

"Oh, praise the Lord. We've been so worried about that quilt, thinking someone stole it."

"I don't think she'll be too happy when she sees it, unfortunately."

"Oh, I think she'll be very happy," I countered. "Someone will try to get there today to retrieve it."

"We'll be here until four o'clock."

"Thanks so very much!"

When I hung up, I was doing a happy dance.

"You received good news, I assume," Grayson noted with a smile.

"Oh, indeed! One of the many headaches we had after the show was a missing quilt from our challenge exhibit. It blew away in the storm but was found by the intersection of 42 and Main."

"Wow, that is good news! That wind must have been gruesome!"

I didn't waste any time calling Cher. She answered right away, and I told her every detail of the phone call. She was delighted, and I could hear her yell to the girls, "The quilt has been found!"

"Did you call Marta?"

"No, you're the first to hear. I think you and I were more concerned about her quilt than she was."

"I'll call her if you want," Cher offered.

"Oh, would you? I have a guest for breakfast."

"Oh, sure you do. That's okay, I'll give her a call. She may want you to retrieve it since you live so close."

"Yes, I'll be happy to."

Grayson grabbed the phone from me then and said, "Good morning, Cher."

"Goodbye, Cher," I said after I took the phone back. "We'll be in touch." Grayson and I burst into laughter, wondering what her face looked like.

In seconds, the phone rang and rang, and we just let it. We continued to sit at the kitchen table until we finished eating. It was the best breakfast ever. Instead of rehashing what we talked about last night, we talked about the show.

"Do you mind if I change into some jeans before I take you home?" I asked as I took my last sip of coffee.

"No, take your time. I'll do what I can to clean up here."

"You don't have to do that," I said, shaking my head.

"Who do you think does most of the cleanup at my house?" he joked.

I smiled and let him do what he wanted as I went upstairs. I couldn't believe what was happening. Did we just make up? I don't remember one kiss or hug last night, but here we were, acting like we hadn't just spent months apart. Neither one of us seemed ready to admit we had made up.

As I pulled up my jeans, I thought about the chances of Grayson coming into Alexander's last night and finding me sitting alone at the bar. Pretty slim, I'd say.

When I returned to the kitchen, I saw not only most of my kitchen cleaned up, but also my cat sitting on Grayson's lap, happy as a lark. Not even Cher was able to get Puff's attention in this way.

"Well, this is a first," I said, looking at the sight.

"At least somebody here likes me," Grayson teased.

We got on our way and pretty much remained silent as we drove. I think we'd said everything we could possibly say to one another last night.

"I'll just drop you off," I suggested when we were within a few blocks of his house.

"No, ma'am. You're coming in the house with me."

"Oh, Grayson. Did you warn Kelly, or has she called to check on you for not coming home?"

"No, not that I'm aware of. I'm a grown-up, you know."

I shook my head in disbelief.

As we stepped inside the front door, Grayson called out Kelly's name to come downstairs. I wanted to hide.

"Kelly! Kelly, we have company!" he said a little louder.

Kelly finally came out of her room and walked down the stairs. I'd never seen her with such a big grin.

"Claire! Oh, gosh! It's good to see you. How did you guys do after the storm?" she asked casually.

"I'm recovering," I said with a smile. "Thanks again for all your help."

"Speaking of helping," Grayson said as he put his arm around me, "I drove Claire's car home last night after she had dinner with some friends."

"Oh, good," she said matter-of-factly. "Wherever your car is, I can take you to get it."

"I can do that as well," I offered. "He insisted I come in to say hello."

"Okay, whatever," Kelly said, shrugging it off.

"I want to change clothes, so you go on, Claire," Grayson directed. "Kelly will take me."

"Okay, great, but I was just thinking ..." Kelly paused. "We were going to have a cookout with some of my friends here tonight, and I could use some help. Dad *tries* to barbeque, but he ends up burning everything. Would you like to come?" I looked at Grayson for his reaction.

"Well, I guess if I'm not intruding on a planned party," I responded shyly.

"Oh, great. Now I'll have two women telling me how to grill," Grayson joked.

"Billy and I are going to a ballgame this afternoon, but we'll be back around four o'clock," Kelly noted. "No one is coming until six o'clock. Will that work for you?"

"It will!" I nodded. "How about I bring some of my brownies that I happen to know are pretty popular around here?"

"Yes!" Kelly grinned. "I had just planned on melon slices, but your brownies sound much better. Thanks so much, Claire!"

Kelly went back upstairs, and Grayson took my hand as we walked out onto his beautiful patio.

"Claire, did you notice how happy Kelly was to see you?" I nodded and smiled.

Grayson then took my hand and placed it on his chest.

"I've missed you, Claire Stewart," he said, now bringing me closer.

"Oh, how I've missed you, too, Grayson Wills. I guess I'll see you tonight."

"I look forward to it. How about I pick you up about five thirty?"

"Oh, I can meet you here."

He shook his head, as if that wouldn't work. "You talk too much," he said, pulling me close for a long, passionate kiss on the lips.

I left Grayson's house on a cloud. When I pulled out of his driveway, I noticed I'd three missed calls from Cher. That made me chuckle. She'd just have to wait a little bit longer. These past several hours had been too perfect. Was I dreaming? Kelly somehow accepted me now. When did that happen? Had I made too much out of her behavior before? Grayson was so sweet, as always. It was just like him to be a gentleman and insist on picking me up tonight.

I pulled up to my cabin, which now looked happier and prettier than it ever had before. Getting news about Marta's quilt was icing on the cake this morning. I sat in my Subaru, trying to adjust to the past several hours. My cell phone rang again with Cher's name on the screen. She was persistent!

"Yes, Cher Bear. You rang?" I teased.

"You've got a lot of explaining to do, Claire Bear!"

WHITE GULL INN'S
Cherry Pancakes

Yields 10 pancakes (4–5 inches in diameter).

1 cup flour

3 tablespoons sugar

1 tablespoon baking powder

¾ teaspoon baking soda

¼ teaspoon salt

2 eggs, slightly beaten

1¼ cups buttermilk

2½ tablespoons melted butter

1 cup pitted tart Montmorency* cherries, drained

In a medium bowl, stir together flour, sugar, baking powder, baking soda, and salt. In a separate bowl, mix eggs and buttermilk. Pour eggs and buttermilk into dry ingredients and stir until smooth. Add melted butter, and stir to combine.

Grease heated griddle if necessary. Test whether the griddle is hot enough by sprinkling drops of water on top. If they skitter, the griddle is ready. Pour about 3 tablespoons of batter from the end of a large spoon or pitcher onto the griddle for each pancake. Cook on that side until the pancakes are puffed and dry around the edges. Sprinkle six or seven cherries over each pancake. Then flip the pancakes and cook the other side until they're golden brown. Remove the cakes from the griddle and garnish with a few more cherries before serving. Serve warm with butter and heated Door County maple syrup.

Thanks to the White Gull Inn in Fish Creek, Wisconsin, for serving such a delicious breakfast and for sharing this recipe with us.

* *For information on where frozen Montmorency cherries are sold near you, please contact Seaquist Orchards in Ellison Bay, Wisconsin, by emailing Robin Seaquist at robin@seaquistorchards.com.*

READER'S GUIDE:
Quilted Cherries

by Ann Hazelwood

1. Miscommunication between Claire and Grayson was certainly hurtful to both of them. Have you ever been in a relationship where there's no going back? Will Claire and Grayson make it work?

2. Claire had mixed feeling about Foster Collins in this novel. Will he still play a role in her life now that she and Grayson seem to have made up?

3. There's no question that Kelly's jealously toward Claire caused Claire to reject Grayson's proposal. How do you see the relationship between Kelly and Claire changing in the future?

4. Doing an outdoor quilt show carries a lot of liability and risk. Will the Door-to-Door Quilt Show survive for another year after what happened with the second show? Why do you think so?

5. Claire and Michael found a new appreciation for each other in this book. What do you attribute that to?

About the Author

Ann Hazelwood is a former shop owner and native of Saint Charles, Missouri. She has always adored quilting and is a certified quilt appraiser. She's the author of the wildly successful Colebridge Community series and considers writing one of her greatest passions. She has also published the Wine Country Quilt series and East Perry County series and is now writing the Door County Quilts series.

booksonthings.com

Cozy up with more quilting mysteries from Ann Hazelwood...

WINE COUNTRY QUILT SERIES

After quitting her boring editing job, aspiring writer Lily Rosenthal isn't sure what to do next. Her two biggest joys in life are collecting antique quilts and frequenting the area's beautiful wine country. The murder of a friend results in Lily acquiring the inventory of a local antique store. Murder, quilts, and vineyards serve as the inspiration as Lily embarks on a journey filled with laughs, loss, and red-and-white quilts.

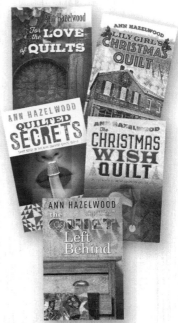

THE DOOR COUNTY QUILT SERIES

Meet Claire Stewart, a new resident of Door County, Wisconsin. Claire is a watercolor quilt artist and joins a prestigious small quilting club when her best friend moves away. As she grows more comfortable after escaping a bad relationship, new ideas and surprises abound as friendships, quilting, and her love life all change for the better.

Want more? Visit us online at ctpub.com